Ma   on's
fina   ous
La   and
fie   oss.
It i   nds
the   ing
of

Th   His
Ur   —an
eig   ear
Av   ood
ho   to
ass

Ma   rful
we   of
St   the
wi   e of
Ro   hen
Ma   the
vir   vel,
is   f a
my

A GOOD YEAR

Peter Mayle

WINDSOR
PARAGON

First published 2004
by
Time Warner Books
This Large Print edition published 2004
by
BBC Audiobooks Ltd by arrangement with
Time Warner Books Ltd

ISBN 1 4056 1014 X (Windsor Hardcover)
ISBN 1 4056 2009 9   (Paragon Softcover)

British Library Cataloguing in Publication Data available

Printed and bound in Great Britain by
Antony Rowe Ltd., Chippenham, Wiltshire

For Jennie, and for all those who work so hard in the vineyards to turn grapes into nectar.

AUTHOR'S NOTE

This is a work of fiction. The characters and their names are inventions, and have nothing to do with real life. Between the lines, however, there were several real people involved.

For his crucial contribution to the book, I would like to thank Ridley Scott, whose nose for a good story got me started. I was also very fortunate to receive expert advice of an alcoholic nature from Allen Chevalier in the Luberon and Anthony Barton in the Médoc. And Ailie Collins was, as always, a joy to work with.

Mille mercis à tous.

One

It was high summer in London, and the raindrops felt almost warm on Max Skinner's face as he ran up Rutland Gate and into Hyde Park. He followed the curve of the Serpentine while the shapes of other people determined to suffer before breakfast came and went in the grey predawn murk, their faces slick with rain and sweat, their progress marked by the moist slap of their footsteps on the path.

The weather had discouraged all but the hard-core joggers. It was too wet for those bouncing, pink-cheeked girls who sometimes provided Max with a little welcome distraction. Too wet for the resident flasher who was usually on duty behind a bush near the bandstand, leer and raincoat at the ready. Too wet even for the pair of Jack Russells whose joy it was to nip at every passing ankle, their embarrassed owner lumbering after them mouthing apologies.

It was too wet, and perhaps too early. Max had been getting into the office late recently, often as late as seven-thirty, and Amis, his boss and nemesis, was not pleased. This morning would be different, Max promised himself. He'd get in first, and make sure the miserable sod knew it. That was the big problem with Max's working life: he liked the job but loathed the people, Amis in particular.

Turning at the top of the Serpentine, Max started back towards the Albert Memorial, his thoughts on the day ahead. There was a deal that he'd been nursing along for months, a deal that

1

would deliver a bonus big enough to pay his infinitely patient tailor and, much more important, get the bank off his back. Occasional murmurs of discontent about the size of his overdraft had turned into letters couched in ever more menacing terms, underlining the fact that it had been a lean year so far. But it was going to change, Max felt sure. With a surge of optimism, he sprinted down Rutland Gate, shook himself like a dog on the doorstep, and let himself into the stucco-fronted Georgian house that a developer had gutted and converted into what he described as highly desirable executive pieds-à-terre.

The janitor of the building, a gnome of a man with a papery, subterranean complexion, looked up from his vacuum cleaner and clucked his tongue at the trail of wet footprints Max was leaving on the carpet.

'You'll be the death of me, you will. Look at that bleeding mud, all over my Axminster.'

'Sorry, Bert. I keep forgetting to take off my shoes before I come in.'

Bert sniffed. They had the same conversation every time it rained, and it always ended with the same question. Bert was a keen follower of the stock market, and longed for the chance to do a little insider trading. 'Got any good tips for today, then?'

Max paused at the door of the elevator and put a finger to his lips before speaking. 'Buy low. Sell high. Don't tell a soul.'

Bert shook his head. Cheeky young git. But then, he was the only one in the building to remember Bert's birthday with a bottle of Scotch, and there was always a nicely filled envelope from him at

Christmas. Not a bad lad, thought Bert, as he pushed the vacuum cleaner back and forth over the traces of wet mud.

Max's second-floor apartment was a work in progress; or, as a decorator friend with his eye on a lucrative assignment had said, an unfinished symphony. At the moment, it was a place used for sleep and very little else. There were two good modern paintings leaning against the wall, a few pieces of spiky avant-garde furniture, a dusty and sorry-looking ficus, a battery of stereo and video equipment. Despite having been there for more than two years, Max had managed to avoid giving the apartment any personal touches, apart from a small pile of running shoes in one corner. He went into the tiny, unused kitchen, opened the refrigerator, empty except for a bottle of vodka and a carton of orange juice, and took the carton with him into the bathroom.

Hot water and cold juice. The after-run shower was a daily reward for one of his few healthy habits. He worked too hard, ate in the irregular way of bachelors, slept too little, and certainly drank more than the five units of alcohol a week decreed, with sanctimonious relish, by the company doctor. But he ran, and he was young. Forty was several years away, and by then, he told himself, he would have his life and his finances in order, ready to settle down and—who knows—make another gallant attempt at matrimony.

He studied his reflection in the shaving mirror. Blue eyes, only slightly bloodshot; dark brown hair, cut short in the current fashion; skin taut over high cheekbones. As yet, no obvious bags or wrinkles. Could be worse, he thought, as he stepped over the

3

wet towel and discarded running clothes on the bathroom floor.

Five minutes later, he was ready to conquer the financial universe, dressed in the uniform and trappings of the modern young executive: dark suit, dark blue shirt, dark tie, a bulky watch designed for deep-sea divers obsessed with punctuality, cell phone and car keys at the ready. He ducked through the drizzle and into the obligatory black BMW for the drive to the City, where today, he felt sure, the long-awaited deal would come through. And then the bonus. He'd finish furnishing the apartment, hire a housecleaner to keep it spotless, take a few days off, and drive down to Saint-Tropez before all the girls went back to Paris. Not even the weather forecast on the radio—scattered showers, followed by outbreaks of heavier rain, with a chance of hail—could dampen his spirits. This was going to be a good day.

At this time of the morning, twenty minutes should have been more than enough to get him into the Lawton Brothers' offices. They were at the top end of Threadneedle Street—'handy for the Bank of England,' as the senior Lawton brother was fond of telling his prospective clients. Established in the late eighties, the company had boomed through the nineties with everyone else, merging and acquiring, ducking and diving, and gaining a reputation for savage asset-stripping that was the envy of its more ethical and kindhearted competitors. Now it was often described in the financial press as a model of tough, efficient management, well suited to today's hard times. Young executives who survived a few years at Lawtons could survive anywhere.

Max's cell phone rang as he was coming down Ludgate Hill. It was just before six-thirty.

'Taking the morning off, are we?' It was the voice of Amis, nasal and aggressive. He didn't wait for Max to answer. 'We need to talk. See if you can get in here by lunchtime. Tracy will tell you the restaurant.'

So much for my good day, Max thought. Although, if he were honest with himself, no day that included Amis could be entirely good. Mutual dislike had been in the air the instant the two men met, when Amis had swaggered in, fresh from spending three years in New York, to run the London office. From the start, their relationship had been tainted, as is so often the case in England, by the simple difference in the way they spoke English. Their accents.

Max was the product of a minor public school, and had grown up in the leafy middle-class comfort of the Surrey hills. Amis was born and raised in the grim outer reaches of south London, neither leafy nor comfortable. In fact, they had grown up less than twenty miles apart, but it might as well have been twenty thousand. Max liked to think that there was not a trace of snobbery in him. Amis liked to think that he didn't have a chip on his shoulder. They were both wrong. But each had a grudging respect for the other's ability, and so, with difficulty, they tolerated one another.

Easing the BMW into its appointed slot in the underground garage, Max tried to guess the reason for today's meeting. Lunch at Lawtons was normally a sandwich at your desk, eyes glued to the screen. Lunch, in a phrase that Amis had picked up in New York, was for wimps. And yet here he was

5

talking about a proper lunch with knives and forks—a wimp's lunch—in a restaurant. It was curious. Max was still puzzling over it as he stepped out of the elevator and made his way through the rows of partitions to his own cubicle.

Lawtons took up the entire floor of a glass and concrete box. With the exception of the mahogany and leather splendour of the large suite shared by the two brothers, the offices had been designed to reflect the spirit of the company: no frills, no aesthetic refinements. This was a factory for making money, and austerity ruled. The Lawtons had a habit of bringing clients on a tour of what they called the engine room for a glimpse of the staff at work. 'There they are, forty of the best business brains in the City. *And they're all thinking about your problems.*'

Not content with his earlier call, Amis had sent Max an e-mail instructing him not to be late for lunch. Max looked up from the screen toward the glassed-in corner office where Amis was normally to be seen striding up and down with a phone stuck to his ear, but this morning the office was empty. The big creep must be at a breakfast pitch somewhere, thought Max; or maybe he was off taking elocution lessons.

Max hung up his jacket and got down to work, running the numbers one final time on TransAx and Richardson Bell, the two companies whose charms he was peddling to one of Lawtons' larger clients. If the deal went through, it was going to earn him a bonus that was, he had calculated, considerably more than the prime minister made in a year. He checked and double-checked, and the right answers came up each time. Now he was ready to present everything to the brothers. They could move in, and he would be six figures richer. He leaned back in his chair, stretched, and glanced at his watch. It was past twelve o'clock, and he realized he had no idea where he was supposed to be for lunch.

He crossed the floor to where Tracy, a brisk and well-upholstered young woman, was on sentry duty outside the corner office. She had recently been promoted from Amis's secretary to his personal assistant (a step up, so office rumour had it, that was the direct result of a dirty weekend with Amis in Paris). Sadly, promotion had spoiled her, making her cocky and self-important.

Max perched on the corner of her desk and nodded toward the empty office. 'Are we still on for lunch, or is he busy causing havoc in the stock exchange?'

Tracy looked as though she'd like to have given him a ticket for parking in a restricted area. 'Mr. Amis will meet you at the Leadenhall Cellars. Twelve-thirty sharp. You're not to be late.'

Max raised his eyebrows. The Cellars, once a storage depot for the old Leadenhall market, had been turned into a gentrified wine bar where the young Turks of the City gathered to eat virile lunches—slabs of red meat and Stilton—drink overpriced claret, and prepare for the rigours of the afternoon with a notoriously powerful port. Despite the bare brick walls and the sawdust on the floor, it was one of the City's most expensive restaurants.

'He's dipping into his savings, isn't he?' said Max. 'Any idea what it's about?'

Tracy looked down at her desk and rearranged

7

some papers. 'Not a clue,' she said. The offhand tone of her voice was unconvincing and, Max found, irritating.

'Tracy, there's something I've been dying to ask you.'

She looked up.

'How was Paris?'

So it was true. Leaving her to her blushes, Max went back to get his jacket and an umbrella, bracing himself for a dash through the rain to Leadenhall Street. He hesitated in the doorway of the building before plunging into the thicket of oversized golf umbrellas—this summer's style accessory—that had sprouted everywhere like multicoloured mushrooms, blocking the pavement and making progress slow and difficult. He was going to be late.

He arrived in the crowded, vaulted room to find Amis already at the table, cell phone to his ear. During his time among the movers and shakers of Wall Street, Amis had picked up some of their more flamboyant sartorial affectations—the aggressively striped shirt with white collar, the scarlet braces, the tie spattered with bulls and bears—decorative flourishes that clashed with his hard, thin-lipped face and convict's haircut. Whatever he wore, he would always look like a thug. But he had a genius for deal making, and for that he was much loved by the Lawton brothers.

He finished his call, and made a point of looking at his watch—gold, and even bulkier than Max's, its face encrusted with a multitude of dials: depth in metres, elapsed time, and, a special feature, the waxing and waning of the Nasdaq. 'What happened to you, then? Lost your way?'

Max helped himself to a glass of red wine from the bottle on the table. 'Sorry about that,' he said. 'Umbrella jam in Leadenhall Street.'

Amis grunted, signalled to one of the waitresses, and became suddenly jovial. 'You know what would make me a happy man, my love?' He gave her a wink and a smirk. 'A nice juicy sirloin, well cooked, none of that blood all over the place. Get enough of that at the office.' The waitress did her best to smile. 'And chips. And then I'll have the crème brûlée for afters. Got that?' His cell phone chirped, and he muttered into it while Max ordered lamb chops and a salad.

Amis put down his phone and took a gulp of wine. 'Right, then,' he said, 'give me the rundown on TransAx and Richardson Bell.'

For the next half-hour, Max went through the figures and projections, his analysis of the management, and the possibilities of corporate loot and plunder that he had been working on since the start of the year. Amis ate his way through the presentation, making notes on the pad by his plate but offering neither question nor opinion.

Max finished talking, and pushed aside the remains of his congealed chops. 'Well? Is this why we're having lunch?'

'Not exactly.' Amis was probing the recesses of his back teeth with a toothpick, examining his discoveries with an air of mild interest as he took pleasure in keeping Max waiting.

The waitress came to clear away the plates, which appeared to be the cue Amis had been waiting for. 'I've been having a chat with the brothers,' he said, 'and they share my concerns.'

'What are you talking about?'

9

'Your performance, my friend. Your productivity. You've been like the walking wounded this year. Pathetic.'

'You know what I've been putting together over the past six months—I've just told you.' Max had to make an effort to keep his voice down. 'And you know bloody well that deals like this don't happen in a couple of weeks. They take time.'

Amis greeted the arrival of his crème brûlée with another wink at the waitress. 'Won't wash, my friend, won't wash. You want to know what's wrong?' He looked at Max and nodded two or three times. 'Personal life's getting in the way. Too many late nights, too much chasing after totty. You've lost the killer instinct.' Taking his spoon, he stabbed his dessert through the heart.

'That's crap, and you know it. Both those companies are ripe. This deal is as good as sewn up.'

Amis looked up at him, a fleck of yellow cream on his chin. 'You've got that right, anyway.'

'What do you mean?'

'I'm taking it over.' Amis spooned in another mouthful, crunching the caramelized sugar between his teeth.

Max took a deep breath. 'We'll see what the Lawtons have to say about that. They're . . .'

'Too late, sunshine. They're sorted. I got the green light from them this morning.'

Max saw months of work wiped out. Even worse, he saw his bonus disappearing into Amis's bank account as his unpaid bills piled up and the bank moved in to tighten the noose around his neck. 'You can't do that. It's bloody daylight robbery. It's stealing.'

'Where have you been living? It's business, that's what it is. Business. Nothing personal, no hard feelings. And I'll tell you what I'll do. I've had a tip about a little engineering firm, but I won't have time for that now. You can take it over.'

A memory came back to Max from many years ago, when his uncle Henry was giving him a lecture about life: *Better to die on your feet than live on your knees*. Max came to a decision. 'I can take it over, can I? I can work it up, and then, when it's all set, I can get screwed again. Is that what you're saying?' Max leaned across the table. 'Well, you can stuff your little engineering firm, and you can stuff your job. I'm not going to work for a thieving prick like you.'

Amis felt a glow of satisfaction as Max pushed back his chair. Lunch had gone according to plan; in fact, it couldn't have gone better. He'd received a detailed, up-to-date brief on the deal, and, since Max had resigned, there wouldn't be any severance to pay. Perfect. 'Suit yourself,' he said. 'Your decision. Make sure your desk is cleared out by this evening, OK?'

Max stood up, but Amis hadn't finished with him. 'Aren't you forgetting something, my friend? The company vehicle?' He held out his hand. 'I'll have the car keys, if you don't mind.'

Max took the keys from his pocket and hesitated for a moment before dropping them carefully into Amis's half-eaten crème brûlée.

Amis watched him go. He reached for his cell phone and punched in Tracy's number.

*   *   *

During the walk back to the office, Max's emotions were a mixture of apprehension at what he'd just done and elation at having done it. This was a bad moment to be out of a job, it was true. But the thought of life without Amis and his constant needling was something of a consolation; unfortunately, it was not nearly enough to make up for the lost bonus. He was in trouble, and he needed to find something else. He decided to spend his last afternoon at Lawtons making a few calls. Might even try New York.

When he got back, however, he found he could barely squeeze into his cubicle. Tracy and two security guards were waiting for him.

'Jesus,' said Max. 'What do you think I'm going to do, nick the carpet?'

'Standard termination procedure,' said Tracy. She turned to the guards. 'Stay with him until he's finished, and then report back to me.' She stopped in front of Max as she was leaving the cubicle and smiled sweetly. 'How was lunch?'

Max looked around the space where he had spent most of his waking hours over the past eighteen months. What did he want to take with him? What would he be allowed to take? His diskettes? Certainly not. His official Lawton Brothers desk diary? God forbid. What else was there? Nothing much. He shrugged at the guards. 'Help yourselves, boys.'

Out on Threadneedle Street, he saw an empty cab throwing up a miniature bow wave as it came toward him through the rain. He raised an arm to hail it, remembered that he had just joined the ranks of the unemployed, and waved it on. He couldn't remember the last time he'd been on the

London Underground. This was going to be a novel experience. He splashed toward the Bank station, feeling the moisture soaking through the soles of his shoes.

There was no solace to be found in his apartment. Max kicked off his shoes and peeled off his socks. A leaden afternoon light, more like winter than summer, seeped through the windows. The answering machine blinked its red eye.

'You bastard! Where *were* you last night? I've never been so humiliated in my life. All those ghastly men trying to touch me up. Don't bother ever . . .'

Max winced and shut off the diatribe before it had finished. Working late the night before, he'd completely forgotten that he'd arranged to meet his caller in the bar of the Chelsea Arts Club. Knowing some of his fellow members, he could imagine that their desire to make a pretty stranger feel welcome might have been expressed too enthusiastically. Oh God. Better send flowers and an abject note.

He stripped off his tie and jacket and slumped on the couch, all energy and optimism gone. The apartment was a mess. His life was a mess. As an alternative to housework or vodka, he turned on the television. A cookery programme. A documentary about salamanders. A man with blow-dried hair presenting the news from CNN. Golf, the instant soporific. Max dozed off, and dreamed of drowning Amis in a vat of crème brûlée.

It was evening when the phone woke him. The golfers on the screen didn't seem to have made any progress since Max had dropped off several hours before. Perhaps it was a long hole. He turned off

13

the TV and picked up the phone.

'There you are, you old bugger. I tried you at the office, but they said you'd left early. Are you all right?'

It was Charlie, his closest friend and ex-brother-in-law.

Max yawned. 'I'm fine. No, actually, I'm not fine. It's been one of those days.'

'It's going to start getting better. Tonight, you and I are celebrating the promotion of Charles Willis, real estate's rising star. It happened this afternoon. Bingham & Trout have made me a full partner. Time for young blood, they said. The property business is changing, we must move with the times, a strong hand on the tiller, all that stuff.'

'Charlie, that's terrific. Congratulations.'

'Well, don't just sit there. Come and help me out with this bottle of Krug.'

'Where are you?'

'An old client of mine just opened this place off the Portobello Road. Pinot, it's called—great bar, great wine list, and even as I speak it is *crawling* with crumpet. All the Notting Hill lovelies, dressed in flimsy garments. I'm fighting them off.'

Max was smiling as he put the phone down and went into the bedroom to change. Ever since they had met at school, Charlie had always been good for morale. And looking out of the window, Max saw that the rain had stopped. His spirits lifted, and he found himself whistling as he went downstairs.

Passing through the lobby on his way out, he stopped to check his mailbox. There was the usual collection of final demands and circulars and one or two of the dinner-party invitations that come the way of every London bachelor; but there was also

14

an intriguing envelope with a French stamp. In the top left-hand corner was a small, stylized image of the statue of Justice, and below was printed the sender's name: *Cabinet Auzet, Notaires, Rue des Remparts, 84903 St. Pons.* Max started to open it, then decided to save it to use as a distraction from the horrors of the tube. He slipped the envelope in his pocket, stuffed the rest of his mail back in the box, and headed for the South Kensington Underground station.

Two

Standing in the crush of humanity as the tube rattled away from South Kensington toward Notting Hill, Max was rediscovering the face of public transport. Almost everyone around him, it seemed, had undergone the modern tribal ritual of piercing. Pierced nostrils, pierced eyebrows, pierced lips, pierced ears, several pallid but prominently displayed pierced navels. Other visible body parts, those that hadn't been pierced, were tattooed. A handful of older, more conservative passengers, without nose jewelry or ear trinkets, looked like relics from a distant, unadorned age. They buried their faces in books or newspapers, carefully avoiding eye contact with those members of the pierced generation jammed up against them.

Max wedged himself in a corner of the lurching carriage and took the letter from his pocket. He read it once, then a second time, his rusty French gradually coming back to him as he went over the formal phrases. Lost in thought, he almost missed his stop, and he was still preoccupied when he pushed open the thick smoked-glass doors of the restaurant.

The hubbub of a fashionable haunt in full cry washed over him like a wave. The long, low-ceilinged room, with its hard surfaces and echoing acoustics, was a giant amplifier, following the popular theory that a high decibel level is essential for the enjoyment of food. It was a place where, if you were romantically inclined, you would have to bellow sweet nothings in your companion's ear. But that was clearly part of the restaurant's appeal, because every table seemed to be taken.

A sinuous young woman, tightly wrapped in what looked like black clingfilm, swayed up to Max, eyebrows raised, eyelashes a-flutter. 'Do you have a reservation with us tonight?'

'I'm supposed to be meeting Mr. Willis.'

'Oh, *Charlie*. Of course. If you'd like to follow me?'

'To the ends of the earth,' said Max. The young woman giggled, and led the way with the undulant strut that none but the runway model or the restaurant hostess can achieve without dislocating a hip.

Charlie was at a corner table, an ice bucket at his elbow. He grinned as he saw Max. 'I see you've met the lovely Monica. Isn't she something? Only girl I know who plays tennis in high heels.'

Monica smiled at them before swaying back to the reception desk, and Max looked at the beaming, rosy face of his friend. Dear old Charlie. Nobody could call him handsome—he was a little overweight, carelessly dressed, his hair perpetually awry—but he possessed abundant charm, liquid

16

brown eyes, and an evident enthusiasm for the company of women that they seemed to find irresistible. He had so far avoided marriage, but with some difficulty. Max had been less fortunate.

He had made the mistake, a few years before, of marrying Charlie's sister Annabel. The marriage had been turbulent from the start, and had ended badly. Much to Charlie's disapproval, Annabel had run off to Los Angeles with a film director, and now lived in a four-million-dollar wooden shack on the beach at Malibu. The last time Charlie had seen her, she had embraced the promise of eternal youth offered by Botox and power yoga. Beyond redemption, Charlie had said to Max. I could never stand her anyway; you're better off without her. And so their friendship had survived the marriage, if anything stronger than before.

'Now then,' said Charlie, pouring champagne, 'listen to this. They've doubled my salary, given me a Mercedes and full partnership shares, and told me the world's my oyster. So tonight's on me.' He raised his glass. 'To London property prices—let's hope they continue to go through the roof.'

'Congratulations, Charlie. It couldn't happen to a nicer crook.' Max sipped his wine and studied the bubbles spiralling up from the base of his glass. Champagne, he thought, was always associated with good times—a drink for optimists.

Charlie looked at him, head cocked to one side. 'You said it had been one of those days. What happened? No assets left to strip?'

Max described his lunch with Amis and the small humiliations of handing back his car keys and then finding two bruisers in uniform standing over his desk. 'So that was the bad news: no bonus, no job,

17

no car. But then this arrived.' He pushed the letter across the table.

Charlie took one look at it and shook his head. 'Wasted on me, old son. My French isn't up to it. You'll have to translate.'

'Remember when we were at school and I used to be packed off to spend the summer holidays in France? My dad's brother, Uncle Henry, had a place about an hour from Avignon—big old house surrounded by vines, not far from a little village. Uncle Henry and I used to play tennis and chess, and in the evenings he'd get me tipsy on watered-down wine and give me lectures about life. Very decent old stick, he was.' Max paused for another nip at the champagne. 'Haven't seen him for ages. Now I wish I'd seen more of him, because he died a couple of weeks ago.'

Charlie made sympathetic noises, and refilled Max's glass.

'Anyway, he never got married, never had any children.' Max picked up the letter. 'And according to the will, I'm his sole surviving relative. It looks as though he's left me everything—house, twenty hectares of land, furniture, the lot.'

'Good God,' said Charlie. 'Twenty hectares is more than forty acres, right? Sounds like an estate to me. A château.'

'I don't remember it quite like that, but it's certainly a big house.'

'With vines, you said?'

'Sure. Vines all over the place.'

'Right,' said Charlie. 'This calls for something a little out of the ordinary.' He raised an arm and made energetic circling motions at a waiter, calling out for a wine list. Turning back to Max, he said,

18

'You know I've always liked a drop of wine. Well, I'm taking it seriously now, starting a cellar. I'm even going to an evening wine-tasting course. This is all most exciting. Ah, there you are.' The sommelier had arrived, and Charlie started to brief him.

'We're celebrating,' he said. 'My friend here has just inherited a château and a vineyard in France, and so we're looking for something appropriate in the way of homemade wine.' He wagged a finger at the sommelier. 'Homemade in Bordeaux, mind you. A classic claret. None of your New World novelties.'

Charlie and the sommelier bent over the list, exchanging knowledgeable murmurs while Max looked around the room—glossy women and prosperous-looking men, London's privileged class, all of them talking at the top of their voices. Max felt a sudden desire to be somewhere quiet, and then thought of his empty apartment. Not that quiet. He looked down at the letter again, and wondered how much the property would fetch if he decided to sell; certainly more than enough to get him out of the hole he was in. He raised his glass in a private toast to Uncle Henry.

'Excellent,' said Charlie. 'That's the one.'

The sommelier pursed his lips and nodded in silent approval before going off in search of the wine.

'There,' said Charlie, pointing to his choice on the list. "The '82 Léoville-Barton. Top bottle. Can't do better than that.'

Max looked at where the pointing finger had stopped. 'Are you serious? Three hundred and eighty pounds?'

19

'That's nothing these days. Not long ago, half a dozen punters—young bankers, I think they were—had dinner at some place in St. James's and went mad. They blew forty-four thousand quid on six bottles of wine. The chef was so tickled he gave them a free dinner. You must have read about it.'

The sommelier returned, and Charlie paused to watch him perform the opening ceremony. The bottle was presented for inspection, in the way a proud parent displays a particularly well-favoured baby. The lead capsule was cut, the long, aristocratic cork withdrawn and sniffed, the dark ruby liquid poured with practised care into a decanter, with a little more than a mouthful going into a glass.

Now it was time for Charlie's performance. 'There are five steps,' he said, reaching for the glass, 'that make all the difference between the art of drinking and the act of swallowing.' The sommelier looked on with the indulgent patience that comes from the thought of a substantial commission. 'First,' said Charlie, 'mental preparation.' He worshipped his glass for a few moments before raising it to the light. 'Next, the pleasure of the eyes.' He tilted the glass so that the differences in colour could be seen—deep red at the bottom, fading into a lighter maroon at the top, with a rim that was faintly tinged with brown. 'Now for the nose.' He swirled the wine gently, opening it up to the air, before dipping his nose into the glass and inhaling. 'Ah,' he said with a slow smile, his eyes closed. 'Ah.'

Max felt like a voyeur spying on a profoundly personal moment. Over the years of their friendship, he had always been amused by the passion with which Charlie attacked his hobbies, from skateboarding when they were at school to last year's preoccupation with karate. Now it seemed that wine had taken over. Max smiled at the expression of purest pleasure that had spread across Charlie's face. 'So far so good?' asked Max.

Charlie ignored him. 'Now for the pleasures of mouth, tongue and palate.' He took a sip of wine, holding it in his mouth while he sucked in a little air, making a discreet lapping sound. For a few seconds his jaw went up and down as though he were chewing, and then he swallowed. 'Mmm,' he said. 'The final step is appreciation. Messages from the palate to the brain. Thoughts of the wine still to come.' He nodded to the sommelier. 'That'll do nicely. You can let it breathe for a while. No, we can do better than that—you can let it regain its composure.'

'Very impressive,' said Max. 'You had me on the edge of my seat. Is that what you learned in the wine-tasting course?'

Charlie nodded. 'Elementary stuff, but it's surprising what a difference it makes—just taking the time to concentrate on what you're drinking. And we're in luck tonight. I had a look at the menu while I was waiting, and there's saddle of lamb. Terrific with a great Bordeaux. And I thought we might start with a few blinis to go with the rest of the champagne. How does that sound?'

The congealed chops of Max's lunch with Amis seemed a long way away. 'Sounds like the ideal diet for an unemployed man.'

Charlie dismissed the problem with a wave of his hand. 'You'll be fine. Anyway, there's your inheritance. You're part of the landed gentry now.

21

Tell me about the château.'

'The house, Charlie, the house.' Max was silent for a moment, looking back into his memory. 'It's quite old; goes back to the eighteenth century, I think, what they call down there a *bastide*, which is a step or two up from a farmhouse. Big rooms, high ceilings, tiled floors, tall windows, thick walls. I remember it was always cool indoors. Cool, and actually a bit of a mess. Uncle Henry wasn't too fussy about housework. A wonderful old dear used to come on a bicycle once a week and rearrange the dust in between drinks. She was always catatonic by lunchtime. There was a little scullery behind the kitchen where she used to sleep it off in the afternoon.'

Charlie nodded. 'Probably still there. Now come on, give me something an estate agent could get his teeth into: number of bedrooms, reception rooms, bathrooms—I take it there's what we in the trade call indoor sanitation facilities—lavish appointments, architectural features, turrets, crenellations, that sort of thing.' He leaned back to allow the waiter to serve the caviar blinis, and the interrogation stopped while they ate the golden savoury pancakes, a perfect foil for the glistening mounds of black, salty bubbles that burst in the mouth.

'I could get used to this,' said Max, as he wiped his plate clean. 'Do you think it would taste as good if it were called fish eggs?'

Charlie dabbed his mouth with his napkin, and finished his champagne. 'Not another drop of wine do you get until you give me some more details. Furnish me with particulars, old son. Furnish me with particulars.'

'Furnish you? God, you're beginning to sound like a property ad in *Country Life*.' Charlie grinned, and nodded in agreement as Max continued. 'It's been a long time since I was there. Years, actually. Let's see. I remember a library with a huge stuffed bear in it, a dining room we never used because we always ate in the kitchen, an enormous vaulted sitting room, a wine cellar . . .'

'Good, good,' said Charlie. 'Always a most desirable feature.'

'. . . a row of attics that ran the length of the third floor of the house . . .'

'Not attics, Max. Staff accommodation,' murmured Charlie. 'Excellent. Plenty of room for the odd maid and butler.'

'. . . I think there were half a dozen bedrooms and two or three bathrooms. Oh, and a grass tennis court and outbuildings, barns and things like that. A courtyard with an old fountain.'

'I can see it now. Sounds to me like a stately home. General state of repair and decoration? Has the refurbisher been around in the last hundred years or so?'

Max shook his head.

'No? Well, they've probably been keeping him busy in the Cotswolds. So how would you describe the interiors?'

'Not great. You know, slightly shabby.'

It was Charlie's turn to shake his head. 'No, no, Max. We don't call it shabby. We call it the patina and faded charm of a bygone age.'

'Of course, right. Well, there's plenty of that.'

The lamb arrived, moist and tender. The wine was poured, admired, and sipped. Charlie, his nose still hovering over his glass, looked up at Max.

'How would you rate it?'

Max took another sip, rolling the wine around his mouth as Charlie had done. 'Bloody good. *Bloody* good.'

Charlie raised his eyes to the ceiling. 'Won't do, old son. You can't describe a work of art like that. You've got to brush up on the jargon, the connoisseur's vocabulary.' He held up one hand, anticipating Max's reaction. 'I know, I know. You're always saying we talk a lot of crap in the property business. But believe me, we're just beginners compared to the wine boys.' He struck a pose, holding his glass by its base and swirling it gently. 'Do I detect faded tulips? Beethoven in a mellow mood? The complexity, the almost Gothic structure . . .' He grinned at the expression on Max's face. 'I've never heard such a lot of twaddle in my life, but that's the way some of them bang on.'

He then told Max about the first meeting of the Young Connoisseurs' Club, which he had been invited to join by Billy, his friend in the wine trade. Half a dozen young men—enthusiastic drinkers, but by no means connoisseurs—had gathered in a set of dignified chambers in St. James's, the headquarters of an old-established firm of shippers. Here, amidst the spittoons and flickering candles, beneath portraits of the bewhiskered gentlemen who had founded the firm, they were to sample wines from a few of the lesser-known châteaux in Bordeaux, and one or two promising upstarts from Australia and California.

Their host Billy was young, as wine merchants go. He had been taken into the firm when his more elderly colleagues had realized that their equally elderly customers were buying less wine, often as a result of natural causes (or, as some would say, death). Billy's mission was to find younger, thirstier souls with a good thirty or forty years of drinking ahead of them, to educate them, and, naturally, to make them faithful clients. Charlie was in the first batch, eager but ignorant, and Billy started the proceedings by demonstrating the basic steps of tasting. Watch me, he told his audience, and do as I do.

The pupils had been rather puzzled to see that the first part of the ritual involved Billy's tie, an ornamental polka-dot creation made of thick Jermyn Street silk. He carefully tucked the end into the waistband of his trousers, advising the others to do the same.

Next, he picked up his glass, not with a nonchalant grab, but delicately, holding the base of the glass between the thumb and the first two fingers. His class stood lined up in front of him, ties tucked in, glasses at the ready but as yet unfilled, waiting for further instructions.

Swirling, said Billy. You must learn to swirl, to let the air in and allow the wine to breathe. The class imitated as best they could the small circular movements of his hand, swirling make-believe wine in empty glasses and beginning to feel faintly ridiculous. It was to get worse before it got better.

The class held their empty glasses up to the candlelight, to appreciate the imaginary subtleties of colour in their imaginary wine. They applied their noses to the empty glasses, breathing in the imaginary bouquet. They took an imaginary mouthful and had an imaginary spit, thankful that their ties were out of the way of any imaginary drops. By this time, everyone was ready for a large Scotch, but it was not to be.

At last, Billy poured out the first of the wines to be tasted as he moved on to part two of wine appreciation for beginners. This was in the nature of an anatomy lesson. Wine had a nose, the class was told. Wine had body, wine had legs. Wine had a robe, a bouquet, a personality, an *essence*. And it was not enough, according to Billy, merely to go through the motions of tasting; one must also know how to describe what one has just tasted. So, as the class dutifully swirled and sipped and spat, Billy provided a running commentary on the wines under review.

The first, so he said, was vigorous and well constructed, even a little bosomy. The second was an iron fist in a velvet glove. The third was a little jagged around the edges, but potentially drinkable. The fourth was a little young to be up so late. And so it went on. As the would-be connoisseurs worked their way through the bottles, the descriptions became more and more outlandish: truffles, hyacinths, hay, wet leather, damp tweed, weasel, hare's belly, old carpet, vintage socks. Music made a brief appearance, with one wine being compared in its lingering finish to the final notes of Rachmaninov's Symphony No. 2 (the Adagio). Surprisingly, there was never a mention of the main ingredient, presumably because grapes, honest and worthy and indeed essential though they may be, were not considered sufficiently exotic to gain a place in the wine lover's lexicon.

'That was just the first session,' Charlie said. 'It got better after that, and I learned quite a bit.' His face became serious as he stared into the dark red heart of his wine. 'It is quite extraordinary, though,' he said, talking more to himself than to Max. 'The most elegant drink in the world. When I've made my bundle, I shall have this every day. I might even buy a vineyard.' He came out of his reverie and grinned at Max. 'And you've already got one. Lucky sod.'

'Not for long. I think I'll have to sell it.'

Charlie winced, then did his best to look stern and businesslike. 'Never, ever make a rushed decision about selling land. They're not making any more of it, or so I'm told. Rent it or sit on it, but don't get rid of it. In any case, you might be able to make a very tidy living with twenty hectares of vines.'

Max remembered the ocean of green that surrounded the old house. In his memory, there was always a man on a tractor somewhere on the horizon. Uncle Henry referred to him as Russell, but that couldn't have been his real name. When he came to the house, he brought with him whiffs of garlic and engine oil. Shaking hands with him was like grasping a warm brick.

'I don't know, Charlie. It's not a game for amateurs.'

Charlie finished a mouthful of lamb and took a long, considered pull at his glass. 'It's changed, no doubt about that. There's a guy taking the course who works for one of the really big shippers, and he's been telling me all kinds of fascinating stuff. Garage wines, for instance. Have you ever heard about garage wines?'

Max shook his head.

'If you want to pull rank, you call them boutique wines, or haute couture wines. Small vineyards, small production, seriously big prices. Le Pin is probably the best-known at the moment. Five thousand pounds a case, sometimes more. And that's wine you won't be drinking for years. Not bad if you're the one growing the grapes, is it?' He looked at Max, a forkful of lamb halfway to his mouth. 'And you can grow a lot of grapes on twenty hectares.' Charlie gave him the kind of long, significant look—head tilted downward, eyes looking up beneath a frowning forehead—that he used to great effect with girls or when describing a particularly enviable property to his clients.

Max began to have the sense that he was being nudged, not too subtly, into a new career among the vines, and as the level of wine in the decanter dropped he became sure of it. At one point, Charlie abandoned rational persuasion altogether in favour of appeals to what he hoped was Max's latent desire to become a French peasant. 'Buy a beret!' he said. 'Take tractor-driving lessons! Get your hands dirty! You'll love it.'

They ate and drank in the companionable silence of old friends, Charlie glancing at Max from time to time as if trying to read his thoughts. In fact, Max was having some difficulty reading them himself. He had always been attracted to change, and the idea of leaving a soggy, jobless London for the warmth and light of the south was immensely appealing. Also, he was curious to see how reality compared to his memories: if the old house was as big as he remembered; if the rooms still had the dry, pungent smell of herbs and lavender; if the sounds of a summer afternoon were the same; if the girls in the village were still as pretty.

Unfortunately, there wasn't any money in the

nostalgia budget. 'The problem is,' he said to Charlie. 'I'm skint. No, worse than skint. Rent, credit cards, debts of one sort or another—I'm a financial disaster. I can't afford to go swanning off to the south of France. I've got to get a job. Simple as that.'

'Let's have a little cheese to go with the rest of the wine, shall we? And I'll tell you why it's not as simple as that.' Charlie leaned across the table, one finger tapping on the cloth to emphasize his words. 'First, you've arrived at a moment in your life of marvellous freedom. No deadlines, no appointments, no responsibilities . . .'

'No money,' said Max.

'. . . a detail I shall come to in a moment. This is a turning point, an ideal time for you to take a break, look at what fate and Uncle Henry have dumped in your lap, and decide what you want to do. The weather down there will be delightful, and the trip will do you the world of good. Put the roses back in your cheeks.'

'Charlie, you don't . . .'

'Hear me out. At the worst, you'll decide to sell the house, in which case you can put it with a local agent while you're down there. At the best . . . well, at the best, you'll decide to stay on and do what I'd like to do: make a really good little wine. Can you imagine a more pleasant life? Agreeable working conditions, the cash rolling in, and as much free wine as you can drink. Heaven.'

As usual when he was in the grip of one of his enthusiasms, Charlie chose to ignore practical problems—in this case, as Max pointed out again, lack of funds. He could barely afford a train ticket down to Brighton, let alone a voyage of discovery

29

in the south of France.

'I was coming to that,' Charlie said. He patted the pockets of his jacket and fished out a chequebook, placing it with a slap on the table between them. 'I'm making so much loot I don't know what to do with it, and there's a lot more in the pipeline. My flat's paid for, they've given me a car, and I'm not interested in yachts or racehorses.' He sat back and beamed at Max.

'Women?'

'Of course. But that's just pocket money.' He took a pen from his pocket and opened the chequebook. 'You can look on this as a bridging loan.' He scribbled out a cheque, tore it from the book, and passed it across to Max. 'There. That should keep you going for a month or two while you sort everything out.'

Max looked down at Charlie's scrawl and blinked.

'Charlie, I can't possibly . . .'

'Don't be bloody stupid. If you sell the house, you can pay me back. And if you keep the house, we can turn it into some kind of mortgage. You can't afford not to give it a go. This is the chance of a lifetime, old son. What do you say to a modest glass of Calvados?'

Max continued to protest and Charlie continued to insist as one Calvados led to another. Unnoticed by them as they talked, the restaurant had become empty and quiet. Standing nearby, Calvados bottle at the ready, the sommelier concealed a yawn and longed for a cigarette. The sound of laughter came from the kitchen, and the waiters started stripping the cloths from the tables. The lovely Monica, now dressed in black leather and carrying a crash

30

helmet, stopped at the table to pat Charlie on the head and wish the two friends good night.

At last, Max gave in, folding the cheque and putting it away with fuddled fingers. Then, with even more difficulty, he wrote out an IOU for ten thousand pounds on his napkin and stuffed it into Charlie's top pocket.

Three

Standing in the shower after his morning run, hot water beating down on a skull tenderized by alcohol, Max reviewed the changes that had occurred during the past twenty-four hours, and found them all good. Lucky, lucky bastard, he thought while he was getting dressed, and caught himself whistling the Marseillaise as he walked up to Knightsbridge for a cup of coffee.

The day was grey but dry, and he sat at one of the tables that had been placed on the pavement as part of London's effort, at least for the summer, to imitate the cafés of Paris. Around him, people were muttering into their cell phones, shuffling documents, and consulting their watches before going off to work. He felt an almost guilty thrill of pleasure that he was no longer one of them. All he had to do today was cash Charlie's cheque, make an appointment with the *notaire*, and book his ticket.

The *notaire* first. It was eight-thirty in England, nine-thirty in France; the office should be open. He took out the letter from the Cabinet Auzet, now dappled with traces of Calvados, and smoothed it

31

on the table, preparing himself for the ordeal of his first French conversation in years. It was just like riding a bicycle, he told himself as he fed the number into his phone. Once learned, never forgotten. Even so, he had a moment of hesitation when he heard a tinny female voice, blurred by static, utter a grudging *'Allo?'* In the French manner, she made it sound as if the call had come at a particularly inconvenient moment.

The voice, which identified itself as belonging to the secretary of Maître Auzet, lost some of its chill when Max explained that he was the nephew of Henry Skinner, and the inheritor of his property. After a number of pauses to allow for consultations with what Max assumed was the *maître* himself, an appointment was made for the following afternoon. He finished his coffee and went in search of a travel agent.

'Air France to Marseille?' The girl at the desk didn't even bother to consult her computer. 'Out of luck there, sir. Air France doesn't fly direct to Marseille from London any more. I could try British Airways.'

Max had developed a deep aversion to all airlines ever since one of them had lost his suitcase and wrongly accused him of having it improperly labelled. It had been returned some days later having been run over, still bearing marks of the tyre that had flattened it. There had been neither apology nor reimbursement. If he hadn't been so impatient to get to Provence, he'd have taken the train.

As it turned out, all direct flights were full anyway, and he had to settle for a short hop to Paris and a connection that would get him into

Marseille around lunchtime. The ticket safely in his pocket, he stopped off at his bank, then spent the rest of the day dealing with domestic chores in preparation for what he was beginning to feel might be a prolonged absence from England.

That evening, packed and ready, he poured himself the last of the vodka and looked through his window at the gloom that had gathered to obscure any glimpse of a sunset. The sense of anticipation and excitement that had been with him all day intensified. Tomorrow he would see the sun and sleep in a foreign bed, perhaps his *own* foreign bed if there weren't any problems taking possession of the house. Feeling slightly lightheaded at the possibility of a new life, he changed the message on his answering machine: 'I've gone to France. Back in six months. Perhaps.'

*   *   *

Heathrow was as depressing and congested as ever, and the weather in Paris was overcast. It wasn't until the Air France *navette* was south of Saint-Etienne that the sky cleared and Max could see mile after cloudless mile of postcard-blue sky. And then, as he walked out of Marignane airport to the car rental area, there was the glorious shock of heat. Taxi drivers in short sleeves and sunglasses loitered in the shade by their cars, eyeing the girls in their summer dresses. A light breeze carried a whiff of diesel, an evocative whiff that Max always associated with France, and every wrinkle of the limestone cliffs behind the airport was crisp and well defined in the brilliant clarity of the light. Artists' light. His London clothes felt heavy and drab.

Driving in his baby Renault toward the Luberon, the scenery was at the same time fresh and yet familiar, reminding Max of the times when uncle Henry had picked him up at the start of his summer visits. He turned off the N7 toward Rognes and followed the narrow road that twisted through groves of pine and oak, warm air coming through the open window, the sound of Patrick Bruel whispering *'Parlez-moi d'amour'* trickling like honey from the radio.

Thoughts of *amour* were pushed aside by an increasingly pressing need to relieve himself. Max pulled off the road, parked next to a dusty white Peugeot, and sought the comfort of a bush. He found the Peugeot's driver already installed, and they nodded to one another, two men with the same urgent mission.

After a while, Max broke the silence. 'Nice day,' he said. 'Wonderful sunshine.'

'C'est normal.'

'Not where *I* come from.'

The man shrugged, zipped, lit a cigarette, and nodded once again before going back to his car, leaving Max to reflect on the insouciant French attitude to bodily functions. He couldn't imagine the same episode taking place on the Kingston bypass back in England, where such activities—if carried out at all—would be conducted in an atmosphere of furtive embarrassment, with many a contorted and guilty glance over the shoulder, in dread of a passing police car and subsequent arrest for indecent exposure.

He took the bridge across the Durance, once a river, now shrunk by the early-summer drought to little more than a muddy stream, and entered the *département* of the Vaucluse. The Luberon was directly ahead—a series of low, rounded humps, softened by a coating of perennially green scrub oak, a cosy, photogenic range that had been disparagingly described as designer mountains. It was true that they were pretty from a distance. But, as Max remembered from boyhood explorations, the slopes were steeper and higher than they appeared, the rocks beneath the scrub oak were as sharp as coral, and the going was hard.

Turning off the main road, he followed the signs to Saint-Pons, and wondered if it had changed much in the years since he last saw it. He guessed not. It was on the wrong side of the Luberon to be considered chic, and, unlike the high-fashion villages—Gordes, Ménerbes, Bonnieux, Roussillon, Lacoste—Saint-Pons couldn't claim the distinction of being a *village perché*, having been built on the plain and not on the top of a hill. Perhaps the lack of altitude had affected the disposition of the inhabitants, because the Saint-Ponnois were known in the region to be more friendly and hospitable than their neighbours to the north who spent their lives perched on crags, and who, several centuries ago, had spent many years at war with one another.

A long avenue of plane trees formed a graceful natural entrance to the village. They had been planted, like every other plane tree in Provence—if one believed the stories—by Napoleon, in order to provide shade for his marching armies. History didn't relate how he had ever found time for war—or, indeed, for Josephine—in the midst of all this frenzied gardening.

Max parked in the shade and strolled into the

main square. It was much as he remembered it: a café, a *tabac*, the Mairie, and a fountain. The only obvious change was a small restaurant, the tables under their umbrellas still filled with people lingering over a shady lunch. What had been there before? It must have been the village hairdresser. Max had dim memories of having his hair cut by a large, scented woman whose bosom, thrust in his ear or close up at eye level, had inflamed his adolescent imagination.

Leading off the square were narrow, shadowy streets, little wider than passageways. Max could see signs hanging over the doors of the bakery and the butcher's shop and, on one corner, another sign with peeling, sun-bleached paint and an arrow marked *Notaire* pointing up the street. He looked at his watch, and saw that he had half an hour to kill before his appointment. The sun beat down on the top of his head. He took his thirst into the café, nodding at the group of old men who had paused in their card game to inspect this stranger in a suit, and ordered a pastis.

The woman behind the bar waved an arm at the shelf behind her. '*Lequel? Ricard? Casanis? Bardouin? Janot? Pernod?*' Max shrugged, and she smiled at his confusion. '*Alors, un Ricard.*' She poured a generous shot into a glass and placed it on the pockmarked zinc bar next to a jug beaded with moisture. Max added water and went to sit at a table on the terrace, where he was joined by the café dog, who put his head on Max's knee and stared at him with large, soulful brown eyes that made him think of Charlie.

Max took his first sip of the cloudy liquid, sharp and refreshing with the bite of aniseed, and wondered why it tasted so much better here than the few times he'd had it in London. The heat, of course; it was a warm-weather drink. But it was also the surroundings. Pastis was at its best when you could hear the click of *boules* and the sound of French voices. It would taste even better, he thought, if he weren't wearing a suit and socks. He took out the *notaire*'s letter and looked at it again as Charlie's words came back to him: *a new life . . . you could be sitting on a gold mine . . . boutique wines are the coming thing.* Max raised his glass and drank to the future.

Looking across the square, he watched the last customers leaving the restaurant, flinching at the heat and adjusting their sunglasses before ambling off in a slow, post-lunch waddle to deal with the business of the afternoon. One of them, a man with a prosperous belly and the remains of a cigar, disappeared up the street leading to the *notaire*'s office. Probably the *notaire* himself, Max thought. He finished his drink and stood up. It was time to go and inherit.

The office was at the top of the street, just before the village ended and the vines began. A small house, its windows shuttered against the heat, a brass plaque on the front door. Max pressed the buzzer.

'*Oui?*' said the tinny voice, querulous at yet another unwelcome disturbance. Max announced himself, heard the latch click, and went in to meet the voice's owner.

She sat behind a large, old-fashioned desk piled with dossiers, a middle-aged woman with the tightly permed hairstyle that had been popular during her mother's youth. Attempting a smile, she

37

waved Max toward the two hard-backed chairs in the corner of the room. Maître Auzet wouldn't be long, she told him, and returned to her files.

He picked up a dog-eared, six-month-old copy of *Coucou* from the table between the two chairs. The magazine, consistent as ever in its choice of editorial revelations, featured all the usual suspects: Stephanie of Monaco, the latest temporary Hollywood legend, Jean-Paul Belmondo's son, Prince William, Johnny Hallyday. In or out of love, it made no difference—they all led the kind of lives that were guaranteed to fascinate people in waiting rooms.

Max was distracted from an exclusive interview with Brazil's top cosmetic surgeon by the sound of an angry raised voice coming from behind the closed door of what he assumed was Maître Auzet's office. There was a final explosive grunt, the door was flung open, and a burly man with the roasted complexion of a farmworker stamped out of the office, giving Max a sidelong glare as he left. The secretary didn't bother to look up from her papers. The man's face seemed vaguely, very vaguely, familiar, but Max couldn't place it. He went back to the cosmetic surgeon, who had apparently achieved an exciting breakthrough in buttock lifting.

Some moments later, there was the click of heels on the tiled floor, and Maître Auzet appeared, smiling a welcome. 'Monsieur Skinner? I'm delighted to meet you. Would you like to come into the office?'

Max needed a moment to recover from his surprise before getting up and shaking the proffered hand. Maître Auzet was, despite the official masculine title, a young woman: slim and olive-skinned, with the deep, burnished henna-red hair that one only seems to see in France. She was wearing a jacket and skirt that wouldn't have been out of place in Paris, and her elegant legs ended in an equally elegant pair of high heels.

'Monsieur Skinner?' She seemed amused by his evident surprise. 'Is something wrong?'

Max shook his head, and muttered something about never having seen his English solicitor, Mr. Chapman, in high heels before following her into her office. In contrast to the secretary's sparse and rather dingy surroundings, the office of Maître Auzet was not unlike her, sleek and modern, beige and dark brown. The desk was bare except for a laptop, a notepad, a vase of peonies, and a crystal tumbler filled with a bouquet of Montblanc pens.

'Could I ask you for some identification?' She smiled again. 'Just a formality.' Max gave her his passport. She put on a pair of reading glasses before comparing the photograph with the real thing sitting opposite her, looking from one to the other, shaking her head. 'Never very flattering, are they? I wonder why that is.' She slid the passport back across the desk and, reaching into a drawer, took out a thick file and a bunch of large, old-fashioned keys tied together with binding twine.

She started to go through the contents of the file, reading out various passages from different documents. Max half-listened, his thoughts far from legal technicalities as he took advantage of her lowered head to study her: the merest, most discreet hint of cleavage where her silk blouse had fallen away from her body as she bent forward; the skin with its rich Mediterranean glow; that

39

wonderful hair; delicate hands, shining, unpainted nails, and, he noticed, no wedding band. Maybe his luck really was changing. He tried to think of a convincing excuse for another, less businesslike meeting.

'. . . and so you don't have to worry about the property taxes. They won't be due until November.' She closed the file, and pushed it across the desk with the keys. '*Voilà.*'

She turned to the pad on which she'd made some notes.

'Unfortunately'—her mouth formed a pout, as if to emphasize the burdens of a *notaire*'s life—'matters of succession are never completely without a few loose ends.' She looked at Max over the top of her glasses and tilted her head prettily. 'You probably saw one of them leaving the office while you were waiting.'

Max thought back to the scowling peasant. 'He didn't seem too happy. Who is he?'

'Claude Roussel. He used to work for your uncle.'

Now he remembered. That was Russell, an older Russell made thicker and balder and more weather-beaten by the passage of the years, but certainly the same man he'd met once or twice at the house. 'What's he upset about?'

Maître Auzet glanced at the wafer of gold on her wrist. 'It's a little complicated to explain, and I don't really have time today . . .'

Max held up a hand. 'I've just had a wonderful idea.'

She looked at him, half-smiling.

'Tomorrow. Lunch. Even *notaires* eat lunch, don't they?'

40

She took off her glasses. There was a moment's hesitation and a twitch of one shoulder. 'Yes,' she said, '*notaires* eat lunch.'

Max stood up and inclined his head in an abbreviated bow. 'Until tomorrow, then.' He turned to leave.

'Monsieur Skinner?' Her smile had broadened. 'Don't forget your keys.'

Max gathered up the keys and the bulky file, stopping at the secretary's desk on his way out. 'I hope you have a truly splendid evening, madame. Champagne and dancing.'

The woman looked up at him and nodded. 'Of course, monsieur.' She watched him go through the front door, whistling as he went. The younger men were often like that after meeting Maître Auzet for the first time.

Four

Max drove out of the village toward the house, finding memories around every bend. The ditches on either side of the road were still as deep and overgrown as they had been when Uncle Henry used to send him down to the baker's every morning on a dilapidated bicycle, with the promise of a five-franc reward if the croissants were still warm by the time he got back. He used to race against himself, legs pumping furiously to break his previous best time and add to the collection of five-franc pieces that he kept in an old mustard pot beside his bed. The pot, empty at the beginning of the holidays, would be full and wonderfully heavy by the end. It had been Max's first experience of feeling rich.

He pulled up in front of the stone pillars, crumbling and stained almost black by two centuries of weather, that marked the entrance to the dirt road leading down to the house. The name of the property could just be made out etched into the stone: Le Griffon, the letters soft and fuzzy with lichen after their prolonged battle against the elements.

Max drove on, through rows of well-kept vines, and parked under the plane tree—a huge tree, pre-Napoleonic—that shaded the long south wall of the *bastide*. In contrast to the clipped and orderly vines, the garden was in a state of some neglect, as indeed was the outside of the house. It made Max think of a distinguished grande dame whose makeup was starting to crack. The handsome façade needed repointing, the closed shutters hadn't seen fresh paint for years, the dark green varnish on the front door was buckled and peeling. In the courtyard, vigorous weeds had pushed through the gravel, and the water in the square stone *bassin* made a viscous, opaque setting for a group of struggling water lilies. Pigeons squabbled in the branches of the tree.

A little sad. And yet, you could see what the house had been, and what it could very easily be again. Max walked around to the two open-fronted barns attached to one side of the house, where he remembered Uncle Henry had kept his dented black Citroën DS. That had gone, leaving only a selection of rusting agricultural implements and two bicycles—old even when Max first saw them—with the red rubber tyres that he had found

42

so exotic.

Returning to the front door, he matched one of the keys to the keyhole, but failed several times to make it turn. Then he remembered that, in typically perverse French fashion, the lock worked in the opposite direction from Anglo-Saxon locks. He shook his head as he pushed open the door. They never made it easy for foreigners, the French. Even the simple things were complicated.

Once inside, he could make out the broad steps of a stone staircase rising up into the shuttered gloom. On either side of the entrance hall, double doors led to the main rooms of the ground floor, the classic *bastide* layout. He let himself into the cavernous kitchen, opening the shutters so that the late-afternoon sunlight flooded in to illuminate the motes of dust floating in the still air. A massive cast-iron range and a bath-sized sink took up one entire wall, glass-fronted storage cabinets another; the big wooden plank table was where it had always been, in the centre of the room. Running his fingers across the table's surface, he found the spot where he had carved his initials. Nothing had changed.

The tall, rectangular windows offered a view to the lower slopes of the Luberon. Between the house and the mountain were more vines, which, as Max could see, were being patrolled by the eternal figure on a tractor, towing a machine that was spraying a blue fog of pesticide over the neat green rows. That must be Roussel, probably still in the foul mood he had displayed in the *notaire*'s office. Max decided that their first meeting could wait until he'd calmed down.

*　　　*　　　*

Out in the vines, Roussel, with a peasant's eye for any change in the landscape, however small, had noticed the opening of the shutters and was on his cell phone, announcing the news to his wife, Ludivine.

'He has arrived, the Englishman. He is in the house now. No, I haven't met him, but I saw him in Auzet's office. He's young.' Roussel broke off while he negotiated his turn at the end of a row of vines. 'Is he *sympa*? How do I know if he's *sympa*? One is never sure with the English.' He looked over at the house as he put the phone back in his pocket, and sighed. Ah, the English. Will they ever stop invading France? He heard a yelp, and glanced at the vines behind him. *Merde*. His dog, who had been following the tractor, had been caught by an errant puff of *bouillie bordelaise*, and now had a pale blue head, which added to his already eccentric appearance.

*　　　*　　　*

Max continued to explore, throwing open all the shutters, peering into armoires and drawers, getting back a sense of the house's geography while he compared the present with the past. It was, if anything, bigger than he remembered. Even Charlie would have to stretch his estate agent's vocabulary to do justice to the six bedrooms, the library, the dining room, the immense living room, the kitchen, the back kitchen, the double pantry, the scullery, the tack room—and surely there was a cellar somewhere at the far end of the house. Max

44

made his way through the living room, footsteps echoing on the stone floor, and paused to look at a group of photographs that had been arranged on the top of an elderly, dust-coated piano. His eye was caught by a faded black-and-white image of a man and a boy, squinting into the sun: Uncle Henry and his young nephew, each holding an old wooden tennis racket.

He moved on, through a small door beside the fireplace and down the short flight of steps that led to the cellar. Unlocking the door, he pushed it open, feeling a current of cooler air on his face as he fumbled for the light switch.

The single bare bulb lit a narrow, practical room. The floor was gravel, the ceiling low, the storage bins constructed of brick. The air smelled of must and damp cobwebs. A vintage enamel thermometer hanging on one wall listed temperatures from 50 degrees Centigrade to minus 15, with cryptic comments by the side of each figure: 50, for instance, was a nice day in Senegal; 35 was apparently a temperature that encouraged bees to swarm; minus 10 was cold enough to freeze rivers, and minus 15 was marked by a single chilly date, 1859. The cellar temperature stood at 12 degrees Centigrade, and Max remembered Uncle Henry telling him that it never varied by more than two degrees, no matter what the weather did outside. An equable temperature, he used to say, is the secret of a healthy, contented wine.

Max examined the bottles. There was a scattering of regional reds and whites—some Châteauneuf-du-Pape, a few cases of Rasteau and Cassis, but the great majority was the wine of the property, decorated with the florid blue and gold

45

label that Uncle Henry had designed himself. Max chose a bottle of Le Griffon 1999, and took it over to the upended barrel that served as a cellar table, where there was a corkscrew and a none-too-clean glass. Shaking the glass to dislodge the remains of a dead earwig, Max wiped it with his handkerchief before opening the bottle. He poured, then held the glass up to the light, allowing himself to have an optimistic moment contemplating the fortunes to be made from boutique wines.

He sniffed. He gargled. He shuddered, and immediately spat before rubbing his teeth with a finger to remove what felt like a thick coating of tannin. The wine was one step up from vinegar, enough to pucker the liver. Awful.

Maybe it was just an unfortunate choice of bottle. Max selected another one, going through the same procedure to arrive at the same undrinkable result. Not quite the gold mine that Charlie had in mind. Max decided to call and tell him the worst.

'I'm in the cellar, and I've just tasted the wine.'

'And?'

'Young, of course.'

'Of course. But promising?'

'Could be. Lacks finesse. Needs some discipline, a firm hand, a smack on the bottom.' He stopped, unable to keep it up. 'Actually, Charlie, it tastes likes a gendarme's socks. I couldn't even swallow it. That bad.'

'Really?' Charlie sounded more interested than discouraged. 'Well, that could be the fault of the maker rather than the grapes. It often is, you know. What we need is an oenologist.'

'We do?'

'A wine expert. I've been reading about them. They're magicians, some of those boys. They fiddle about with the blending of grapes from different parts of the vineyard until they get the right balance. It's like a recipe, really, except that it's for wine instead of food. They can't turn plonk into Pétrus, obviously, but they can make a huge difference. Ask around. There must be a few not far from you. Anyway, how's the château? No, don't tell me. I'll pop down for a couple of days when I can get away. Line up the ladies.'

Max was pensive as he left the cellar. Where would he find a wine magician? It was not the kind of listing you'd see in the Yellow Pages. Perhaps Maître Auzet would know. He'd ask her when they met for lunch.

At the thought of food, his stomach reminded him that he hadn't eaten since his rubber airline breakfast that morning. He took his suitcases up to the rather grand bedroom—large fireplace, several bad oil paintings—that had been Uncle Henry's, and after changing out of his suit, he went down to the village for an early dinner.

It was happy hour in Saint-Pons. Leather-faced men dusty from the fields were lined up at the bar of the café, loud and talkative, their accents as thick as the smoke from their cigarettes. Max ordered a Ricard and found a seat in the corner, feeling pale and foreign. Through the open door of the café he could see a game of *boules* in progress, the players moving slowly and noisily from one end of the court to the other. The evening sun slanted across the square, painting the stone houses with a coat of honey-coloured light, and the café jukebox was having an Aznavour evening. Max found it hard to believe he'd been staring out of his window at a grey London sky only twenty-four hours before. This could be a different planet. And, he had to admit, a much more pleasant planet. The only blots on an otherwise sunny landscape were the disappointing quality of the wine and the prickly disposition of Monsieur Roussel.

A few kilometres away, Roussel and his disposition were engaged in a heated discussion over dinner with Madame Roussel, an admirable woman who had somehow managed to retain her optimism despite many years of marriage to a resolute pessimist.

'. . . it cannot be anything but trouble,' Roussel was saying. 'Change is always bad, and he is young. He will want to take out the vines and make *un golf* . . .'

'More couscous? Or are you ready for the cheese?'

Roussel held out his plate for another ladle of the spicy stew without interrupting his gloomy predictions '. . . or maybe he will turn the house into one of those hotels . . .'

'What hotels?'

'You know, those little chichi places with old furniture, and all the staff in waistcoats. Or maybe . . .'

'*Eh beh oui!* A nuclear power station, no doubt. Clo-Clo, how can you say such things? You haven't even met him. He might have more money than the old man to spend on the vines. He might even consider selling the vineyard to us.' Madame Roussel leaned forward to wipe a spot of gravy from her husband's chin. 'In any case, the only way to find out is to go and speak to him, *non*?'

48

Roussel's grunt could have been taken as yes or no. Madame persisted.

'You know I'm right, Clo-Clo. But for heaven's sake don't go with a face like a boot. Go with a smile. Go with a bottle. And while you're there, don't forget to tell him about my sister.'

Roussel rolled his eyes and reached for the cheese. 'How could one ever forget your sister?'

* * *

Max finished his drink and left the café, stopping to watch the *boules* game. Uncle Henry had once explained the niceties of the *point* and the *tir*, the *raspaille* and the *sautée*—funny how the words came back to him without any recollection of their meaning—and had demonstrated the correct way to stand and throw one sunny evening on the gravel in front of the house. But the most important asset for any player, he used to say, was a talent for dispute. Argument was vital to the proper conduct and enjoyment of the game.

One of the players was about to throw. Feet together, knees bent, brow furrowed in concentration, he pitched his *boule* in a long and deadly arc that knocked aside two other *boules* before coming to rest within a hairbreadth of the small wooden target ball, the *cochonnet*. It looked to Max like a clear winner, but it was nothing of the sort; it was merely the signal for a heated debate between the two teams. The distance in millimetres and fractions of millimetres between *boule* and *cochonnet* had to be measured, then measured again, then challenged, which of course required yet another measurement. Voices were raised,

49

shoulders were shrugged, arms spread wide in disbelief. There seemed to be no immediate prospect of the game continuing. Max left them to it and walked across the square to the restaurant.

Chez Fanny, with its tiled floor, cane chairs, paper tablecloths and napkins, and posters of old Marcel Pagnol films on the wall, was small and unpretentious. But the restaurant possessed two secret weapons: an old chef who had learned his trade at l'Ami Louis in Paris, and who cooked accordingly; and Fanny herself, who provided the *ambiance*, that intangible ingredient vital to any restaurant's continuing success.

It has been said that you can't eat atmosphere, which is true, and that the cooking is all that counts, which isn't. Eating is, or should be, a comforting experience, and one cannot be comforted eating in chilly, impersonal surroundings, a fact that was very well understood by Fanny. She made her customers—all of them, not just the men—feel loved. She kissed them when they came in and again when they left. She laughed at their jokes. She was incapable of having a conversation without physical contact—a touch on the arm, a squeeze of the shoulder, a pat on the cheek. She noticed everything, forgot nothing, and appeared to like everyone.

She had, of course, heard about the new owner of the big house. Anyone in Saint-Pons with ears had heard about him, either from the official village information service, the butcher's wife, or from the wise men of the café. She watched Max walking across the square and saw that he was heading for the restaurant. She turned to a mirror, making minute adjustments to her hair and *décolleté* before stepping outside.

Max had started to study the framed menu that was nailed to the trunk of a plane tree.

'*Bonsoir*, monsieur.'

Max looked up. 'Hi. Oh, sorry. *Bonsoir*, madame.'

'Mademoiselle.'

'Of course. Excuse me.' For a few seconds they looked at one another in silence, both smiling. An observer would have guessed that they liked what they saw. 'Am I too early?'

No, monsieur wasn't too early. He had come just before the rush. Fanny placed him at a table on the small terrace, brought him a glass of wine and a saucer of sleek black olives, and left him with the menu. It was short, but filled with the kind of dishes Max liked: a choice of deep-fried sliced zucchini, vegetable terrine or a pâté to start; *bavette aux échalotes*, roasted cod, or *brochette de poulet* as a main course; cheeses, and those two reliable old standbys, *tarte aux pommes* and *crème brûlée*, for dessert. Simple food of the kind that attracted customers rather than Michelin stars.

Max made his choice and settled back in his chair, his feelings a mixture of contentment and anticipation as he watched Fanny embracing a group of four that had just arrived. Somewhere in her family, he thought, there must have been some North African blood. It would explain her coffee-coloured skin, her mop of black curls, and her dark eyes. She was wearing a sleeveless, close-fitting top that accentuated the slender column of her neck and the curve of a jaunty bosom. From the waist down, she was wearing jeans and espadrilles. Max wondered if her legs were as long and well shaped

51

as the rest of her.

She caught him looking at her, and came over to his table, smiling. *'Alors, vous avez choisi?'* She sat down opposite him, pad and pencil at the ready, and leaned forward to take his order.

With some difficulty, Max kept his eyes on the menu, to prevent them from their natural inclination to stray, and ordered zucchini, the steak, and a carafe of red wine.

Fanny noted down the order. 'Is there anything else you'd like?'

Max looked at her for a long moment, his eyebrows raised and his imagination churning.

'Pommes frites? Gratin? Salade?'

Later, sitting over a Calvados and a second cup of coffee, Max reviewed the first day of his new life. With the optimism induced by a good dinner and the soft warmth of the evening breeze, he could see that his initial disappointment over the wine was nothing. That, according to Charlie, could be fixed; as for Roussel, he would probably require some diplomatic handling, and Max would have to tread gently. But the other discoveries of the day were all encouraging—a potentially wonderful house, a delightful village, and two of the prettiest women he'd met for months. And perhaps more important, there were the first stirrings of a sense that he could happily fit in down here in Provence. Another of Uncle Henry's nuggets of advice to the young came drifting back into his mind from years ago: *There is nowhere else in the world where you can keep busy doing so little and enjoying it so much. One day you'll understand.*

He paid the bill and overtipped. The restaurant was still busy, but Fanny found time to come over to wish him good night with a kiss on each cheek. She smelled like every young man's dream.

'*A bientôt?*' she said.

Max smiled and nodded. 'Try to keep me away.'

Five

God's alarm clock, the sun, came streaming through the bedroom window and woke Max after the best night's sleep he'd had in years, even though sleep had not come instantly. In London, there had always been the lullaby of distant traffic, and a glow in the sky from the city's lights. In the country, there was total silence, and the darkness was thick and absolute. It would take some getting used to. Now, half-conscious and at first not sure where he was, he opened his eyes and looked up at the plaster and beam ceiling. Three pigeons were conducting an interminable conversation on the window ledge. The air was already warm. Glancing at his watch, he could hardly believe he'd slept so late. He decided to celebrate his first morning in Provence with a run in the sun.

Although many foreign habits, such as tennis, were now familiar to the inhabitants of Saint-Pons, the sight of a runner was still enough to cause a flicker of interest among the men who spent their lives in the vines. A small group of them, trimming off overgrown shoots, paused to watch as Max ran by. To them, voluntary physical exercise in the midmorning heat was an incomprehensible form of self-torture. They shook their heads and bent their backs and resumed their trimming.

It seemed to Max that he was running more easily than he had ever done in Hyde Park; probably, he thought, because he was breathing sweet air instead of the fumes from a million exhaust pipes. He lengthened his stride, feeling the sweat run down his chest, and moved onto the shoulder of the road as he heard a car coming up behind him.

The car slowed down to keep pace with him. Glancing over, he saw Fanny's curly head and wide smile. She overtook him, then stopped and pushed open the passenger door.

'*Mais vous êtes fou,*' she said, and cocked an approving eye at his legs. 'Come. Let me take you into the village. You look as if you need a beer.'

Max thanked her but shook his head, not without some reluctance. 'This is what I do to get rid of the Calvados. You know what the English are like. We love to suffer.'

Fanny considered this national peculiarity for a moment, then shrugged and drove off, watching the running figure grow smaller in the rearview mirror. What an odd lot they were, English men; uncomfortable with women, most of them. But that was hardly surprising when one considered their education. The public school system had once been explained to her—all boys together, cold baths, and not a female in sight. What a way to start your life. She wondered if Max would settle in his uncle's house, and found herself hoping he would. The selection of unattached young men in Saint-Pons was severely limited.

After the third mile, Max was beginning to regret that he'd turned down her offer. The sun seemed to be focused on the top of his head, and the air was still, with no breeze to relieve the heat. By the time he got back to the house he was melting, his shorts and T-shirt black with sweat, his legs like jelly as he climbed the stairs to the bathroom.

The shower was a classic example of late-twentieth-century French plumbing, a monument to inconvenience, no more than a vestigial afterthought attached to the bath taps by a rubber umbilical cord. It was a hand-held model, thus leaving only one hand free for the soap and its application to various parts of the body. To work up a satisfactory two-handed lather, the shower had to be placed, writhing and squirting, in the bottom of the bath, and then retrieved for the rinsing process, one body part at a time. In London, it had been a simple matter of standing under a torrent; here, it was an exercise that would tax the ingenuity of a contortionist.

Max stepped out gingerly onto the flooded tile floor and dripped dry while he was shaving. Among the BandAids and aspirin in the medicine cabinet above the basin, he found a small flask, still half-full of Uncle Henry's eau de cologne. It was a relic from the old Turkish baths in Mayfair, with a label like an ornate banknote and a scent that made Max think of silk dressing gowns. He splashed some on, combed his hair, and went to choose something suitable to wear for lunch with Maître Auzet.

She had suggested, for the sake of discretion, a restaurant in the countryside, a few miles away from the prying eyes and wagging tongues of Saint-Pons. Max found it without difficulty, rural France often being more generously supplied with restaurant signs than road signs, and arrived a few

55

minutes early.

The Auberge des Grives was a two-storey building in the concrete blockhouse style of architecture, rescued from ugliness by a magnificent run of wisteria that stretched the length of a long terrace. Groups of local businessmen and one or two middle-aged couples were murmuring over their menus. There was no sign of Maître Auzet, although, as the waiter told Max, she had reserved her usual table overlooking the sweep of vines to the south.

Max ordered a *kir*, which was delivered with a dish of radishes and some sea salt, together with the menus and the wine list—a tome bound in tooled leather, bulging with expensive bottles. Not surprisingly, Max failed to find any mention of the wine from Le Griffon. He called the waiter over.

'I was told the other day about a local red. I think it's called Le Griffon,' he said.

The waiter looked impassive. *'Ah bon?'*

'What do you think of it? Any good?'

The waiter inclined his upper body toward Max and lowered his voice. *'Entre nous*, monsieur'—he applied his thumb and index finger delicately to the end of his nose—*'pipi de chat.'* He paused to allow this to sink in. 'May I recommend something more appropriate? In the summer, Maître Auzet is partial to the rosé of La Figuière, from the Var, pale and dry.'

'What a good idea,' said Max. 'It was on the tip of my tongue.'

The arrival of Maître Auzet was marked by a flurry of deference from the waiter, who escorted her to the table and eased her into her chair. She was wearing another of her suits, black and severe,

56

and carried an anorexic briefcase. She had clearly decided that this was to be a strictly business lunch.

'*Bonjour*, Monsieur Skinner . . .'

Max held up his hand. 'Please. Call me Max. And I can't possibly keep calling you *maître*. It makes me think of some old man with a white wig and false teeth.'

She smiled, took a radish from the dish, and dipped it in the salt. 'Nathalie,' she said, 'and they're my own teeth.' She bit into the radish, a pink tongue darting out to lick a grain of salt from her lower lip. 'So tell me. You found everything in order at the house? Oh, before I forget . . .' She opened her briefcase and took out a folder. 'A few more bills—house insurance, some work the electrician did, the quarterly account from the *Cave Co-opérative*.' She slid the folder across the table. '*Voilà*. That's all. No more disagreeable surprises, I promise you.'

Before Max could reply, the waiter reappeared with an ice bucket and the wine. With the first glasses poured, a light meal of salad and fillets of *rouget* ordered, and the social niceties out of the way, Nathalie began to describe the situation with Roussel and the vines.

In Provence, she explained, as in most other wine-producing regions, there was an arrangement known as *métayage*. Roussel and Max's uncle had adopted this system many years ago, whereby Roussel did the work on the vines, Uncle Henry paid for the cost of upkeep, and the two of them shared the wine. With Uncle Henry's death, the change of proprietor had made Roussel anxious. He wanted the arrangement to continue, and was worried that Max might be thinking of ending it.

57

Max asked if that were technically possible, and Nathalie admitted that it was. But, she said, it would be difficult and perhaps legally complicated to change things. As legal people love to do, she then cited a precedent—a local precedent, in fact. The owners of a nearby vineyard had worked with the same family of peasants for nearly two hundred years. A few generations ago, after a dispute, the owners tried to cancel the arrangement. The peasants resisted. After a prolonged and bitter argument, the peasants won the right to continue working the land, which they still did. But the two families hadn't spoken to one another since 1923.

Max finished a mouthful of *rouget* and shook his head. 'Unbelievable. Is that really true?'

'Of course. There are hundreds of histories like that, feuds over land and water, even within the same family. Brothers against brothers, fathers against sons. It's good, the fish, no?'

'Terrific. But tell me something. I tasted some of the wine—Le Griffon—at the house last night. It was undrinkable. And your friend the waiter here thinks it's terrible.' If he was expecting any sympathy from Nathalie, he was disappointed.

Nothing but a shrug. *'Dommage.* But this isn't the Médoc.'

'But if the wine is that bad, it can't be very profitable to sell, can it?'

'I'm a *notaire.* What do I know about selling wine?'

Probably a lot more than I do, Max thought. 'What I'd really like to know is this: if the wine is as bad as it seems to be, why is Roussel so anxious to carry on making it?'

Nathalie wiped some sauce from her plate with a

58

piece of bread. 'It's his habit. It's what he's been doing for twenty-five years, and he's comfortable doing it.' She leaned forward. 'What you must understand is that people down here don't like change. It upsets them.'

Max raised his hands in surrender. 'Fine. I've got no objection if he wants to go on working the vines. But what I would like is some decent wine at the end of it. That's reasonable, isn't it?' He paused, trying to remember the word Charlie had used. 'Actually, what I want to do is get someone to come in and take a look at the vines. An *oenologiste*.'

The word was hardly out of his mouth before Nathalie was wagging a finger at him, a gesture the French cannot resist before correcting a foreigner who commits a hiccup in their language. '*Oenologue*.'

'Exactly. A wine doctor. There must be quite a few around here.'

There was a moment's silence while Nathalie considered the wine in her glass, the hint of a frown on her forehead. 'I don't know,' she said. 'Roussel might feel . . . how shall I say . . . threatened? Not trusted? I'm sure he's like all the rest of them. They don't like outside interference. It's a rather sensitive situation. It always is where vines are concerned.' She shook her head at the delicacy of it all.

Max practised his shrug. 'Look. He stands to benefit as much as I do if we improve the wine. You don't have to be a genius to see that. What has he got to lose? Anyway, I've made up my mind. That's what I'm going to do.'

Nathalie was saved from having to give an immediate reply by the arrival of the waiter to clear away their plates and sing the praises of the cheese board in general and the Banon in particular, a goat cheese that he informed them, kissing the tips of his fingers, had just been awarded Appellation Controlée status. The interruption seemed to help Nathalie come to a decision. '*Bon*,' she said. 'If you're sure that's what you want to do, I can ask some friends. They might be able to help you find someone who can do it without stepping on any toes.'

'You're a princess.' Max leaned back, feeling that he had won a minor victory. 'You wouldn't like to help me with another problem, would you?'

The frown had disappeared, and Nathalie was smiling. 'That depends.'

'I found all this furniture in the attic. Old stuff, but one or two pieces might be worth selling, and I could do with some cash to take care of the bills. You wouldn't happen to know an honest antique dealer, would you?'

For the first time since she'd sat down, Nathalie laughed. 'Of course,' she said, 'and I believe in Father Christmas, too.'

'I thought so,' said Max. 'You look the type.' He poured the last of the wine. 'So they're all villains, are they?'

Nathalie's lips formed a dismissive pout, an answer that needed no words. 'What you should do,' she said, 'is spend one Sunday at Isle-sur-Sorgue. You'll find more dealers there than anywhere except Paris. See if you like the look of any of them.' At this, Max sucked in a deep breath and shook his head. Nathalie looked puzzled. 'What's the matter?'

'Well,' he said, 'look at me. I'm naive, innocent,

60

and trusting. And I'm a foreigner, alone in a strange land. Those guys would have the shirt off my back in five minutes. I couldn't possibly go without some local protection, someone who knows the ropes.'

Nathalie nodded, as if she couldn't see what was coming. 'Do you have anyone in mind?'

'That's my other problem. I don't know anyone except you.'

'So what are you going to do?'

'I'm hoping that my enormous charm and the promise of a good lunch will be enough to persuade you to come with me. *Notaires* don't work on Sunday, do they?'

Nathalie shook her head. '*Notaires* don't work on Sunday. *Notaires* do occasionally have lunch. In many ways, *notaires* are very similar to people. Or hadn't you noticed?'

Max winced. 'Let me start again. I'd be the happiest man in Provence if you would care to join me on Sunday. That is, if you're free.'

Nathalie put on her sunglasses to signal that lunch was over and it was time to go. 'As it happens,' she said, 'I am.'

Driving back from the restaurant, Max twice caught himself nearly falling asleep at the wheel. The road in front of him had a hypnotic shimmer in the heat, the temperature inside the car was in the nineties, and by the time he'd reached the house the lunchtime wine was whispering to him, telling him to go straight upstairs, lie down, and close his eyes.

His instinctive reaction was to resist, remembering with a smile the oft-repeated words of Mr. Farnell, his history master at school. The

61

siesta, according to Farnell, was one of those pernicious, self-indulgent habits, typical of foreigners, that had sapped the will and contributed to the downfall of entire civilizations. This had enabled the British, who never slept after lunch, to move in and accumulate their empire. QED.

But the interior of the house was delightfully cool, and the endless scratchy serenade of the *cigales* was delightfully soothing. Max went to the library and picked a book from the shelves. He would read for half an hour before attacking the rest of the afternoon. He settled into one of the old leather club chairs and opened the book, a threadbare copy of E. I. Robson's *A Wayfarer in Provence*, first published in 1926. On the very first page, Max was fascinated to discover that Provence had been invaded by 'cruel ravishers'. Alas, despite this promising beginning, he never reached page two.

He was jolted awake by what he thought at first was thunder, then realized it was merely someone trying to break down the front door. Shaking his head to clear away the cobwebs of sleep, he pulled open the door to find, staring at him with undisguised curiosity, a man with a deep red face and a dog with a pale blue head.

Six

The two men stood examining one another for a moment before Roussel put on the smile he'd been practising on the way over and stuck out a meaty

62

paw.

'Roussel, Claude.'

'Skinner, Max.'

Roussel pointed downward with a jerk of his chin. 'My dog, Tonto.'

'Ah. Roussel, Tonto.' Max bent down and patted him, raising a puff of blue dust. 'Is he always this colour? Most unusual. I've never seen a blue terrier before.'

'I was spraying the vines, the wind changed . . .' Roussel shrugged as Tonto slipped past Max and into the kitchen.

'Please,' said Max. 'Come in.' Roussel took off his flat cap and followed Max through the door.

They reached the kitchen in time to see Tonto, in the way of small and self-assured dogs, christening a leg of the kitchen table. Roussel shouted at him and apologized profusely, but then added: 'It's a sure sign he likes you.'

Max put down an old newspaper to blot up the puddle. 'What does he do if he doesn't like you?'

Roussel's smile barely faltered. 'Oho,' he said, *'le sens de l'humour anglais*. My tailor is rich, eh?'

Max had never understood how that particular phrase had become embedded in the French language, nor why the French seemed to find it so amusing, but he smiled dutifully. There was something about Roussel that he warmed to; besides, the man was so obviously doing his best to be agreeable.

And even helpful. 'Now, as to the plumbing,' Roussel was saying, 'there can sometimes be complications when the level in the well is low. The pump is old, and needs encouragement. Also, there is the *histoire* of the septic tank, which can be

63

capricious when the mistral blows.' He lowered his head, peering up at Max from beneath an overgrown tangle of sun-bleached eyebrows, and tapping his nose. The *histoire* was clearly not a pleasant one.

'These things I attended to for your uncle Skinner during his last few years, when his sight was failing.' Roussel assumed a pious expression and crossed himself at the mention of the old man's name. '*Un vrai* gentleman. We became very close, you know. Almost like father and son.'

'I'm happy that you were here to take care of him,' said Max, shaking his left leg free from Tonto's amorous clasp.

'*Beh oui*. Almost like father and son.' Emerging from his memories, Roussel bent down and ran a finger across the surface of the table. He seemed surprised at the result, as though dust were a rarity in empty, uncared-for houses. '*Putain*,' he said. 'Look at that. This place could do with a good *femme de ménage* to give it a spring-cleaning.'

Roussel displayed the dusty fingertip for inspection, and then clapped a hand to his forehead. 'But of course! Madame Passepartout, the sister of my wife.' He slapped his palm on the table for emphasis, displacing more dust.

Max and Tonto looked at him, both heads cocked.

'A veritable tornado in the house. Not a speck escapes her, she is *maniaque* about her work. She sees dirt, she destroys it. *Tak zak!*'

'Sounds like the answer to a young man's prayer. But I imagine she's . . .'

'*Mais non!* She is resting between engagements at the moment. She could start tomorrow.' And not a moment too soon as far as I'm concerned, thought Roussel. Fond as he was of his sister-in-law, she could be something of a trial when at a loose end, always at his house scrubbing anything that didn't move, rearranging the furniture, polishing and titivating. He always had the feeling that she wanted to dust him.

Max could see that there was to be no denying Madame Passepartout if he wanted to establish a good relationship with Roussel. He nodded his agreement. 'That would be great. Just what I need.'

Roussel beamed, a man who had successfully completed a ticklish negotiation. Madame his wife would be delighted. 'We must celebrate our meeting,' he said, heading out of the kitchen. 'Wait here.'

Tonto resumed his courtship of Max's leg. What was it about small dogs that made them leg-molesters? Was there a link, however unlikely and distant, between that and the preference that very short men have for very tall women? Or perhaps the enthusiasm was because Tonto had never been exposed to a young English leg before. Max shook him free for a second time and gave him the end of a baguette to distract him.

When Roussel returned, he was carrying a bottle that he presented to Max. '*Marc de Provence,*' he said. 'I made it myself.'

The bottle was unlabelled, and contained a pale brown liquid that had a thick, oily look about it. Max hoped it travelled well. He filled two glasses, and the two men toasted one another.

Wiping his watering eyes after the first explosive swallow, Max was reminded of the equally foul-tasting wine in the cellar. 'Tell me,' he asked

65

Roussel, 'what do you think of our wine, Le Griffon?'

Roussel wiped the back of his hand across his mouth to remove any residue of *marc* before it could cause blisters to form on his lips. *'Une triste histoire,'* he said. 'I have to admit that the wine is perhaps a little naive, a little unfinished around the edges.' He paused, shook his head, and smiled. 'No, I must be honest. It's worse than that. Unkind people have called it *jus de chaussette.* At any rate, it leaves something to be desired.' He took another nip of *marc,* and sighed. 'It is not for lack of care. Take a look at the vines. Not a weed to be seen. Not a sign of *oïdium*—you know, the vine mildew. I cherish those vines as if they were my children. No, it's not lack of care that's the problem.' He raised his hand, rubbing the tips of his first two fingers against his thumb. 'It's lack of money. Many of the vines are old and tired. They should have been replaced years ago, but your uncle Skinner was not in a position to invest. *Hélas*, the wine has suffered.' He stared into his glass, shaking his head. 'I can't work miracles. I can't make an omelette if I have no eggs.'

Max overcame his faint surprise at the sudden evocation of an omelette in the vineyard, and turned the conversation back to grapes. 'Well, you'll be pleased to hear I'm getting someone in to look at the vines, the grapes, everything. An *oenologue.'*

Roussel's head snapped up from its contemplation of the glass. 'What for?'

Max made calming motions with his hands, stroking the air in front of him. 'Now, this is no criticism of you, none at all. You've done all you can. But if we get some professional advice about making improvements, I'm sure I can get hold of the money to pay for them. Then we'll make better wine, and that will be good for both of us. Makes sense, doesn't it?'

From Roussel's expression, he was far from convinced as he reached for the bottle of *marc*.

'I talked to Maître Auzet about it. She thinks it's a great idea,' Max said. 'In fact, she's going to find somebody. She told me she has friends in the wine business.'

That seemed to meet with Roussel's approval. A swig of *marc* found its target, and he grunted like a boxer taking a punch to the stomach. 'Maybe it's not a bad idea. You took me by surprise, *c'est tout.*' He looked over at Max, his face the colour of old ochre, with a strip of white across the part of his forehead normally covered by his cap. 'So you want to keep the vines. That's good. Can you cook?'

Max shook his head. 'Eggs and bacon, the English breakfast. That's about it.'

'You must come to the house next week for dinner. My wife makes a *civet* of wild boar—a *civet* made in the correct fashion, with blood and red wine. Not like English food.' He grinned as he put his cap on. 'You know what they say? The English murder their meat twice: once when they shoot it and once when they cook it. *Drôle, n'est-ce pas?*'

'Very comical,' said Max. 'Almost as funny as my tailor is rich.'

This set Roussel off, and his shoulders were still quaking with laughter when Max showed him out. Both men felt that it had been an unexpectedly pleasant start to their relationship.

Roussel waited until he was some distance from

the house before making the call. 'He says he's going to bring in an *oenologue*, someone that you're finding. Is that true?'

Nathalie Auzet looked at her watch, her fingers tapping the desk. The one day she was hoping to leave the office early, and now Roussel wanted to have his hand held. 'That's right. Don't worry about it. You're quite safe. He's not going to throw you out.'

'Well, I don't know. Do you think . . .'

She cut him off. 'Roussel, trust me. I will arrange someone sympathetic.'

'If you're sure.'

'Quite sure. I must go.'

The phone went dead. Roussel looked at it and shrugged. He hoped she knew what she was doing.

Max rinsed the *marc* glasses, the harsh, pungent smell reminding him of the harsh, pungent taste. An evening on that stuff would give him brain damage. He thought of emptying the bottle down the sink, then decided to keep it for Roussel. He'd be back. Max liked what he had seen of the man so far, which was fortunate. In cities, neighbours were people with whom you occasionally shared an elevator. In the country, they could affect every day of your life, and it was important to be on good terms with them.

His thoughts turned to Madame Passepartout, who would be arriving in the morning, and he walked through the succession of rooms, trying to decide where to tell her to start cleaning. Or was she as sensitive about housework as Roussel was about vines? Perhaps it would be more diplomatic to let her decide for herself. God knows she had plenty of choice. He came to a stop by the grand

68

piano, with its impressive layer of dust and dead insects. The silver frame with its old photograph of him and Uncle Henry, caught in a slant of evening sunlight, looked particularly tarnished and dingy. As Max picked it up for a closer look, the worn velvet back of the frame came away in his hand. Another photograph, tucked behind the first, was revealed, and with it a previously hidden chapter in Uncle Henry's life.

The second photograph also featured Uncle Henry, but this time a younger version. He was standing next to some kind of truck with his arm around the shoulders of a good-looking blonde woman. They appeared to be joined at the hip, both smiling at the camera, and the woman had one hand resting on Uncle Henry's chest, a gesture at the same time casual and possessive. There could be little doubt about the intimacy of their relationship.

Max looked more closely at the photograph. Judging by the clothes, it was obviously taken in the summer. But judging by the truck, probably not in France. He took the photograph over to the window where the light was better, and was able to distinguish more detail: the glint of a wedding ring on the woman's hand, the Chevrolet emblem above the truck's radiator, and, blurred but just legible, the California licence plate. What was Uncle Henry doing running around with blondes in California? The old devil.

Seven

Another glittering morning, another run, another slippery session of acrobatics in the shower. Max pulled on shorts and a T-shirt and was hoping that yesterday's bread would still be edible when he heard the sound of a car pulling up outside the house, then three imperious toots on the horn.

He went downstairs and opened the door to see a brightly coloured bottom and two sturdy legs protruding from the back of an old but highly polished Renault 5. The bottom's owner withdrew from the car and straightened up, clutching a vacuum cleaner and a plastic bucket, which she placed on the ground next to an array of mops and brushes and cleaning products. Madame Passepartout had arrived.

'I haven't deranged you?' she asked, pumping Max's hand up and down as though she were trying to detach it from the rest of his body. 'But I wanted to get here before you had breakfast.' She plunged back into her car and reappeared with a paper bag. '*Voilà*. They're still warm.'

Max thanked her, and stood nursing his croissants while Madame Passepartout brought him up-to-date on the current state of French bread (not what it used to be), and the morals of the baker's daughter (not what they should be). A reply clearly wasn't expected, and while Max helped Madame Passepartout carry her equipment into the kitchen he had time to study this voluble new addition to his life and household.

At a guess, she was in her early fifties, but

despite her age and her substantial build she was not yet ready to abandon the clothing of youth. Tight and bright was the Passepartout style, with an orange tank top and turquoise leggings, stretched to the maximum, relieved by a pair of sparkling white tennis shoes on surprisingly dainty feet. Her black hair was cut almost as short as a man's, her dark eyes bright with curiosity as she now looked around the kitchen.

There was a sharp intake of breath. *'Ho la la! Mais c'est un bordel.* An old man living alone. One can always tell.' She stood with her hands on her hips, her lips clenched in disapproval. 'This won't do for a nice boy like yourself. Dust everywhere! Mice, no doubt! Probably scorpions! *Quelle horreur.'* She filled the kettle to make coffee and took a cup and saucer and a plate from the dresser, looking at them with deep suspicion before rinsing them in the sink. Shaking her head and clicking her tongue, she wiped the table free of dust and told Max to sit down.

Breakfast was served, a novelty for Max that he found very enjoyable. And while he ate his croissants and drank his coffee, Madame Passepartout's stream of chatter continued without a break. She would arrange everything, she told him, from lavender essence (a sure protection against scorpions) to furniture polish to toilet paper—doubtless Monsieur Max preferred the refinement of white to the more common pink—and while she chattered she prepared her weapons for an assault on the stove, which in her professional opinion hadn't been cleaned since the Revolution.

'Bon,' she said finally, pulling on a pair of rubber

71

gloves that matched her leggings. 'By lunchtime, you will see a difference here. Now you must go. I cannot clean around you. *Allez!*'

Feeling as though he were back at school under the thumb of a benign but dominant matron, Max was more than happy to do as he was told. His instincts told him that Madame Passepartout might prove to be a treasure once he had found a way of turning down her volume.

Distracted by Roussel's visit the previous evening, Max had put off his intended tour of the property. Now, like any new landowner, he wanted to explore his land, and his exile from the kitchen provided the impetus he needed. In the dossier he'd been given by Maître Auzet was a copy of the *plan cadastral*, a detailed map showing the various parcels of land, each meticulously numbered, that made up the twenty hectares surrounding the house. Taking the plan with him, he stepped outside and stood in the courtyard for a moment, listening to the *cigales* and the muttering of pigeons, the heat of the day coming down on him like a blanket.

For once, there was no sign of Roussel and his tractor, and the vines—*his* vines, he reminded himself with a sudden prickle of excitement—extended in an unbroken sea of green in every direction. Behind the house, an alley of cypress trees, untrimmed and shaggy, led down to the tennis court. All those years ago, it had seemed so big, and the net so high. Now it had shrunk to a scruffy patch, the net sagging on its posts, the whitewashed lines on the balding court faded to near invisibility.

He moved on into the rows of vines, his feet

kicking up puffs of dust. The soil was thin and dry, marked by a network of fissures, but the vines looked healthy enough, with bunches of grapes beginning to form in pale clusters. Bending down, he picked a couple of grapes and tasted them: bitter, and filled with pits. It would be weeks before they would be juicy and swollen with sunshine, and probably years before they would become drinkable wine. He began to get a sense of the patience required to be a winemaker; patience, and luck with the weather. And an *oenologue*. He wondered if Nathalie Auzet was having any luck finding someone.

By now, he was several hundred metres from the house, and had come to a low stone wall that separated one parcel from the rest. He checked with the plan and found that the land beyond the wall formed the limit of his property. In contrast to the other level parcels, this one sloped away gently down to the east before ending at the road.

Hopping over the wall, Max found a noticeable difference in the soil—or, rather, the lack of it. The texture of the land had changed abruptly, from sand and clay to rock, and the surface appeared to consist entirely of jagged limestone pebbles, blinding white in the sun, warm to the touch, an immense natural radiator. It seemed unlikely that even the most undemanding of weeds could find sufficient nourishment to grow here. And yet the vines appeared to be healthy, the leaves a bright green, the tiny grapes coming along nicely. He made a mental note to ask the *oenologue* how the vines could flourish in such inhospitable surroundings.

He was turning to go back to the house when he

felt the electronic tickle of his phone vibrating in his pocket. He took the call sitting on top of the wall, the heat from the stone coming up through the cotton of his shorts.

'What's the weather like down there?' There was a wistful tone to Charlie's voice as he asked the question that so often begins a conversation between someone in the north and someone in the south.

'Oh, the normal. I was going to send you a postcard. You know, the old chestnut: "The weather is here, wish you were beautiful." Let's see. It's about eighty-five and sunny. How is it in London?'

'Don't ask me. I think I'm getting webbed feet. Listen, I think I'll be able to slope off for a day or two at the end of the month. There's an international real estate symposium in Monte Carlo on the future of luxury properties.' There was a dismissive snort from Charlie. 'A bunch of wide boys seeing what they can unload on the Russians, I expect. Anyway, I've been delegated to represent Bingham & Trout, and I thought I could drive over afterwards and take a look at the château.'

'Great, Charlie. That's terrific. You'll love it here. I'll alert the staff.'

'You do that. What's happening with the grapes? Any joy on the wine doctor?'

'As a matter of fact, I'm seeing someone on Sunday who has contacts in the business. Could be promising.'

'Hmm. What are you up to today?'

'Well, I'm in the vines at the moment, getting to know the grapes. Then I've got some tidying up to

74

do in the courtyard. And then I'll probably go down to the village for lunch. Not exactly hectic.'

'Max?' Charlie's voice sounded almost serious. 'Tell me the worst. Is it really wonderful down there?'

Max looked across the vines toward the Luberon and the great sweep of blue sky, and thought of life without suits or meetings or office politics, without traffic jams or polluted air. 'Yes,' he said. 'Yes, it is.'

'Lucky bastard.'

*　　　*　　　*

Max spent the rest of the morning starting to sort through the contents of the barns, clearing a blocked drain in the stone *bassin*, making a list of supplies that he was going to need to restore the courtyard to its previous respectability: weed killer, a truckload of the fine gravel that he remembered were called *grains de riz*, pruning shears, a rake. He'd never had a house before, let alone a large country house, and he found himself enjoying the simple, unfamiliar chores. His hands, now smelling of ancient pond life, were filthy from clearing the drain and beginning to blister from dragging fallen branches into the barn for firewood. He added a saw to his list.

'*Peuchère!* How can you support the sun without a hat?' asked Madame Passepartout as she emerged from the kitchen, finger wagging. 'Do you want grilled brains?'

For the second time that morning, he felt like a guilty schoolboy. He added a hat to his list.

It was noon, and Madame Passepartout was leaving for lunch. But before she left, Max was

75

summoned to come inside and inspect the results of her efforts. He made admiring and grateful noises as he was shown the gleaming stove, the burnished copper saucepans, the scrubbed and spotless stone floor. It was, as far as he could see, a total transformation.

'You've done a huge amount in one morning,' he said. 'It's brilliant.'

Madame Passepartout allowed herself to preen for a moment before modesty took over. '*Bof*. It's a start. At least you could eat in here without poisoning yourself.' She gave him a sideways look, stern and accusing. 'That is, if you had any food. There is not enough here to feed a rat. Nothing. What are you going to do about lunch?'

'Oh, I thought I'd go to the café in the village. *Steack frites*, something like that.'

Again the warning finger. '*Attention*. The steak is announced as beef, but it is not. It is horse. You are better with the omelette.' With that, and a promise to be back in the afternoon, Madame Passepartout drove off.

Max cleaned himself up, left the front-door key under a pot of geraniums in the courtyard, and drove down to the village. En route, thoughts of a café omelette gave way to a desire for something a little more substantial—he was finding that Provence made him permanently hungry—and he decided to eat at Fanny's.

But it was not to be. Fanny was *désolée, désolée*, squeezing his arm and gazing into his eyes to emphasize her regret, but it was Saturday, and, as so often at this time of year, the entire restaurant had been booked by a wedding party. Max took his disappointment to the café.

As it turned out, the omelette was excellent, plump and runny, the salad fresh and well dressed, and the *pichet* of pink wine cool and crisp. From his seat outside the café, Max had a clear view of the celebration that was taking place across the square.

The provincial French at play are often a surprise to visitors who have been brought up with the myth that Parisians, with their reserve and their chilly good manners, are representative of the way the rest of France behaves. The crowd on Fanny's terrace was mostly young, with a scattering of children and older adults—all of them, from the sound of it, well supplied with wine. Bursts of laughter came rolling across the square, as did fragments of speeches, complete with interruptions and applause, and a quavering rendition of 'La Vie en Rose.' This started as a solo by an elderly man, standing with one hand on the shoulder of the bride and the other conducting the other guests, as they joined in, with a glass of champagne.

Max sat over an espresso and a Calvados, a sense of well-being spreading through him like a soothing drug. He hadn't yet had a chance to feel lonely; that would probably come in time. But for the moment, with the sun high in a blue sky, a full stomach, and the thought of tomorrow's excursion with Nathalie Auzet, he was at peace with the world. He tilted his face up to the sun, closed his eyes against the glare, and gave in to the impulse to doze.

He was shocked into consciousness by a pandemonium of car horns. The square had filled up with cars, each decorated for the occasion, according to tradition. Strips of chiffon, white, blue or pink, were tied to radio antennae, wing mirrors, or, in one case, the driver's sunglasses, and the obligatory sound effects had turned the peace of the afternoon into bedlam. After a triumphal tour of the square, the blaring cavalcade swept off for what promised to be an ear-splitting start to the honeymoon.

Max rubbed his eyes, and felt a slight tenderness on his eyelids where they had caught the sun. Silence and emptiness were returning to the square as the village closed its shutters and prepared to take its siesta.

When he got back to the house, it was to find that Madame Passepartout and her vacuum cleaner were in full cry. He left her to it and spent the rest of the afternoon in the barns, trying to restore a semblance of order to the chaos of fertilizer sacks, oil drums and old tractor tyres that littered the beaten mud floor. It was heavy, dirty work, and by seven o'clock he was more tired than he'd been in years, his muscles aching pleasantly from the exercise. He took a glass of wine and sat on the parapet of the *bassin*, watching the sun dip slowly toward the western horizon as it turned the sky into a lurid bonfire of pink and lavender.

Too weary even to consider eating, he took a long hot bath, and then dropped almost instantly into the welcome oblivion of sleep.

Eight

Sunday morning felt different from weekday mornings; even quieter than normal, as though the countryside itself were taking the day off. Max hadn't seen a living soul during his run. There were no cars on the roads, no tractors on the horizon, no figures in the vines, just perfect stillness, bathed in sunshine, wherever he looked. And today, there was no chance of that peace being shattered by a domestic symphony conducted by Madame Passepartout.

He opened one of the kitchen windows, dislodging an indignant pigeon, and heard the distant tolling of the church bell summoning the villagers to mass, an interlude of piety before the indulgence of Sunday lunch. He remembered once reading an article claiming that members of the Catholic faith ate better and more copiously than Protestants, the reason being that they could confess to any sins of gluttony committed at the table and so absolve themselves of any guilt. Looking inside the refrigerator, he found little to lead him into temptation, and had to make do with a bowl of *café crème*.

The kitchen smelled of Madame Passepartout's attentions, of cleanliness and wax polish and lavender essence. She had restored the surface of the old wooden table to a healthy gleam, and had placed in the middle of it a bowl of dusky pink roses cut from the bush in the courtyard. Next week, Max thought, he must talk to her about wages. Whatever she asked would be worth it, if only for the pleasure of having coffee every morning in such polished and fragrant surroundings.

Max himself was polished and fragrant in preparation for his outing with Nathalie Auzet. He had shaved with extra care, and dressed in dark blue cotton trousers and an old but still presentable

79

silk shirt that a girlfriend of long ago had given him one Christmas. On his way to the front door, he caught sight of himself in the hall mirror, and saw that his London pallor had been replaced by the beginnings of a tan—a café tan, confined to his face and forearms, but a start. He left the key under the pot of geraniums and drove off, whistling.

Nathalie's house was a commuter's joy, only two doors up the street from her office. A glossy black Peugeot 305 convertible, top down, was parked outside, and the door to the house was ajar. Whatever journalists wrote with such horrified relish in the newspapers about rising crime statistics obviously didn't yet apply to Saint-Pons.

Max raised the heavy bronze knocker and gave two tentative taps.

'*Oui?*' The voice came from the top of the house, cutting through the buzz of a hair dryer.

'Nathalie, it's me. Max.'

'Are you always early?'

'I promised my mother never to be late for meetings with *notaires*, specially when they drive convertibles.'

The hair dryer stopped. 'Come in. I'll be down in a minute. '

Max went through a tiny hall and into an L-shaped room, the sitting area divided from the kitchen by an old zinc-topped bar. A leather chesterfield, with a silk shawl thrown over the back, and two club chairs were arranged around a coffee table piled with books, and a handsome oriental carpet, its colours muted with age to a soft glow, covered the tiled floor. A large nineteenth-century Provençal mirror, in a massive frame of gilded gesso, hung above the fireplace, reflecting a vase of lilies on the mantelpiece. A group of Lartigue photographs—all of them signed, Max noticed—decorated one wall. Everything spoke of quiet good taste and no shortage of money.

Perched on the edge of the chesterfield, Max inspected the books on the coffee table. They were mostly on art or photography, from Caillebotte and Botero to Atget and Erwitt, although one pile seemed to be devoted to wine—volumes on Yquem, on Burgundy, on the legendary champagnes. And on top of the pile, there was an old copy of *The Great Wine Châteaux of Bordeaux*.

Max picked up the book, a little foxed but still handsome, and started to leaf through the pages. If it were still in print, he thought, he'd get a copy for Charlie, a man who would appreciate the mixture of fine wines and what he would call highly desirable real estate. Remembering the glorious bottle they had shared in London, Max turned to the index to look up Château Léoville-Barton.

As the pages fluttered open, a bookmark fell to the floor. Max picked it up and saw that it was a wine label; a wine among hundreds of others that he'd never heard of, but he liked the simplicity of the label's design and the thick cream stock on which it was printed. It was discreet and clean without being too modern, exactly the kind of label he would choose for his own wine, if he could ever get anything drinkable out of the vineyard. He put it back as he heard Nathalie coming down the stairs, replaced the book, and stood up to greet her.

She had left her *notaire*'s uniform in the closet, and was wearing close-fitting white trousers with a black top that left her arms bare, and the sunlight

81

slanting through the window picked out the sheen of her copper hair. Max started to shake hands, but to his surprise she leaned forward and kissed him on both cheeks, her scent warm and spicy. The morning was starting well.

'Well,' she said, 'are you ready to *chiner*?'

'Sounds like fun. Is it legal?'

Nathalie laughed. 'It means to go looking for antiques, for bargains.' She picked up a big leather shoulder bag. 'Although you won't find any bargains today. We'll take my car. I like to drive.'

And Max had always liked the idea of having a pretty chauffeur; it had been one of his executive fantasies. Even so, he soon found himself jamming one foot hard on the floor, searching for a nonexistent brake. Nathalie drove in the classic French manner—fast, with impatience, and testing the outer limits of safety—and she had a cavalier disregard for the advantages of keeping both hands on the wheel. That is not to say the nonsteering hand was idle. When it wasn't shifting gears, it was kept busy brushing back the shining hair, adjusting the sunglasses, or adding touches of visual punctuation to the conversation.

As the kilometres flew by, she told Max a little about the development of Isle-sur-Sorgue from a sleepy little town with a Sunday-morning bric-a-brac market to an internationally known antiques centre. 'Now they all come here,' she said. 'Dealers from New York and California, London, Munich, Paris, decorators and their smart clients with houses in the Alpilles . . .' She paused while she executed a particularly ill-advised burst of speed, passing the car in front on a blind bend and narrowly missing an oncoming cyclist. She glanced

82

over at Max, and grinned. 'You can open your eyes now. We're nearly there.'

Max offered up a silent prayer of thanks to the patron saint of terrified passengers and began to relax as traffic slowed to a crawl, cars nudging along in a search for parking spots by the side of the river. Nathalie saw a couple loading a large and very gloomy religious painting into a Volvo; sign language established that they were about to leave. She stopped, forcing the rest of the traffic to back up. Almost immediately, a blare of horns began, building up to a crescendo of irate honks from the car immediately behind her. Nathalie ignored the noise, taking her time to ease into the spot left vacant by the Volvo before waving on the car behind with a gesture of her hand, ending with a flip of the fingers that was just this side of an insult. The driver accelerated away, returning the gesture with interest.

Max got out of the car and stretched. 'Is it always like this on a Sunday?'

Nathalie nodded. 'The winter's a little quieter, but not much. There's no off-season for shopping.'

They started walking toward the line of stalls where the *brocanteurs* had set out this week's priceless relics—old linen, crockery, ragged posters, café ashtrays, chairs on their last legs, amateur Cézannes, the contents of a hundred bygone households. 'This side is mainly for tourists,' Nathalie said, 'people looking for a souvenir to take home. Over there, on the other side of the street, are some of the serious dealers. The rest are further on, in the old station. We'll start with them.' She took Max's arm, and steered him onto a narrow footbridge that led across the river. 'But first, coffee. If I don't have coffee, I shall become a foul-tempered *salope.*'

More stalls sprawled along the other bank of the river, these laden with cheese and flowers, olive oil and herbs, the cheap clothes and sturdy pink brassieres and corsets that only seem to be sold in provincial French markets. Max was silent, taking in the colours, the smells, the good-humoured jostling of the crowd, enjoying the light pressure of Nathalie's guiding hand.

They found a table at a café overlooking the river and ordered two *grands crèmes*. Nathalie seized her cup with both hands, took a long, greedy swallow, and sat back with a sigh of satisfaction. '*Alors*,' she said, 'before I forget.' She started to search through her bag. 'Lunch.'

Max watched her, a frown on his face. She didn't seem the kind of girl who would bring sandwiches. But, as Uncle Henry used to say, you never can tell with the frogs, slaves as they are to their bellies.

Nathalie looked up and saw his quizzical expression as she took her cell phone from her bag. 'What is it?'

Max shook his head. 'Nothing. Actually, I just remembered something my uncle used to say about the French and food. I thought for a moment you were going to pull out a picnic. You know, lunch.'

Nathalie's eyebrows went up at the absurdity of such an idea, and she clicked her tongue. 'Do I look like a *bonne maman*?'

He gave her a long, appraising look. It was difficult to imagine her sweating over a hot stove. 'No, I suppose not. You haven't got the build for it. And an apron wouldn't go with the handbag. Tell me, did you know him? My uncle?'

'I met him once. A very English man.'

'Is that good or bad?'

Nathalie cocked one shoulder and smiled. 'That depends on the man.' She left Max to consider that as she scrolled through some numbers, picked one, and put the phone to her ear. *'Jacques? C'est Nathalie. Bien, et toi?'* She laughed at the reply. *'Oui, deux. Dans le jardin. A tout à l'heure.'*

They finished their coffee, and Nathalie looked at her watch. 'We have plenty of time before lunch. Who do you want to see first? The expensive dealers, or the ridiculously expensive dealers?' She slung her bag over her shoulder and led the way through the crowd, hair and hips swinging in a way that put all thoughts of antique furniture out of Max's mind.

After nearly two hours spent looking at commodes, armoires, four-poster beds, marble baths and a variety of overdecorated chairs and tables attributed to the various Napoleons and the even more numerous Louis, one thing had become abundantly clear to Max: the clutter in his attic would be of little interest to these lovers of fine *marqueterie* and the belle époque. Feeling a little let down, he went over to Nathalie, who was chatting to a willowy young man standing amidst a collection of chandeliers, and waited for a pause in the conversation.

'It's been an education,' he said to her when the young man had drifted off, 'but I don't think my stuff is in this league. Not enough ormolu.'

'Ah bon? Maybe what you need is . . .'

'A drink. And then lunch. And a junk dealer to come and take it all away.'

Nathalie laughed. 'No Rembrandts in the maid's

room? No Poussins under the bed? Poor Max.' She took his arm. 'Never mind. A glass of wine will cheer you up.'

She had chosen a small restaurant owned by a friend, popular with dealers and decorators who sought relief in its cool, walled garden after the rigours of a morning's haggling. She led Max to the only free table, in a corner shaded by the leaves of a giant fig tree that appeared to be growing out of the wall.

A burly man in billowing white shirt and trousers appeared with menus, two noisy kisses for Nathalie, and a handshake for Max: Jacques the owner, scolding Nathalie for not coming more often as he waved to a waiter to bring wine. He recommended the *plat du jour* with the passionate enthusiasm of a man who was worried that he might have bought too much of it, and wished them a pleasant lunch.

The wine arrived in a thick carafe beaded with moisture, an irresistible sight on a thirsty day. Max poured, and they touched glasses, a small politeness that, with Nathalie, he found oddly intimate. Like most Englishmen, he was accustomed to drinkers keeping their distance from one another, with only an impersonal, mumbled 'cheers' before the first sip.

'So?' Nathalie had pushed her sunglasses up into her hair, her fine dark eyes wide and amused. 'You won't be retiring on the proceeds of the treasures in your attic?'

'Afraid not. But thanks for bringing me. You must have had better things to do today.' The unspoken question hung in the air for a moment.

'Max,' she said, 'I think you're fishing.'

86

Max grinned. 'Well, what do you usually do on weekends? Apart from motor racing?'

'Ah.' Nathalie smiled, but refused to be drawn out. She retreated into her menu. 'The lamb is always good here, and so is the salmon. They serve it with a sorrel sauce. And you should start with the *pissaladière*.'

Max abandoned his menu and leaned back in his chair. 'Fine. Anything you say.'

Nathalie gave a dismissive wave of her fingers, as though she were batting away an insect. 'Do you always do what women tell you?' She looked up, half-smiling.

'Depends on the woman.'

They ordered, and ate, and one carafe of wine led to another as they talked on into the afternoon, exchanging the kind of edited life histories that strangers reveal to one another on their way to friendship. Max noticed that Nathalie listened—attentively, and laughing in all the right places—much more than she spoke. But lunch had been a success, he felt; so much so that it wasn't until they were walking back to the car that he remembered to ask if she'd had any luck in her search for a wine doctor.

'I think so,' she said. 'Didn't I tell you? He's supposed to be one of the top men, but he's very busy.' She shrugged. 'All the good ones are. If they're not in Burgundy, they're in California or Chile. Anyway, his office promised me that he'd call next week.'

They reached the car. Max stopped, putting his hand on his heart and what he hoped was a winning expression on his face. 'Nathalie,' he said, 'can I suggest the perfect way to end a lovely afternoon?'

She had turned her head away, and looked back at him with a sideways, wary glance. He had so far behaved like a civilized man, but one could never tell. The English were not always what they seemed. Her eyebrows went up.

'Let me drive.'

Nine

This was Mr. Chen's third visit to Bordeaux, a city he found increasingly agreeable. As on his previous visits, he was particularly taken by the elegance and human scale of the eighteenth-century buildings, which made a refreshing change from the glass and steel towers of his native Hong Kong. He admired the architectural set pieces—the Place de la Bourse, the Esplanade des Quinconces, the Grand Théâtre, the fountains and statues—and he delighted in the tranquil surface of the broad, slow-flowing Garonne. And, telling himself that there should always be a place in a man's life for recreation, Chen had begun to appreciate some of Bordeaux's less publicized attractions, the exotically dressed young ladies who patrolled the back streets of the old town. In fact, he was thinking of increasing his visits to two a year.

It was in his nature to make himself well informed, and in the course of doing his homework he had discovered, among many other things, that Bordeaux was the first place in France where tennis had been played; that the novelist François Mauriac had invented 'the aristocracy of the cork' to describe the multinational mix of French,

English, Irish, German and Swiss wine grandees; and that their original cellars had been built next to the river, on the quai des Chartrons.

And it was here, where the rue Ramonet joined the quai des Chartrons, that Mr. Chen told the driver of his taxi to drop him off. A stroll, and a breath of cool river air, would clear his head before he tackled the business of the day. He had made his arrangements with the bank. He had dropped a few discreet hints to his clients. All that remained was to hope that this year's price wouldn't be too exorbitant.

He turned off the *quai* and into the cours Xavier Arnozan, a broad street of trees and graceful houses, and saw that the others were arriving. He quickened his pace to join them as they made their way through an unmarked front door.

In the sober gloom of the entrance hall, a small party of businessmen, all of them Asian, conservatively dressed in the dark suits and quiet ties of their trade, were exchanging bows and business cards and handshakes with their host, a tall Frenchman in well-cut tweeds that could only have come from a London tailor. Their common language was English, spoken in a variety of accents. Their common interest was wine.

'This is not an ordinary tasting,' the Frenchman was saying. 'In fact, you will already have noticed something unusual.' He paused to brush back a wing of greying hair that had fallen over his forehead after one bow too many. 'Normally, with the great wines of Bordeaux, tastings are held *sur place*, where the grapes are grown. In this case—this unique case, if I may say so—the vineyard is too small to offer comfortable facilities, or indeed any facilities at all. Except for the grapes, of course.' He looked at the attentive faces around him, and shook his head. 'We cannot offer even a miniature château, and there are no plans to build one. The land is far too precious to waste on bricks and mortar. That is why the tasting is being held here in Bordeaux.'

The businessmen nodded, their dark heads bobbing as one.

'Now, gentlemen, if you'd like to follow me.' He led the way down a narrow corridor lined with portraits of stern-faced men, their features partly obscured by the luxuriant facial hair popular in the nineteenth century. The Frenchman waved a manicured hand at the paintings. 'Honourable ancestors,' he said, with a smile that was echoed by the group.

They reached the tasting room, small and dim, dominated by a long mahogany table. Arranged along its polished length were shining rows of glasses, silver candlesticks with lighted candles, and a trio of open, unlabelled bottles, each identified by a hieroglyphic scrawled in white chalk. Ornate copper *crachoirs* had been placed at either end of the table in readiness for the ceremonial spitting that would take place later on, in the course of the tasting.

The Frenchman adjusted his already perfectly displayed shirt cuffs and clasped his hands in front of his chest, a slight frown on his face to indicate the importance of what he was about to say. 'As you all know, this is a tasting by invitation only, restricted to the highest level of international buyers, the crème de la crème.' Around the room, heads were inclined in recognition of the compliment. 'In other words, those who can appreciate the extraordinary qualities of this remarkable wine.'

As if programmed, the eyes of the buyers turned to look at the three bottles on the table while the Frenchman continued. 'Our vineyard is tiny, and we can produce only six hundred cases of wine a year. Six hundred cases, my friends.' He took from his pocket a newspaper clipping. 'Less wine than the Gallo brothers can produce in California in a morning. And now that they have acquired the Martini winery'—he held up the clipping—'it's probably less wine than they can produce before breakfast. What we are offering here is a mere drop in the wine ocean. You can understand why we can't afford to waste it on amateurs and thirsty journalists.'

The buyers smiled and nodded again, flattered to be included in such elite company. One of them raised a hand. 'What is current Gallo production? Do you have a figure?'

The Frenchman consulted his clipping. 'About six million cases a year.'

'Ah so.'

The Frenchman continued. 'We have two problems. The first is that, as I have explained, we don't possess a château, and so our wine cannot claim an illustrious name. We call it Le Coin Perdu, the godforsaken spot, because that is the old local name for the vineyard my family took over and rescued from neglect more than a generation ago. Their faith in the land, those years of work nursing the vines, have now been justified. The wine is exceptional. But that brings us to the second problem.'

He spread his hands wide and raised his tweed-clad shoulders in a slow-motion shrug. 'There is not enough of it. In a good year, six hundred cases. And when you have quality combined with scarcity, it is a sad fact that prices rise. Fortunately, we have not yet reached the six figures—in dollars, mind you—that were paid some years ago for a single bottle of 1787 Château Margaux, but the price of this year's wine will be—how can I put it?—*impressionnant*: around forty thousand dollars a case.' He shrugged again, the picture of a man overtaken by sad but uncontrollable events. 'However, as we say in France, only the first bottle is expensive.'

There was an audible intake of breath. His attempt at humour was lost on the buyers, who, to a man, produced pocket calculators.

'While you do your sums, my friends, think of Pétrus. Think of Latour, of Lafite-Rothschild. These wines can outperform the stock market, particularly today. They are not mere bottles of liquid, however glorious. They are *investments*.'

At the mention of that thrilling word, the mood of the room lightened, and the buyers watched as the Frenchman went to the table, adjusted the set of his cuffs once again, and picked up one of the bottles. He poured no more than a mouthful into a glass and inspected its colour against the flame of a candle. He gave a slow nod of satisfaction, then lowered his head, swirled the glass, and brought it to his nose, closing his eyes as he inhaled. *'Quel bouquet,'* he murmured, just loud enough to be heard. The buyers maintained an appropriately reverent silence; they might have been observing a man lost in prayer.

'*Bon.*' The spell was broken as the Frenchman began to pour the wine, mouthful by mouthful, into the other glasses as he resumed his sermon.

'This is our first series of tastings for this vintage, and you, our friends from Asia, are the first to taste. Next week, our friends from America will be here, and then our friends from Germany.' He gave a sigh. 'Let us hope there will be enough for everyone. I hate to disappoint true connoisseurs.'

Unnoticed by the group, another figure had slipped quietly into the tasting room: a svelte, young blonde woman dressed in a tailored grey suit that was saved from severity by a breathtakingly short skirt.

'Ah,' said the Frenchman, looking up from his pouring, 'allow me to present my assistant, Mademoiselle de Salis.' Heads turned briefly, then returned for a second look at the legs. 'Perhaps, my dear, you would help me distribute the glasses.'

Each of the buyers clustered around the table took his glass, careful to adopt the taster's grip, with the thumb and the first two fingers holding the base. Like a synchronized team, well rehearsed in the movements of the ritual, they swirled their wine, raised their glasses to the candlelight, and peered respectfully at the colour.

'A darker robe than usual Bordeaux,' pronounced one of the buyers.

The Frenchman smiled. 'What an eye you have, Monsieur Chen. It is altogether richer, an oxblood ruby. Velvet rather than wool.'

Monsieur Chen filed the comparison away in his memory, to be used later. His less sophisticated clients were always impressed by this kind of language, the more gnomic the better.

'Time to put your noses to work, gentlemen.' The Frenchman led by example, bowing his head over his glass, and the room was silent except for the sound of wine-scented fumes being funnelled up into twenty receptive nostrils. And then, tentatively at first but with increasing confidence, came the verdicts, delivered in accents that had their origins in Hong Kong, Tokyo, Seoul and Shanghai. Violets were mentioned, and vanilla. One outspoken soul, more imaginative than the rest, was heard to murmur 'wet dog,' causing a momentary elevation of the Frenchman's eyebrows.

But this was little more than a prelude to the verbal acrobatics that followed once the wine had been taken into the mouth, chewed, rolled around the tongue, allowed to irrigate the back teeth and infiltrate the palate before being consigned to the *crachoirs*, with Mademoiselle de Salis waiting behind the table armed with a supply of linen napkins for the less accomplished spitters.

How does one describe the indescribable? The buyers, now that they had tasted, did their best with evocations of leather and chocolate, pencil shavings and raspberries, of complexity and depth, of backbone and muscularity and hawthorn blossom—of almost anything, in fact, except grapes. Notepads were produced, and scribbled on. The buyer from Shanghai, evidently a gentleman with dynastic interests, offered the opinion that the wine was undoubtedly more Tang than Ming. And through it all, the Frenchman nodded and smiled, complimenting his guests on the perspicacity of their palates and the felicity of their comments.

Some time later, when he judged the moment to

94

be ripe, when the gargling and spitting seemed to have run its course, he directed a discreet flutter of his fingers at Mademoiselle de Salis.

Putting aside her napkins, she picked up an oversized Hermès notebook, bound in black crocodile, and a Montblanc pen of the kind normally used to sign international treaties, and began to make her rounds. Like a perfectly trained sheepdog, she separated the buyers from the flock, one by one, taking them in turn away from the table so that their orders could be noted down in as much privacy as the size of the room allowed.

The capping of the pen and the closing of the notebook acted as a signal to the Frenchman. With many a pat on the shoulder and squeeze of the arm, he shepherded the group out of the room and down the corridor before giving his farewell address in the hall.

'I must congratulate you on the wisdom of your decisions,' he said, 'decisions I know you won't regret. Your orders will be dispatched very shortly.' He raised a hand and tapped his nose. 'Perhaps I could offer you a little advice. First, that you restrict this wine to your most trusted clients, those who prefer to keep their drinking habits to themselves. Publicity would inevitably spoil the intimacy of the relationship that we have built up. And second, I would suggest that you keep a few of your cases in reserve.' He smiled at his partners in future prosperity. 'Prices have a habit of going up.' On that reassuring note, with the bowing and shaking of hands completed, the group filed through the front door and into the bright sunlight of the street.

Hurrying back to the tasting room, the

Frenchman found Mademoiselle de Salis seated at the table, her blonde head lowered over her notebook and a calculator. He came up and stood behind her, and began to massage her shoulders. '*Alors, chouchou?* What's the score?'

'Chen took six cases, Shimizu took a dozen, Deng took four, Ikumi eight, Watanabe and Yun Fat . . .'

'The total?'

Mademoiselle de Salis gave the calculator a final stab with a crimson-tipped finger. 'Altogether, forty-one cases. Just over one and a half million dollars.'

The Frenchman smiled and looked at his watch. 'Not too bad for a morning's work. I think we've earned our lunch.'

Ten

This sunny morning, Madame Passepartout had chosen to attack the sitting room, in particular the cobwebs that festooned the lofty vaulted ceiling. A fear of heights ruled out the use of a stepladder, but to compensate for this she had added to her armoury a new, improved feather duster with a telescopic handle. She was using it like a lance, bringing down great swags of dusty grey filament, when she heard the sound of a car pulling up outside the house. Pausing in mid-thrust, she cocked her head.

'Monsieur Max! Monsieur Max!' Her screech echoed through the room and out into the hallway.

In response there was a muffled reply, and then

the sound of hurried footsteps on the stairs. Max appeared in the doorway, one side of his face covered with shaving cream. 'Are you all right, madame? Is something wrong?'

She pointed the feather duster in the general direction of the outdoors. 'There is a person.'

'A person?'

The duster pointed again. 'Outside. I heard a car.'

Max nodded. From the panic-stricken sound of her voice, he had thought that she had met with a terminal domestic accident, or at least been menaced by a mouse. But, as he was beginning to find out, every aspect of life for Madame Passepartout was steeped in drama. 'Don't worry,' he said. 'I'll go and see who it is.'

The car was small and nondescript and unoccupied. Max walked through the courtyard, reached the end of the house, turned the corner, and bumped into something soft and surprised. A girl.

'Oh!' she said, stepping backwards. And then, 'Hi.' She was in her mid-twenties, sweet-faced, blue-eyed, golden-haired, and golden-skinned. And when she smiled, she revealed her nationality. The only country where they issued teeth like that—so regular, so blindingly white—was America. Max stared at her, his mouth open.

'Do . . . you . . . speak . . . English?' She asked the question with the slow, exaggerated clarity that is often used with children and foreigners.

Max pulled himself together. 'Absolutely,' he said. 'Like a native.'

The girl was visibly relieved. 'Great. My French is about that much?' She held up one hand, the

97

thumb and index finger curled to make a zero. 'Maybe you can help me? I'm looking for the owner of the property? Mr. Skinner?' The American intonation turned every sentence into a question.

'That's me.'

The girl laughed and shook her head. 'You're kidding. You can't be.'

'Why not?'

'I don't think you're old enough to qualify.'

Max rubbed his chin and found his fingers coated with foam. 'Ah. I was shaving.' He wiped his hand on the back of his shorts. 'Old enough to qualify for what?'

'Mr. Skinner's my dad.'

'Henry Skinner?'

The girl nodded. 'You missed a bit.' She tapped her cheek. 'Right there.'

They looked at one another in silence while Max wiped his face. 'Better?'

The girl was shifting her weight from one leg to the other. 'Look, this is kind of embarrassing, but it's been a long drive and I really need a bathroom. Can I . . .'

'Right. Of course. A bathroom.' He led the girl into the house, and pointed up the stairs. 'Second on the left. The door's open.'

Madame Passepartout emerged from the sitting room, her face a question mark as she watched the girl take the stairs two at a time. She turned to Max. '*Eh alors?*'

'Coffee,' said Max. 'That's what we need.'

Madame Passepartout, feeling that this could provide a fascinating break from the cobwebs, led the way into the kitchen and started to fuss with the

98

kettle and the *cafetière*, laying out three cups and saucers on the table. 'An unexpected friend,' she said, and gave Max an arch look. 'Perhaps a *copine*?'

'Never met her in my life.'

Madame Passepartout sniffed. In her experience, young women never turned up at the homes of young men by accident. There was always *une histoire*. She poured boiling water over the ground coffee, impatient for the return of the stranger. She sensed the prospect of revelations.

Which there were, but unfortunately for Madame Passepartout they were in English, a language that she found almost completely impenetrable. Nevertheless, she sat at the table as the two began to talk, her head swivelling from one to the other like a spectator at a tennis match.

'Right,' said Max, 'first things first. This is Madame Passepartout. And my name's Max.'

The girl stretched across the table to shake hands. 'Christie Roberts. From St. Helena, California.'

That would explain the teeth and the tan, thought Max. 'You're a long way from home. Is this a holiday for you?'

'A vacation? Not exactly. Well, it's kind of a long story.' She dropped two sugar lumps into her cup and stirred her coffee while she collected her thoughts. 'I was raised by my mother. She never talked much about my dad, but she did tell me he died in a car crash when I was a baby. Then a couple of years ago, she got sick, and last year she died. A stroke.' Christie shook her head. 'Does it bother you if I have a cigarette?'

'Go ahead. You're in France, smoker's heaven.'

99

Max fetched an old Suze ashtray and pushed it across the table while Christie took a pack of cigarettes from her bag and lit one. 'Dumb habit. I've got to be the only person in California who does nicotine instead of dope.' She blew a plume of smoke up at the ceiling. 'So. After the funeral, I had to go through all my mom's papers—bank statements, insurance policies, the usual stuff. Anyway, I found this letter, really old, from some guy called Henry, saying he missed her and wanted her to come out to be with him in France. And in the same envelope was a fuzzy photograph of him—well, I guess it was him—sitting outside a bar in the sun.'

'Really? Do you have it with you?'

'It's in my bag in the car. But it got me curious, and I started asking around in St. Helena, people who'd known my mom when she was young. Well, it turns out that this Henry had spent some time in California, and he and mom were, you know, seeing each other.' She finished her coffee, smiling her thanks when Madame Passepartout refilled her cup. 'That made me even more curious, so the next thing I did was get a copy of my birth certificate from Sacramento. And there was my father's name.'

'Henry Skinner?'

She nodded. 'That's why I'm here. I thought it was about time I met my dad.' Stubbing out her half-smoked cigarette, she shrugged. 'But I guess I'm too late.'

Max shook his head. 'Afraid so. I'm very sorry. He died last month. Tell me, how did you know where to come?'

'An old friend of my mom's works in

Washington, for the State Department. It took a few weeks, but those guys can find out anything.'

Max stood up, still shaking his head. 'Let me show you something.' He went to the sitting room, and came back with a silver photograph frame. Removing the back, he took out the concealed second photograph, brown and cracked with age, and placed it on the table in front of Christie.

She studied it for a long moment. 'Wow. This is really weird.' She looked up at him, and back at the photograph. 'That's my mother. And I guess that's my father.'

'My uncle,' said Max.

Madame Passepartout used the pretext of clearing away the coffee cups to lean over and peer at the photograph, which only added to her frustration. 'Monsieur Max,' she said, *'Qu'est-ce qui se passe?'*

Max scratched his head. 'I'm not sure.' Turning to Christie, he began to tell her his side of the story—his boyhood visits to the house, the death of his uncle, the will. And as he mentioned the will, something that Nathalie Auzet had told him came into his head.

He picked up the old photograph and stared at it. 'My God, I'd forgotten all about that. I wonder . . .' He looked at Christie. 'Listen, I have to make a phone call.'

Christie smiled. 'Go ahead.'

Max got through to the *notaire*'s office, only to be told by the secretary that Maître Auzet was in Paris for a few days. He put down the phone and slumped back in his chair. 'The thing is,' he said to Christie, 'there's this inheritance law in France. When you die, your property has to go to your next of kin—your husband, your wife, your children. You have no choice. Now, when Uncle Henry made his will, he thought that I was his only surviving relative. He didn't know about you.' Max frowned. 'That's strange, isn't it? Why didn't he know about you?'

'Mom married—a guy called Steve Roberts—but it didn't work out. After that, I guess she felt she couldn't . . . you know, come back to your uncle with a surprise package. Or maybe she didn't love him. Who knows?'

Max looked at his watch—the Englishman's inevitable reflex before the first drink of the day—and got up to fetch glasses and a bottle of rosé from the refrigerator. 'You see what I'm getting at, don't you? If you're Uncle Henry's daughter, it might make his will invalid.' He poured the wine and gave Christie a glass. 'Which would mean that the property would legally have to go to you.'

'That's crazy.' Christie laughed. 'Just crazy.' She took a sip from her glass, holding the wine in her mouth before swallowing. 'Hey, this is good. Nice and dry. What's the mix? Grenache and Syrah?' She reached for the bottle and looked at the label. 'Makes our Zinfandel taste like cough syrup.'

'You know a bit about wine?'

'Sure. I grew up in the Napa Valley, and I work in a winery. Public relations. I do the winery tours.'

Max nodded, his thoughts elsewhere. It was dawning on him that what he had just said to the girl—even if she didn't believe it—was more than likely true. According to the serpentine dictates of French law, an illegitimate daughter would quite possibly take precedence over a legitimate nephew.

102

All at once, just as he was beginning to ease into the life of gentleman *vigneron*, his future began to look uncertain. Extremely uncertain. And it was a fundamental uncertainty. He couldn't ignore it, and it wouldn't go away. Did he have a future here, or didn't he?

'Look,' he said, 'we're going to have to sort this out.' He got up, went to a drawer of the dresser, pulled out a phone directory, and started leafing through the Yellow Pages. 'Better to do it now, before things get any more complicated.'

Christie watched, a puzzled half-smile on her face. 'I don't understand. What's going on?'

'I think we should get a legal opinion.' Max found what he was looking for, and reached for his phone.

'Oh, come on. Do you really think . . .'

'I'm serious. Do you have anything against lawyers?'

'Doesn't everyone?'

As Max tapped in the number, Madame Passepartout, saucer-eyed and bursting with frustrated incomprehension, looked at Christie and shrugged. Christie could do nothing but shrug back. They waited for Max to finish his call.

'OK. We've got an appointment in Aix at two o'clock.'

Lunch was a swift, informal affair of bread and cheese and salad in the kitchen. Max was preoccupied, his head filled with depressing possibilities: losing the house, having to go back to London and find a job, scraping together the money to pay back Charlie. Christie was thoughtful, a little bewildered, and saddened by the realization that she never would meet her father.

103

Madame Passepartout had given up the linguistic struggle and had gone home, promising to return to do battle with the cobwebs in the afternoon.

They were about to get into the car when Christie paused as she was opening the door. 'Max? Do we really need to do this?'

Max looked at her across the roof of the car. 'I do. I couldn't stay not knowing if the house were mine or yours. Suppose you did something silly, like marry a Frenchman? You might want to come and live here.'

She shook her head. 'Not on my agenda.'

'You never know. Agendas have a habit of changing.'

The drive down to Aix was marked by the kind of safe, impersonal conversation two people resort to when they don't want to discuss what is really on their minds. They compared jobs: Max's time in the City, Christie's in the winery. They shared an admiration for the spectacular countryside they were driving through—like Napa, but greener and somehow older-looking—and by the time they had found a parking spot in Aix they were starting to feel as comfortable with one another as they could under the curious circumstances.

One of the most attractive corners of Aix is the Place d'Albertas, a miniature eighteenth-century cobbled square built around a fountain. Once an architectural prelude to the palace behind it, the square is now largely taken over by discreet offices filled with more or less discreet members of the legal profession. Maître Bosc, the lawyer Max had chosen at random from the extensive selection in the Yellow Pages, occupied the ground floor of one of the best-kept buildings, his brass plaque twinkling in the sun.

The secretary placed Christie and Max on two hard chairs while she disappeared to announce their arrival. Five minutes passed, then ten. Finally, when enough time had passed to establish that the *maître* was a busy and important man, the secretary reappeared and ushered them into his office.

It was a large, beautifully proportioned room—a high ceiling, tall windows, and delicately moulded cornices—desecrated by the kind of modern office furniture one finds in catalogues that offer a discount for buying in bulk. Maître Bosc stood up behind his faux-rosewood desk and gestured at them to sit down. He was a thickset, rumpled man, shirtsleeves pushed up above his elbows, hair awry, his reading glasses dangling from a cord around his neck, a cigar smouldering between his fingers. He looked at them with a pleasant smile. '*Alors?* What can I do for you?'

Max described the odd situation in which he and Christie found themselves while Bosc made notes, interrupting from time to time with a murmured question. Christie's exposure to lawyers had been limited to the California variety, sharply dressed and aggressive. Bosc, although she couldn't understand him, seemed cozy and sympathetic. But he had a lawyer's instinct for a lengthy and lucrative assignment, something that was apparent from his first words after Max had finished speaking.

He let his glasses drop from his nose, and began to swivel his chair slowly from side to side. 'It's a grey area,' he said.

Max knew little about law, but he had enough experience to know that whenever that invaluable

105

legal accessory, the grey area, was invoked, substantial bills were sure to follow. The lawyer's next words confirmed this.

'The problem is not quite as straightforward as it might appear.' Bosc rekindled his cigar, brushing the fallen ashes from his tie. 'One must search for precedent. But perhaps there is no precedent.' He watched to see how Max received this cheerful news. 'In which case, the highest judicial authorities will have to be consulted.'

Max translated for Christie. 'He says it could be complicated.'

'Yeah, right,' she said. 'Why am I not surprised? Max, we don't need this.'

Max shrugged. 'We're here. We might as well see what else he has to say.'

Bosc swivelled slowly, waiting for them to finish. 'Then there is the question of establishing that mademoiselle is indeed Monsieur Skinner's daughter; a love child, but his daughter nevertheless. Nowadays, there is DNA, of course—one remembers the *affaire* concerning the child of Yves Montand some years ago—but again this is not straightforward. Monsieur Skinner's remains are in a cemetery, and disinterment is an extremely sensitive business requiring permission from a number of different authorities.' He rolled his next phrase around his mouth with evident pleasure. 'There could be formidable complications. Quite formidable. But it's a fascinating case, and I shall be delighted to take it on.'

Max turned again to Christie. 'The complications have just got more complicated. I think I'd better tell you the details afterwards.'

106

Christie rolled her eyes and took out her cigarettes.

Bosc looked from one to the other, not knowing which of them would end up as his client. He hoped it was the one who spoke French. On the other hand, the girl was very pretty. Also, as the young man had told him, American, and therefore extremely rich. He decided to offer them a constructive piece of advice. 'To safeguard your positions,' he said, 'it would be prudent if both parties were to maintain a physical presence in the property while the matter is being resolved. Absence could possibly be interpreted as giving up legal rights. French law can sometimes play these tricks.'

Max was silent for a moment as the words sunk in. 'Let me get this straight,' he said. 'What I think you're saying is that we're going to have to live together. Is that right?'

The lawyer nodded. 'Under the same roof, yes. But not in the romantic sense. Unless, of course . . .' He looked from Max to Christie, signalling all kinds of delightful possibilities with his eyebrows.

'What?' asked Christie.

'Later,' said Max.

The meeting ended with Bosc promising to institute inquiries. But, as he told Max, these would take time. They would have to be patient. He saw them to the front door and stood watching as they went out into the sunlit square, mentally rubbing his hands at the prospect of fat fees to come.

Christie blew out a long, loud gust of air. 'OK. Is that all settled?'

'Not exactly. I think a beer would help me

explain. You're not too fond of lawyers, are you?'

'I used to live with one.'

They walked in silence down the rue de Nazareth to the Cours Mirabeau, and took the last empty table on the terrace of the Deux Garçons. Christie looked around at the crowd, most of them studying maps and guidebooks, many of them in the American vacationers' uniform of baseball caps, baggy multipocketed shorts, and sandals made from strips of black industrial webbing. She turned back to Max with a grin. 'Where's the guy with the beret and the accordion?'

The waiter, impassive and bored, put two beers on their table and waited to be paid, his eyes focused on something far away, perhaps his retirement. He glanced down to assess the size of his tip, acknowledged it with an almost imperceptible tilt of the head, and moved off on feet as flat as the crêpes being eaten at the next table.

Max began his explanation, but he could sense that it was a struggle for Christie to stay interested in precedents and judicial consultations, and when he came to disinterment and DNA tests, she shuddered and shook her head.

'Look,' said Max, 'I'm just telling you what he said.' Before he could continue, Christie put up a hand to stop him.

'Right at the end,' she said, 'when he was looking at both of us, all that stuff with the eyebrows, what was that all about?'

'Good question. I was coming to that. Well, what he was suggesting—no, what he was advising, only as a legal thing, you understand—was that you should, as he put it, "maintain a presence".'

108

'Maintain a presence?'

'Yes. In the house.'

'With you?'

'Well, yes. I mean, I'd be there, obviously. Maintaining a presence as well. Just until this is all sorted out.'

'Max, I only met you this morning. I don't know you. And now you're suggesting I come and live with you?'

She looked comically earnest, her blue eyes wide with concern, a young American woman face to face for the first time with European turpitude. Max gave up trying to take the situation seriously. It was too bizarre.

'It's a big house,' he said. 'We could have three bedrooms each.'

Eleven

'Ah,' said Madame Passepartout, 'it is as I thought. The young *Américaine* is moving in.' She watched approvingly as Max struggled to manoeuvre Christie's bag, an enormous sausage-shaped canvas holdall, through the front door. 'Everything is ready, Monsieur Max,' adding, with a smirk, 'I've put flowers in your bedroom and changed the sheets. I'm sure you'll both be very comfortable.'

Max dropped the bag on the floor. 'No, madame. No. You don't understand. She's staying here, but not with me. Well, with me, but not in the same bedroom.'

Madame Passepartout received this news with a look of astonishment, as though the idea of two

109

healthy and unattached young people choosing not to share a bed was odd, even unnatural. She cocked her head and put her hands on her hips. '*Ah bon? And why not?*'

'I'll explain later.' Turning to Christie, Max nodded toward the stairs and heaved the bag onto his shoulder. 'Let's get you settled in.'

They made a tour of the upstairs rooms, with Madame Passepartout flinging open shutters and flicking any surface she suspected of harbouring dust, pointing out the views through the tall windows and muttering, not quite under her breath, about the waste of Max's perfectly good bedroom. Christie looked with apprehension at the sagging beds, the ancient, lopsided armoires, the uneven tiled floors. Apprehension turned to disbelief when they came to one bathroom even more medieval than the others, with a shower attachment linked to the tub by twisted coils of cracked and faded pink rubber tubing. She shook her head slowly. 'Far out,' she said. 'Incredible.'

'Not exactly the Ritz, I know,' said Max. 'But bags of charm. You won't find anything like this in the States.' He perched on the lavatory seat and stretched both arms out toward the window. 'I mean, you could spend many happy hours here. The view's fantastic.'

A half-smile couldn't conceal Christie's obvious dismay, just this side of horror, and Max tried to imagine the palatial sanitary arrangements she must have been accustomed to in California. Hygiene, as he knew, was one of the minor religions of America. He took pity on her. 'Look,' he said, 'why don't you have my room and bathroom, and I'll go somewhere else?'

110

And so it was decided. Leaving Christie to unpack, Max and Madame Passepartout went downstairs to the kitchen, Max to seek comfort in a glass of wine, Madame Passepartout to seek enlightenment.

'But why not?' she asked again. 'It is the best room. The bed is large enough for two. You could be together. *Très cosy.*'

'We've only just met.'

'So? You'll get to know each other.'

'She's my cousin. At least, I think she's my cousin.'

Madame Passepartout dismissed that trifling accident of birth with a wave of the hand. 'Half the aristocrats in France have *liaisons* with their cousins.' She poked Max in the chest for emphasis. 'And many of the peasants. Why, even here in the village, it is well known that . . .'

Max cut her off in mid-revelation. 'Look, the truth of it is . . .'

'Ah. The truth.'

'. . . the truth of it is that I've never really fancied blondes. I prefer brunettes. Always have.'

'*C'est vrai?*'

'Absolutely.'

Madame Passepartout couldn't help a hand going up to touch her acceptably brunette hair, even as she shrugged. She had proposed what she considered to be a sensible and convenient arrangement—a potentially very pleasurable arrangement—and it had been declined for no other reason, as far as she could see, than the girl having been born a blonde. Absurd. How strange men were, Englishmen in particular. She wished Max an agreeable evening and went off to discuss

111

him and his foibles at length with her sister, Madame Roussel.

Max waited until her car had disappeared up the drive before taking a bottle of rosé and two glasses out into the courtyard. He put the bottle under the flow of the fountain to keep a chill on the wine, and fetched two tattered wicker chairs from the barn, putting them beside the *bassin* so that they faced the sunset. He was, he thought, performing all the duties of a considerate host. But as he sat down to review the events of the day, he couldn't ignore the thought that his days as a host might be numbered. Was the house really his, or would some arcane wrinkle in a law established centuries ago by Napoleon decide otherwise? Had he been stupid to bring up the problem in the first place? Possibly. But he liked to think of himself as a man with one or two basic principles, and a voice from the grave came back to remind him of something that Uncle Henry had often told him: a principle isn't a principle until it costs you money. Not only money, in this case, but a new life.

'Hi.'

Max turned from the contemplation of his future to see Christie, dressed in fresh jeans and white T-shirt, her wet hair brushed straight back. She looked about eighteen.

'Congratulations. You worked out how to use the shower.' Max poured a glass of wine and held it out to her.

'Thanks. Is that all you ever get? A trickle?'

'The French aren't great at showers. But they do wonderful sunsets.'

They sat for a moment without speaking, looking at a sky streaked with gold and pink and

112

decorated with small, rose-coloured clouds that could have been painted by Maxfield Parrish in one of his more extravagant moods. Water splashed from the fountain, the sound mingling with the chirrup of *cigales* and the creak of frogs calling out to one another across the *bassin*.

Christie turned to look at Max. 'What was he like, my dad?'

Max stared into the distance, consulting his memory. 'I think what I liked most about him was that he treated me like an adult instead of a schoolboy. And he was funny, especially about the French, although he loved them. "Our sweet enemy," he used to call them; or, if they were being particularly obstinate and difficult, "bloody frogs". But he rather admired their superiority complex and their good manners. He was a great one for good manners. I suppose nowadays he'd be considered very old-fashioned.'

'Why's that?'

'He was a gent. You know, honourable, fair, decent—all those things that have rather gone out of style. You'd have liked him a lot. I did.' Max sipped his wine and glanced at his watch. 'I thought we might go down to the village to eat. I'll tell you more about him over dinner.'

Chez Fanny was noisy and already crowded with people from the village and a handful of tourists, these easily identified by their sun-flushed faces and their logo-spattered clothes. Fanny came over to greet Max, a look of surprise on her face when she saw he was not alone.

'It's been so long,' she said, patting Max on the arm as she kissed him. 'At least two days. Where have you been? And who's this?'

113

Max made the introductions and watched the two women sizing one another up as they shook hands, a searching mutual inspection that neither bothered to conceal, almost like two dogs meeting in a park. Why was it that men were never as open in their curiosity? Max was smiling as they sat down at their table.

'What's so funny?' asked Christie.

'You two,' he said. 'I thought for a moment you were going to start sniffing each other.'

Christie's eyes followed Fanny as she snaked her way through the tables. 'They wear their clothes pretty tight over here, don't they? If she sneezed she'd be out of that top.'

'I live in hope,' said Max. Seeing Christie raise a censorious eyebrow, he hurried on. 'Now, what would you like? Have you ever had rabbit stuffed with tapenade? Wonderful.'

Christie seemed unconvinced. 'We don't do rabbit in California. Is it, you know, gamey?'

'Tastes like chicken. You'll love it.'

The topic of uncle Henry occupied most of dinner, and Max told Christie as much as he could remember of those summers long ago. His uncle had given him what amounted to a haphazard education, introducing him to tennis and chess and wine, good books and good music. Max recalled in particular one endless rainy day devoted to the *Ring* cycle, preceded by his uncle's comment: 'Wagner's music isn't as bad as it sounds.'

There had also been lessons on elementary tractor maintenance, gutting chickens, and the care and handling of a pet ferret whose job it was to keep the rats down. Tossed into this informative stew were other diverse ingredients, such as the

114

unpredictable nature of red-haired women, the virtues of Aleppo soap, the importance of a good blue suit—'Remember your tailor in your will; it's the only time you should pay him'—and a proven system of winning at backgammon.

'I loved those summers,' said Max. 'It was just like being with an older boy who knew a lot more than I did.'

'Where were your parents?'

'Oh—Shanghai, Lima, Saudi Arabia, all over the place. My father was a kind of minor diplomat. Every four years he'd be sent somewhere they didn't play cricket and where it was considered generally unsuitable for little English schoolboys.'

Evening had given way to night, and the terrace was lit only by the flicker of candles on each table and the line of coloured bulbs that had been strung along the front of the restaurant. Most people had finished eating, and were sitting over coffee, smoking, chatting quietly, and listening to the Edith Piaf album that Fanny had put on—hymns to heartbreak, a sob in every song.

Max could see that Christie was getting drowsy, ducking her head as she tried to stifle a yawn. The wine, the food, and her long day were catching up with her, and he signalled for the bill, which Fanny brought over with a glass of Calvados.

She pulled up a chair and sat down. 'Your *petite amie*,' she said, nodding at Christie, who seemed to be two seconds away from sleep. 'I think you've worn her out.' Fanny's expression was amused and curious, her eyes almost as black as her hair in the glow of candlelight.

Max tasted the Calvados, like apples on fire, and shook his head. First Madame Passepartout, now

115

Fanny, both leaping to the same conclusion. Perhaps he should feel flattered. 'It's not like that,' he said. 'She's come all the way from California. Long flight.'

Fanny smiled, and leaned across to ruffle Max's hair. 'Better luck tomorrow then, *hein*?' Her hand dropped to his shoulder and rested there, warm and light. Without thinking, he ran his fingertips along the inside of her bare, caramel-coloured arm, tracing the fine line of the vein that led from wrist to elbow. Their heads were close enough for him to feel her breath on his cheek.

'Am I interrupting something?' Christie had roused herself, and was watching them with half-open eyes.

Max cleared his throat and sat back. 'Just paying the bill.'

Driving back to the house, Max could still feel the touch of Fanny's skin, as if his fingers had their own memory. Christie yawned again. 'Sorry I pooped out. But thanks a lot. It was a nice evening. And you were right about the rabbit.' Max smiled in the darkness. 'Glad you enjoyed it.'

Although neither of them knew it at the time, this was the high point of their relationship for several days to come.

*   *   *

The enforced proximity of two strangers is frequently awkward, because having a guest in your life demands a certain consideration that may not come naturally. And sometimes, if old habits are sufficiently entrenched, it may not come at all. That is how it was between Christie and Max.

By its nature, it was a strange and slightly uneasy arrangement for both of them, and one that wasn't helped by what Christie later described as a clash of lifestyles. Max was an early riser; Christie liked to sleep in. She would come down to the kitchen to find that Max had eaten the last of the croissants and finished off the orange juice. Christie was tidy by nature; Max was not. He liked Mozart; she preferred Springsteen. Neither one of them could cook, a daily problem. Christie found Madame Passepartout nosy and intrusive; Max considered her a jewel beyond price.

There were also the minor inconveniences common to many old houses in rural France: the erratic water supply, by turns scalding, freezing, or almost nonexistent; the unpredictable quirks of electricity that falters and dims and, for no apparent reason, extinguishes itself; the racket of a tractor under the bedroom window at six a.m.; the odd taste of the milk; invasion by insects—all of these quickly began to chafe at the nerves of a girl used to the comfort and efficiency of life in the more modern, cushioned and opulent surroundings of the Napa Valley. And then there were the French: formal one minute, familiar the next, talking like machine guns, obsessed with their stomachs, perfumed with garlic, and, in Christie's opinion, suffering from a permanent attack of arrogance.

Max found himself taking a perverse pleasure in disagreeing with her, defending France and the French, occasionally fanning the flames of argument with mild criticisms of America. These were never well received. Although Christie was too intelligent to swallow the doctrine of 'either for us or against us', she was puzzled and sometimes angered by what she thought of as the Europeans' tendency to bite the hand that had fed them so generously after World War Two. And she was angered still further when Max, talking about the shelf life of gratitude, reminded her of Lafayette, and America's debt to the French. And so the atmosphere in the house became increasingly strained. Madame Passepartout sensed the tension, and even she was uncharacteristically subdued. It was inevitable that the constant bickering would have to come to a head.

It started in public. Driven by hunger, Christie and Max had declared a hostile truce and were having dinner in the village. Fanny, it has to be said, behaved in a way that did nothing to improve a delicate situation, fussing over Max while ignoring Christie, who watched with an ever more baleful eye. The final straw came with the arrival of dessert.

Christie speared her poached pear with a murderous jab of her fork. 'Does she have to give you a massage every time she comes to the table?'

'Just being friendly.'

'Yeah, right.'

'Listen, that's the way she is. You don't have to watch.'

'Fine.' Christie pushed back her chair and stood up. 'Then I won't.' And she marched off into the night, her back stiff with anger.

Max caught up with her a few minutes later on the road outside the village. Slowing the car down to walking speed, he leaned over and opened the passenger door. Christie ignored him, looking straight ahead as she quickened her pace. After a hundred yards of crawling along beside her, Max gave up, slammed the door shut, and accelerated.

Back at the house, he tossed the car keys onto the kitchen table and searched for something to take the edge off his temper. Roussel's evil-tasting *marc* matched his mood, and he was on his second glass by the time Christie came through the door.

He looked up at her set face, hesitated, and should have thought better of it. But in his irritation he said it anyway. 'Nice walk?'

Those two words opened a floodgate. Christie's complaints, after a passing swipe at Fanny, moved on to the real focus of her dissatisfaction: Max, or rather, his attitude—unsympathetic, self-centred, smug, a twisted sense of humour. *Typically English*. She paced back and forth in front of the stove, glaring at him while she waited for him to erupt, or at least react. But he had already wrapped himself inside that cocoon of chilly condescension which the Englishman will often assume in the face of emotional outbursts, particularly those coming from women and foreigners. Nothing could have been more infuriating to a girl spoiling for a fight.

'You're entitled to your opinion,' Max said, 'however offensively you express it.' He pointed to the bottle on the table. 'Care for a drink?'

No, she wouldn't care for a goddamn drink. But she would care for the basic consideration that should be given to someone in her position—someone far away from home, not speaking the language, surrounded by strangers, *living* with a stranger.

Max swirled the last mouthful of oily liquid around in his glass before tossing it back with a shudder and getting to his feet. 'I'm off to bed,' he said. 'Why don't you grow up? I didn't ask you to come.'

He never made it to the kitchen door. Christie snapped, seized the nearest weapon to hand, and let fly. It was unfortunate that the weapon was a six-inch cast-iron skillet, even more unfortunate that her aim was true. The skillet caught Max full on the temple. There was an explosion in his head, a burst of pain, then blackness. His legs buckled and he collapsed, unconscious, on the floor.

Christie stood in shock, looking down at the prone figure. Blood was beginning to seep from Max's head, leaving a thin red line as it dribbled down the side of his face. He made no sound, and lay still; ominously still.

Remorse and panic took over. Christie got down on the floor and cradled Max's head in her lap while she tried to stop the flow of blood with a wad of paper towel torn from a kitchen roll. She felt his neck and thought she detected his pulse, a moment of relief quickly cancelled out by thoughts of possible consequences: trauma, brain damage, multimillion-dollar lawsuits, arrest for causing grievous bodily harm, years spent rotting in a French prison cell.

A doctor. She must call a doctor. But she didn't know how to call a doctor in France. The police? The fire department? Oh my God. What had she done?

The head on her lap moved, no more than a cautious inch. There was a groan, and then one of Max's eyes opened slowly, looking up past the curve of her blood-stained bosom at her frowning, anxious face.

'Where did you learn to throw like that?'

Christie exhaled, a great gust of relief. 'Are you OK? Listen, I am *so sorry*. I don't know what happened. I guess I must have—God, the blood. Tell me you're OK.'

Max moved his head gingerly. 'I think I'll live,' he said, 'but I can't be moved.' He let his head fall back on her lap, folded his arms across his chest, closed his eyes, and groaned again. 'Although there is something that might help.'

'What? Anything, anything at all. A doctor? Aspirin? A drink? Tell me.'

'You wouldn't happen to have a nurse's uniform, would you?'

Christie looked down at her victim's face. Max opened both eyes, and winked. 'I've always had a thing about nurses.'

They were both laughing as Christie helped him up and sat him down at the table, where she went to work on his wound with a bowl of water and more paper towels. 'It's not as bad as I thought,' she said when she had cleaned the gash above his eyebrow. 'I don't think you're going to need stitches. But what a dumb thing to do. I'm sorry. I really am.'

'I probably deserved it,' said Max.

She squeezed his shoulder, took the bowl of bloody water, and emptied it down the sink. 'OK. Now what I need is some antiseptic. What do they use here? Do you have any iodine?'

'Never touch it,' said Max. He reached across the table for the bottle of *marc*. 'Try this. It kills all known germs. Unblocks drains, too.'

She dabbed the alcohol on his head, then made a makeshift bandage with strips cut from a clean dish towel. 'There,' she said. 'Are you sure we shouldn't call the doctor?'

Max started to shake his head, then winced. 'Why spoil a nice evening?'

Twelve

The following morning, Max confronted his battered reflection in the shaving mirror, lifting the strip of dishcloth to inspect the livid welt above his left eye. Apart from some tenderness, and a throb of discomfort if he moved his head abruptly, the damage didn't seem too bad. Doctor Clerc in the village could clean the wound up and dress it in no time. He crept down the stairs, hoping to avoid Madame Passepartout, who, given her love of drama, would undoubtedly want to call Médecins Sans Frontières and a helicopter full of paramedics.

He crept in vain. She was lying in wait for him outside the kitchen door, with an apprehensive Christie hovering at her side.

'I couldn't sleep,' said Christie. 'I was so worried. I thought you might have, you know, complications—shock, post-accident trauma. I brought you a couple of Advil, but you were asleep. How do you feel?'

Before he could answer, Madame Passepartout clapped both hands to her cheeks in horror. *'Oh la la la, le pauvre!* What has happened to your head?'

Max touched the dishcloth cautiously. 'Nothing to worry about. Gardening accident.'

'Last night you were gardening?'

'I know. Silly of me. Mistake to do it in the dark.'

'Don't move.' Madame Passepartout plucked

her cell phone from the pocket of her trousers, today a luminous jungle green. 'I will call Raoul.'

'Raoul?'

'Of course Raoul. He has the ambulance.'

Max began to shake his head and regretted it. 'Please. I'll be fine.' He turned to Christie and changed languages. 'I'm going to let the doctor in the village take a look at it.'

Christie insisted on driving him, and they left Madame Passepartout on the doorstep, clucking with concern and muttering about concussion and that redoubtable French panacea, the antibiotic.

Half an hour and a tetanus shot later, the blood-stained dishcloth replaced by a more conventional dressing, Max came out of the doctor's office clutching a sheaf of prescriptions to find Christie in the waiting room. 'Don't ever get sick in France,' he said. 'The paperwork's enough to put you in bed for a week.'

She looked at him and couldn't help grinning. 'I guess the doctor didn't have a white bandage. Or did you ask for pink?'

They walked down the street to the café, arriving just as Roussel was leaving after a restorative early-morning beer. As they shook hands, he peered at Max's head. *'Eh alors?* But what . . .'

'Gardening accident,' said Max. He cut short the inevitable questions by introducing Christie to Roussel, who removed his cap with a flourish and bobbed his head. 'Enchanted, mademoiselle. So you are staying with Monsieur Max? Then I hope you will be coming with him to dinner tonight. My wife has made a *civet* of wild boar.' He kissed the tips of his fingers. 'With Châteauneuf-du-Pape, and blood pressed from the carcass, in the correct

123

fashion.' Seeing the blank look on Christie's face, Roussel turned to Max and shrugged.

'Mademoiselle doesn't speak French,' said Max, 'but I know she'd love to come. She likes blood.' With an uncertain smile and a sideways look at Christie, Roussel stumped off, leaving them to their coffee and croissants.

Christie wiped a flake of pastry from her mouth and cradled her cup in both hands, breathing in that wonderful morning smell of coffee and hot milk. 'Max, can I ask you a question? What are you saying when they ask what happened to your head? I mean, are you telling them . . .'

'Gardening accident. I thought it would cut a long story short.'

She leaned over to touch his arm. 'Thanks. That's nice of you.'

It was amazing, Max thought, how a little bloodshed had cleared the air between them. 'I hope you don't mind,' he said, 'but Roussel asked us over for dinner tonight, and I accepted. Quite unusual, actually. The French don't normally invite foreigners into their homes until they've known them for at least ten years. It'll be an experience. Not like dinner in California.'

Christie didn't answer, her eyes looking past Max at a figure making a beeline for their table. 'Better get your gardening story ready. Here comes another one.'

Max looked around to see Nathalie Auzet, sleek in her suit and heels, wearing an amused expression. 'I've just seen Roussel,' she said. 'He told me you'd had a fight with a tree.' She kissed Max lightly on each cheek, and looked at him over the top of her sunglasses. 'The pink suits you.

124

Nothing too serious, I hope?'

'I'm fine, but the tree's in pretty bad shape. Nathalie, I'd like you to meet a friend, Christie Roberts. She's over from California.'

Nathalie removed the sunglasses to get a better view of Christie before taking her hand. 'I might have guessed. Just like the photographs one sees of California girls. They always look so innocent.' Still holding Christie's hand, she turned to Max. '*Très jolie.*'

Max nodded. Christie coughed. Nathalie let go of her hand.

'Now Max, I have some news for you.' Nathalie had put on her sunglasses and a businesslike expression. 'I have engaged an *oenologue*—one of the best—to come and take a look at your vines. I'm waiting for him to call and confirm, but he's hoping to come down from Bordeaux tomorrow. We were lucky to get him; he's almost never in France.'

Max made suitably grateful noises as Nathalie continued. 'I have to go to Marseille tomorrow, but that doesn't matter. Maybe we could have lunch when I get back, and you can tell me all about it.' She turned to smile at Christie. 'If you brought your little friend, I could practise my English on her.' She gave them a playful wave of her fingers. 'Bye-bye.' And with that, she swayed up the street, heels clicking on the pavement.

Christie blew out a gust of air and shook her head. 'Frenchwomen. They're always hitting on somebody.'

'Flirting,' said Max. 'It's an old French habit, like dangerous driving.'

'But with me? I had to fight to get my hand

back.'

'What do you mean?'

'What do you think?'

'Funny. It never occurred to me.' Max was thoughtful as he watched Nathalie turn off the square and head up towards her office.

* * *

That afternoon, Max took Christie on a tour of the land around the house. The explosion of the previous evening had made them more relaxed in one another's company, the bickering forgotten as they made their way through the vines, planning a route for the *oenologue*'s visit. A vineyard was familiar territory for Christie—a wine brat, as she called herself—and she looked at the vines with an informed eye, noting the absence of weeds and mildew, comparing the pruning and tying with the way these things were done in California. It was much the same on the whole, although, as she said to Max, there was more of a manicured finish to the Napa vines, often with a rosebush at the end of each row.

'I've seen photographs of that in Burgundy and Bordeaux,' said Max, 'but down here they don't seem to go in for decoration. I suppose they feel you can't drink rosebuds, so why bother?'

'Actually, it's not for decoration. It's more like the canary in the coal mine, a kind of danger signal,' said Christie. 'If there's any disease about, the rose will usually get it before the vines. So you have time to treat them before it's too late. Neat idea, even if the French did think of it first.' She cocked her head and looked at Max. 'On the other

126

hand, there wouldn't be any vines in France if it hadn't been for America.'

'It was that beetle, wasn't it?'

Christie nodded. 'Phylloxera. Back in the 1860s, it killed almost every vine in France. Then they found that some American vine was resistant to the bug, and they brought over millions of vinestocks and grafted the European vines onto them. There you go—the basic history of modern wine in thirty seconds.'

'That's what you tell them back at the winery, is it? But I seem to remember that the beetle came over from America in the first place.'

Christie grinned. 'We don't go into that.'

They climbed over the wall and into a stony field at the edge of the property. Max kicked at the pebbles to see if there was anything underneath that resembled earth. 'Not much to look at, is it? I'm amazed anything can grow here.'

But Christie didn't answer. She had pushed her sunglasses back into her hair, and had squatted down between the rows of vines. Looking up at Max, she held out a tiny, wilted bunch of embryonic grapes, none of them much bigger than the head of a match. 'Take a look at this.'

He took the bunch from her and weighed it in the palm of his hand.

'Notice anything?' asked Christie. She didn't wait for him to answer. 'It hasn't fallen off. It's been clipped off. See the diagonal cut on the stem? That's a cut made by secateurs. And look—there are bunches all the way along this row.' She stood up and peered over the vines. 'Same there, as well. I'll bet it's the same through this whole patch.'

Max couldn't imagine Roussel spending hours

127

cutting off grapes that he'd worked hard to cultivate. It didn't make sense. 'That's strange,' he said. 'I bet they don't do that in California.'

'Sure they do,' said Christie, 'but not everyone—only the really serious guys. They cut off maybe two out of every three young bunches so that the bunch that's left gets all the nourishment. That makes it more concentrated, with a higher alcoholic content. The fancy name for it is the *vendange verte*. It's slow and expensive, because machines can't do it, but in theory you get a better wine. This must be a special part of the vineyard. What's the grape?'

Max shrugged. 'I'll ask Roussel this evening. And we can ask the wine man tomorrow. Seems like a lot of trouble to go to for that dreadful stuff in the cellar.'

Christie was looking out across the vines, a speculative expression on her face. 'You know, this is a great spot. The exposure's right; facing east, the stony ground warms up slowly, which is better for the roots, and there's a perfect slope for drainage. You should be able to grow some good wine here. Land like this would fetch a small fortune in Napa.'

'How small?'

'Well, to give you an idea: Coppola paid $350,000 an acre a couple of years back when he bought the Cohn winery.'

Max whistled.

'Yes,' said Christie. 'It's crazy. But that's the wine business. Have you ever heard of a wine called Screaming Eagle? Not long ago at the Napa Wine Auction, one bottle went for half a million dollars. One bottle.'

'Mad,' said Max. 'How could you ever drink a bottle of wine that cost half a million dollars?'

Christie laughed. 'You don't understand America. The guy who bought it will never drink it. It's for show, like a painting. He probably has it on a pedestal in his living room, along with the price tag.'

'You're right,' said Max. 'I don't understand America.'

They walked through the rest of the stony patch, and it was as Christie had thought, with those unobtrusive, neatly clipped bunches lying at the foot of the vines. Eventually, they would rot and disappear back into the earth. Next year, thought Max, the cycle would start again. He hoped he would still be there to see it.

*　　　*　　　*

Early evening found Max watching the sun slide down while he waited for Christie to finish getting ready for dinner *chez* Roussel. It had been an instructive day, and he was on the phone, reporting back to Charlie in London.

'. . . and so by the end of tomorrow, if this guy's any good, we should know what we have to do to sort out the vines. Now, is that property thing still on? Are you still coming down?'

'Next week. I've just been looking at the programme. You won't believe this, but "Whither the luxury villa?" is one of the subjects for a panel discussion. I ask you. Can you imagine anything more dreary? Anyway, I'm going to rent a car in Nice and get away as soon as I can. Do you good to have some company after being on your own in that bloody great château. What sort of kit will I need? White tie and tails? Shorts and sun hat?'

Max was about to answer when he saw Christie come out of the front door—a transformed Christie, with her hair swept up, wearing a slim black dress and a pair of scarlet high heels that hinted at a previously hidden side of her personality.

Without thinking, Max called across the courtyard, 'You look terrific.'

'What?' Charlie's voice on the other end of the line sounded puzzled.

'Not you, Charlie. Actually, it's a bit of a long story.'

'It's a babe, isn't it? You've got a babe there. Bastard.'

*   *   *

The Roussel mansion came as a surprise. Max had been anticipating a dilapidated collection of farm buildings, but instead he found himself driving up to a Provençal hacienda. True, it was constructed of concrete, that special raw pink concrete which is forever raw and pink, impervious to the softening effects of time and weather. But it was vast, with long, low wings extending on either side of a central two-storey block, steps leading up to an enormous tiled terrace, a meticulously landscaped front garden, and enough decorative wrought ironwork—trellises, gates and curlicued railings—to open a showroom. For a peasant with an ancient tractor, Roussel seemed to be doing rather well for himself.

They found him on the terrace, a cell phone

130

pressed to his ear, a frown on his face. Seeing them climbing up the steps, he finished the conversation and walked across to greet them, putting on a smile as he came. This evening, it was Roussel *en tenue de soirée*, wearing black trousers, crisp white shirt and black waistcoat, for all the world like Yves Montand about to do a turn on stage. The pale strip of untanned skin across the top of his forehead was the only sign that he spent most of his life outdoors with his cap on.

'Monsieur Max! Mademoiselle! Welcome!' He was clearly rather taken with Christie's outfit, lingering with exaggerated gallantry over her hand as he gave her bosom a surreptitious appraisal. 'We must have an *apéro*—no, first I show you my little property.'

He took them round to the back of the house, where they were greeted by a chorus of squeals and barks coming from a squirming pack of mud-coloured hounds. They were in a long, fenced-off run with a large wooden hut at one end built in the Alpine style, decorated with fretwork flourishes, more like a chalet than a kennel.

'*Chiens de chasse*,' said Roussel, waving a proprietorial arm. 'They are impatient for September, when the season starts. Nothing eludes them—boar, snipe, partridge . . .'

'Postmen?' said Max.

Roussel winked at him. 'Always the *blagueur*. But you should see them hunt, a magnificent sight.' He led them away from the kennel to an area enclosed by a stone wall that framed a picture of cultivated perfection—row upon row of vegetables, separated from one another by low box hedges and pathways of raked gravel. 'My *potager*,' said Roussel. 'I was

131

inspired by a photograph of the gardens at Villandry. This is more modest, of course. Would you care to see my black tomatoes?'

They marvelled at the black tomatoes, admired the small grove of truffle oaks, and exclaimed with wonder at Roussel's pride and joy, a lifesized sculpture of a wild boar rampant—*le sanglier rose*—executed in the same emphatic pink concrete as the house. Everything was immaculately maintained, and the property had evidently cost a considerable amount of money. Perhaps an inheritance, Max thought, or it might be that Roussel had made a lucrative marriage. That must be it. In any case, it was not what one would expect from a man who habitually dressed like a scarecrow down on his luck.

The glories of the garden dealt with, Roussel took them back to the terrace to meet madame, a swarthy, smiling woman with the shadow of a moustache and a taste for bright orange accessories. She distributed pastis, they clinked glasses, and stood in amiable silence, searching for conversation. Max congratulated them on their view while Christie, recovering from her first-ever encounter with pastis, did her best with smiles and sign language to compliment madame on her unusually vibrant earrings.

And then, with a rumble of wheels, the Roussels' daughter, a more delicate version of her mother, emerged from the house with a moveable feast—a trolley laden with slices of fat-dappled sausage, wedges of pizza, tapenade on squares of toasted bread, slivers of raw vegetables with an *anchoïade* dip, olives both green and black, radishes with white butter, and a thick earthenware terrine of

132

thrush pâté, with the unfortunate bird's beak protruding from the dark meat.

'Ah,' said Roussel, rubbing his hands, 'a few small mouthfuls to encourage the appetite.'

Max nudged Christie. 'Pace yourself.'

She looked at the trolley. 'This isn't dinner?'

Max shook his head. 'Afraid not.'

For a few moments, nothing was heard except murmurs of appreciation at the display of food, which seemed to act as a signal for Madame Roussel to excuse herself and return to the kitchen with her daughter. Roussel took a knife to the thrush pâté and spread some on a small square of toast, which he presented to Christie. She took it with barely concealed reluctance, her eyes still on the beak as she whispered to Max: 'What else is in there? The head? The feet?'

Roussel smiled at her, pointing to his mouth and nodding his encouragement. 'Jolly good,' he said, drawing on the limited English vocabulary he had picked up from Uncle Henry. 'Stick it to your ribs.'

'Claude,' said Max, 'there's something I wanted to ask you. You know the vines at the end of the property, beyond the wall? I took a look at them today, and I noticed that a lot of the young grapes have been cut off. Is that a good idea? I mean, I'm no expert, but it seems like a bit of a waste.'

Roussel took his time to answer, his tan and white forehead crinkled in thought, his lower lip out-thrust. He sighed, a melodramatic gale of air that made his lip tremble. 'People will tell you,' he said, 'that vines must suffer, but that poor parcel of land is beyond suffering. Nothing but stones and dust'—he paused to shake his head—'*putain*, even the weeds complain. If I didn't thin out the bunches, we wouldn't have grapes; we'd have pinheads. Pinheads,' he repeated, holding up a forefinger and thumb a millimetre apart.

He drained his glass, and searched the trolley without success for the bottle. Muttering about his wife letting them die of thirst, he went indoors to fetch more pastis.

Max took the chance to tell Christie what Roussel had said about the grapes. Looking around, she tipped the remains of her drink into a glazed urn containing a neatly tailored shrub, and shook her head. 'I don't buy that,' she said. 'Nobody goes to that kind of trouble unless . . . you know what? Why don't you ask him . . .'

But he was back, brandishing a bottle and some of his best cocktail-party English. Refilling their glasses, he beamed, and with an accent that had very little to do with any known tongue, cried, 'Bottoms away! Air of zer dog! Pip pip!'

Christie edged closer to the glazed urn, waiting for an appropriate moment to jettison at least part of the mixture—forty-five degrees of aniseed-flavoured alcohol—that was already starting to make her head swim.

Before Max had a chance to return to the subject of the grapes, Roussel moved closer to him, putting one weather-beaten paw on his shoulder. 'Tell me, Monsieur Max,' he said, 'just between us, of course: what are your plans for the house?'

Max considered the question for a moment, tempted to provide Roussel with some grist for the village gossip mill: a weekend love nest for the Marseille soccer team, an ostrich farm, a school for wayward girls. 'I don't know,' he said finally. 'I'm still settling in. Anyway, there's no need to rush

134

things.'

Roussel patted his shoulder and nodded. 'Very wise. A place like that, right in the heart of the Luberon, is impossible to find nowadays. English, Germans, Americans, Parisians—they're all looking for houses down here.' He removed his hand from Max's shoulder and used his index finger to stir the ice cubes in his glass. 'Best to take your time. Be sure to let me know if you should decide to sell. And *attention.*' The dripping finger was wagged in Max's face. 'Never trust a real estate agent. They're all bandits. I could tell you stories you wouldn't believe. But where are my manners? We are ignoring mademoiselle.' He looked across at Christie, standing by her urn, smiling. Roussel nodded approvingly at the sight of her empty glass, offered her his arm, and the three of them went into the house for dinner.

The interior of the house was as perfectly maintained as the garden, with an equally impressive array of ironwork—over-wrought iron, even more complicated in its twirls and entanglements than the selection in the garden. The tiled floors and the dark wooden furniture gleamed with care and polish. No wall was without its niche, and no niche was without its framed photograph—portraits, for the most part, illustrating the Roussel dynasty, with several studies of camouflage-clad men, chests thrown out, displaying their furred or feathered victims.

Roussel led them through to the dining room, where an entire wall was dedicated to the pleasures of the hunt. There was an iron-barred cabinet, fully stocked with rifles; a stuffed fox snarling from the confines of its glass-fronted prison; an enormous *sanglier* head, mounted on a wooden shield and surrounded by more photographs of Roussel and his fellow warriors; and, hanging over the long dining table like a pungent shroud, the reek of garlic.

'A simple meal,' said Roussel as they all sat down, 'such as a man might have after a day's work in the fields.' It began with *caviar d'aubergine*, a cold purée of eggplant, and a plate piled high with the rolled, stuffed parcels of meat known in Provence, for some reason, as larks without heads. Roussel made a tour of the table, pouring heavy red Châteauneuf from an embossed bottle, and the sight of wine reminded Max of the next day's rendezvous with the man from Bordeaux.

'I'm sure Nathalie Auzet told you about tomorrow,' he said. 'She's found an *oenologue* to come and look at the vines.'

Roussel finished pouring the wine into his own glass, with a roll of the wrist to catch the last drop, and sat down. 'She called me tonight, just when you were arriving.' He shook his head and sighed. 'These Bordelais—they think they can drop in whenever it suits them. But don't you worry about it. I'll deal with him. I'm sure you have better things to do. Leave it to me.' He raised his glass, aiming it first at Christie, then at Max. 'To America! To England! To the *entente cordiale*!'

Christie was hungry, and being unused to Provençal hospitality—which refuses to take no for an answer—made the mistake of finishing her first headless lark rather too quickly. Madame Roussel replaced it at once, serving with it another dollop of aubergine, and giving her a thick slice of bread to mop up the juice. This time, alas, there was no

136

urn to come to her rescue. She noticed that Max was eating very slowly, nodding and smiling as he listened to one of Roussel's monologues.

'People will tell you,' Roussel was saying as he uncorked two more bottles, 'that if you eat the tops of five raw cabbages before drinking, you can take as much wine as you like without suffering.' He made a tour of the table, topping up glasses. 'Roasted goats' lungs are supposed to do the same, although I personally have never tried them. But best of all, so they say, are the beaks of swallows, burnt to a cinder and then ground to a fine powder. You put a pinch or two of the powder in your first glass of wine, and anything you drink afterwards will have no effect on you at all. *Voilà*.'

'Fascinating,' said Max. 'I must make a note to buy some beaks.' He caught Christie's eye and translated for her, seeing her smile gradually freeze when he came to the swallow's beak recipe.

She shuddered, and took a long swallow of wine. 'These guys and their beaks. Haven't they heard of Alka-Seltzer?'

The meal moved slowly on to the main event, brought ceremoniously to the table in a deep iron casserole: a stew of wild boar, almost black with wine and blood-thickened gravy, accompanied by a *gratin* of cheese and potatoes and a further topping-up of Châteauneuf. Christie looked with dismay at the steaming plateful put in front of her, enough for an entire pack of famished dogs. Max loosened his belt. The Roussels attacked their food with undiminished enthusiasm.

There were, inevitably, second helpings. There was cheese. There were great wedges of *tarte aux pommes*, shiny with glaze. And finally, with the

137

coffee and diamond-shaped almond biscuits, there was a compulsory snifter of Roussel's venomous homemade *marc*.

By this time, Christie was anaesthetized. She had arrived at that stage of overeating reached by certain species prior to hibernation and was barely capable of movement or thought, conscious only of an instinct to curl up in a quiet, dark place. Max was little better, and even Roussel had begun to show signs of wear, making only a token effort to persuade them into another glass of *marc*.

It had been, as Max assured Madame Roussel on the doorstep, a memorable evening. After a round of kissing and handshaking, he steered an unsteady Christie across the terrace and folded her into the car.

'I thought you did very well,' he said as they were driving home. 'California would be proud of you. I'm sorry to have put you through all that—I had no idea it was going to be such a marathon. Are you feeling OK?'

There was no reply. And when they reached the house, Max had to carry her, a dead weight smelling faintly of *marc* and almond biscuits, from the car. He took her upstairs, laid her on the bed, took off her shoes, and pulled a blanket over her. As he was putting a pillow under her head, she stirred, and whispered from the depths of her stupor, 'No more. Please. No more.'

Thirteen

Max sat on the raised rim of the *bassin*, his head between his knees, wondering if the heart attack would come before or after breakfast. The heat of the morning sun and the overindulgence of the night before had turned what was normally a pleasant run into an exercise in masochism. He groaned, went over to the fountain, and put his head under the flow of cool water.

A screech from Madame Passepartout, who had been watching him from the kitchen window, cut through the fog in his brain. 'Monsieur Max! Are you mad? That water! There are *microbes* in every drop. Come inside!'

Max sighed, and did as he was told. Madame Passepartout had taken it upon herself to assume medical responsibility for the cut on his head—his wound, as she called it—and had equipped herself with an interesting variety of salves and dressings, which she now laid out on the kitchen table. Muttering about the perils of infection and the virtues of sterility, she removed the old pink bandage and doused the cut with Mercurochrome.

'How does it look?' he asked.

'Silence,' said the great healer. 'This part is extremely delicate.' With her tongue protruding from the corner of her mouth, she applied ointment and a covering of gauze before sealing off the area with an excessively large adhesive pad. 'There,' she said. 'I thought you'd prefer white this time. The pink was most unsuitable.'

Max smiled his thanks. 'Have you seen Christie

this morning?'

'No.' There was a pause while Madame Passepartout stood back to admire her handiwork. 'But I have heard her.'

'That bad, is it?'

Madame Passepartout nodded. 'That brother-in-law of mine, he has a head like a stone. He forgets that others are not used to these things.' She counted them off on her fingers. 'Pastis, wine, and marc—a recipe for catastrophe. C'est fou.'

There was the sound of footsteps making their slow and uncertain way down the stairs, and Christie appeared in the doorway, her face half-hidden by very large, very dark sunglasses. 'Water,' she said. 'Lots of water.' Like a sleepwalker on Valium, she made her way to the refrigerator and took out a bottle of Vittel.

At the sight of someone who so obviously felt closer to death than himself, Max immediately began to feel better. 'Must have been something you ate,' he said. 'Those almond biscuits are killers.' The sunglasses and the clearly unamused face turned toward Max for a moment, then turned away. 'Seriously, it would do you good to get out,' he said. 'Fresh air, birdsong, sunlight on the slopes of the Luberon . . .'

'Coffee,' said Christie. 'Lots of coffee.'

*   *   *

Sitting outside the café after a litre of water and almost as much coffee, Christie was sufficiently recovered to take an interest in what was going on around her. It was market day in Saint-Pons, and stalls had been set up under the plane trees in the

140

square. It seemed as though half of Provence had come to shop, or to look, or to be looked at.

A system of colour coding helped to identify the swarm of humanity moving between the stalls: the locals, most of them deeply tanned, with their faded clothes and well-worn straw shopping baskets; the summer visitors, their skin tones running from northern white to brick red, their new outfits bright with this season's colours; the dark caramel complexions of the North African jewelry sellers; the blue-black of the Senegalese, with their trays of watches and leather goods. A well-tuned nose could pick out the scent of spices, of spit-roasting chickens, of lavender essence, of cheese. And the attentive ear could recognize snatches of at least four languages—French, Arabic, German, English—in addition to the Franco-tourist dialect, a kind of commercial Esperanto spoken by most of the stall holders.

Christie's eye was caught by a group of middle-aged cyclists at the edge of the market taking a break from their exertions. Their gleaming bicycles bristled with gears and gadgets, including cell phone holders fixed to the handlebars, and attached to the back of each saddle was a slender pole from which bravely fluttered a triangular white flag. The owners of these splendid machines, gentlemen encased in too-tight Lycra, resembled plump, multicoloured sausages topped off with lightweight crash helmets the shape of insects' heads. They all wore the fingerless gloves and the narrow, wraparound sunglasses favoured by riders in the Tour de France, and they were verbally slapping one another on the back for completing their gruelling morning spin. Their voices easily

141

carried above the din of the market.

Christie winced. 'Why are Americans always the loudest? It's so embarrassing.'

'They're in pain,' said Max. 'It's those tight shorts. Actually, I'm not sure I agree with you. Have you ever heard the English in full cry? World-class bellowers, some of them.' He watched as one of the cyclists performed a complicated stretching ritual before getting back on the saddle. 'The fact is, we're always tougher on people from our own country. There are lots of wonderful Americans. One of them married my ex-wife, bless his heart.' He sat back and looked at Christie. 'How about you? Is Mr. Napa waiting for you back in the valley?'

Christie shook her head. 'I just broke up with a guy after two years. A lawyer. It's one of the reasons I wanted to get away from California for a while.'

'Heart broken?'

'His more than mine, I guess. I think he wants to get back together.' She grinned at Max. 'So with a bit of luck, he won't sue.'

As Max was looking for the waiter to pay the bill, Fanny came past the café on the way to work, carrying a long brown paper sack stuffed with oversized restaurant loaves. She stopped to be kissed and to fuss over Max's bandaged head. 'Have you seen Roussel?' she asked. 'He was looking for you. Something about a rendezvous at the house this afternoon. A private matter, he said.' She stood smiling at him, her dark eyes bright with curiosity. 'As if anything in this village could be private.'

'Nice outfit,' Max said, taking in the abbreviated

142

cotton vest and low-slung jeans that set off several inches of bare tanned midriff. 'Probably the septic tank,' he said. 'There's a bit of a problem.'

'*Merde*,' said Fanny.

'Afraid so.'

Christie watched as Fanny left and made her way through the crowd. 'It's pretty obvious from seeing the two of you together,' she said. 'You should do something about it. You know? A date?'

Max clapped his hand to his heart and put on a rueful expression. 'All I can do is admire her from afar,' he said. 'It's those impossible restaurant hours. Bloody unsociable. I suppose I could offer to help with the dishes.' He left some change on the table and stood up, looking at his watch. 'Come on. I thought we could buy some stuff in the market and have lunch at the house, in case the wine man turns up early.'

They joined the crush moving slowly through the square, and stopped first at a stall festooned with sausages, its counter covered with *confits* and pâtés that Christie peered at over her sunglasses. 'Could I make a menu request?' she said. 'Nothing with a beak, OK?'

They picked out a rough country pâté, watching the deft hands of the stall holder cut two thick slices and wrap them in waxed paper. He counted out their change with fingers as rosy pink as a well-boiled ham while he advised them on a suitable wine, and the necessity—the absolute necessity—of buying a few *cornichons* to go with the pâté. Then to the cheese stall, and a discussion about the ripeness of the goat cheeses from Banon; each plump disc was wrapped in chestnut leaves that, so they were assured, had been soaked in eau-de-vie.

143

They went on to buy salad and fruit, bread and oil, and a flask of balsamic vinegar, finishing off at the flower stall to pick up a bunch of vivid parrot tulips for the table.

Christie was fascinated by the novelty of it all—the talkative stall keepers, the small courtesies that accompanied each transaction, the general air of easygoing good humour, the lack of haste.

'It beats pushing a shopping cart through the local supermarket,' she said. 'That's for sure. But something like this couldn't happen back home. I mean, there are dogs everywhere, people are smoking, and the guys behind the stalls aren't even wearing plastic gloves. The hygiene police in California would have a field day. They'd shut everything down.'

'And arrest the dogs for loitering with intent, I'm sure,' said Max. 'Amazing that we're not all dropping like flies, really. Yet people seem to live as long here as they do in the States, or longer. You must have read some of those statistics.'

'Sure. We send them out as press releases. You know—the French Paradox: a bottle a day keeps the doctor away. Every time the figures are published, sales of red wine go through the roof. Americans love the quick fix.'

Laden with plastic bags, they were on their way to the car when they came to the village church, and Max stopped to read a notice pinned to the door. He smiled and shook his head. 'Provençal logic. It's wonderful.' He translated the contents of the message. *Please note: The meeting scheduled for today has been changed. It took place yesterday.*

Arriving back at the house, they found a note from Madame Passepartout informing them that a

Monsieur Fitzgerald from Bordeaux had called to say that he would be with them in the early afternoon; that Max was under no circumstances to get his head wet, or too hot; and that she was unable to return to work after lunch due to a *crise de chat*.

'A cat crisis,' Max said in explanation. 'She has this old moggy who sometimes gets fur balls and has to have her paw held. Actually, it's better that she won't be here. She'd be telling the *oenologue* what to do.'

They unpacked the food and Max went to the sink to wash the salad, while Christie perched on the edge of the kitchen table with a glass of wine and a cigarette. 'It doesn't seem like real life down here,' she said. 'Is it always like this? What's it like in the winter?'

Max laid the washed salad out to dry on a strip of paper towel. 'I've never been here in the winter. Uncle Henry always used to say it was a great time of the year for writers and alcoholics—cold, quiet, empty, nothing much to do. I'm rather looking forward to it.' If I'm still here, he couldn't help thinking, as he reached up to the shelf for a battered olive wood salad bowl. He pushed the thought away. 'Now then. This is one of the few things I can manage in the kitchen without chopping bits off my fingers or breaking something: *la sauce vinaigrette à ma façon*. Watch closely.'

He put black pepper and two generous pinches of sea salt into the bowl, grinding them together with the back of a fork until he'd made a coarse black and white dust. A few drops of balsamic vinegar—a deep, deep brown—went in next, and then a long stream of olive oil, greenish yellow in

145

the sunlight. Finally, a cherry-sized blob of full-strength Maille mustard from Dijon. Max picked up the bowl and held it against his stomach while he whisked the mixture with his fork, checking its consistency two or three times before he was satisfied. Putting the bowl down, he tore off a piece of baguette, mopped it in the brown puddle he had prepared with such care, and offered the dripping bread to Christie. 'Some people add lemon juice,' he said, 'but I prefer it like this. What do you think?'

He watched as Christie took the bread and bit into it, wiping a dribble of dressing from her chin with the back of her hand and chewing for a few moments in silence.

'Well?'

Christie looked at the ceiling, nodded her head. 'Shows promise,' she said, in her best wine taster's voice. 'Do I detect a hint of Hellman's?' She looked at Max's stricken face. 'No, it's great. You could bottle it and make a fortune.'

'It's never the same from a bottle. Here, take this tray and I'll bring the rest. We'll eat outside.'

*   *   *

An hour later, they were sitting at the stone table over the remains of lunch and the last of the pink wine when the clatter and wheeze of a weary engine announced the arrival of Roussel's van, which was followed a moment later by a gleaming bottle-green Jaguar. As the dust thrown up by their wheels settled, a tall, elegant man, dressed in a putty-coloured linen suit, got out of the Jaguar. He removed his sunglasses, smoothed his jacket, and

146

brushed back a wing of greying hair from his forehead before walking over to Max.

'Jean-Marie Fitzgerald. *Très heureux.*' The two men shook hands, and Max introduced Christie. Muttering again how happy he was, Fitzgerald performed the ritual of the near-miss kiss—*osculum interruptum*—still favoured by Frenchmen of a certain age and a certain class, ducking his head low over Christie's hand but not quite touching it with his lips before straightening up.

'Fitzgerald,' said Max. 'That's a name I'd associate with Dublin; certainly not with Bordeaux.'

The Frenchman smiled. 'I'm what the English sometimes call a "bog frog"—half-Irish, half-French. There are quite a few of us scattered around in southwestern France. Our Irish ancestors must have liked the climate and the local girls.'

'I imagine your English is pretty good, then?'

Fitzgerald gave Max a rueful look, shaking his head. 'Unfortunately, my English studies didn't get much further than a few phrases—"My tailor is rich," that kind of thing.'

For once, this gem of Gallic humour didn't bring a smile to Roussel's face. He seemed uncomfortable, far from the relaxed, expansive soul of the previous evening. He was virtually ignoring Fitzgerald, and Max wondered if there was a problem between them, or whether it was just the instinctive mistrust that tends to exist between peasants and strangers in suits.

'Do you two know each other?' he asked Roussel.

A vigorous shake of the head. 'Only since half an

147

hour. Monsieur Max, are you sure you want to bother yourself with this? It's hot, and I can easily show him what he needs to see.'

'No, no, it's fine. Part of my education.'

They set off into the fields, Fitzgerald picking his way daintily up and down the rows of vines, stopping from time to time to cup a bunch of grapes in his hand, to ask the age of the vines, or to take a pinch of earth between his fingers, jotting down the occasional thought with a gold pen in a leather notebook. After an hour or so of this, his sadly wrinkled linen suit was showing the effects of the heat, and a drop of perspiration was decorating the tip of his patrician nose.

'Of course,' he said to Max, 'this afternoon is merely a reconnaissance to familiarize myself with the lay of the land.' He stared out across the orderly green rows shimmering in the heat and mopped his face with a silk handkerchief. 'Which, I have to say, seems to be well kept. I will need to take samples of the soil for analysis—*argilo-calcaire*, I would imagine; your man Roussel can help me with that. And naturally I will have to come back to see the *cave*: the condition and quality of your barrels, the details of your *assemblage*—how much Syrah, how much Grenache, and so on—also even the nature of your corks and your choice of bottles. *Bref*, I shall need to take everything into account before making any kind of recommendation.' He closed his notebook with a snap. 'I hope you're not in a hurry, monsieur. But today we can say we're making a start.' He looked at his watch. 'And now, if you'll excuse me, I have a rendezvous on the other side of the Luberon.'

Roussel, who had been silent and attentive, turned to go back with Fitzgerald to the house.

'Hold on,' said Max. 'We haven't finished here yet. There's the other vineyard.' He pointed to the land beyond the stone wall. 'I think Monsieur Fitzgerald should take a look at it.'

Roussel threw up his hands. *'That?* That catastrophe? Just the sight of it would plunge monsieur into despair.' He turned to Fitzgerald. 'Nothing but rocks and grief. Pitiful, pitiful.'

'Even so,' said Max, 'I'd like him to see it while he's here.'

Roussel and Fitzgerald led the way across the field, and Max continued with the translation he'd been providing for Christie during lulls in the conversation. '. . . So Roussel's not too keen on him seeing that patch beyond the wall. Tell me, what do you think of Fitzgerald?'

Christie shrugged. 'It would help if I could understand him. But I'd expected someone—oh, I don't know, someone a little more earthy. He never does any work in the vines, that's for sure. His hands are too soft.'

They watched as the two men in front of them reached the wall. Roussel heaved himself up until he was sitting on top, and then swung his legs across, swivelling on his bottom. Fitzgerald, giving more thought to the well-being of his trousers, negotiated the wall in a tentative, crablike fashion, and stood on the other side, dusting himself down and pushing back the wing of hair that kept flopping onto his forehead.

Roussel waited for Christie and Max before delivering once again his low opinion of the land on which they were standing. 'More like a quarry than a vineyard.' He bent down to pick up a handful of white stone chippings, holding them out to Fitzgerald. 'Call this earth? One might as well try to grow asparagus in the Sahara.' Fitzgerald shook his head in sympathy, his lower lip thrust out as a sign of regret at what he saw.

Turning to Max, Fitzgerald smiled. 'Well,' he said, 'at least there is the rest of the land. I'm sure we can make some progress there. All it takes is time and money.' He started back toward the wall.

'Max,' said Christie, 'ask him why all those bunches have been clipped. I mean, if it's such lousy land, why bother?' She kept her eyes on Fitzgerald as she spoke.

He paused at the sound of her voice, then bent his head to listen to Max's translation. 'A good question. It is common practice, of course, to do it in Bordeaux, but here? In this rubble?' The eyebrows went up in silent inquiry as he looked to Roussel for the answer.

Roussel tossed the handful of chippings back onto the ground. 'As I have already explained to Monsieur Max, it is my little experiment, my last try.' He dusted his hands against his trousers. 'I'm hoping that the size of the grapes can be increased.'

Fitzgerald's expression changed to amused astonishment. '*Incroyable,*' he said to Max. 'I thought I'd never live to see a peasant who is also an optimist.' He patted Roussel on the shoulder. 'I wish you luck, monsieur, with your giant grapes. Or better still, a miracle. And now, I really must go.'

While Max was translating the exchange for Christie, Fitzgerald strode off in the direction of the house, with Roussel a few paces behind. Clearly, as far as they were concerned, the

150

reconnaissance was over.

'Well,' Max said to Christie, 'that wasn't too encouraging.'

'You know something?' she said. 'I think that guy understands English. I was watching his face, and when I asked about the grapes, he couldn't stop himself from looking at them. Just a glance, but I'm sure he knew what I was saying.'

Had there been a flicker of understanding, quickly disguised? Max couldn't say; he'd been looking at Christie when she asked the question. 'I don't know,' he said. 'But he didn't seem to be all that interested. It might be a good idea to get a second opinion. I'll talk to Roussel.'

'Wouldn't hurt,' said Christie. 'There's something not right about that guy. I've never seen a real wine man with a manicure before.'

Fourteen

Sitting in his office high above the harbour, Mr. Chen lit a cigarette and reached for the phone. He was about to confirm his reputation as Hong Kong's most exclusive wine merchant, the *négociant* to know if you were looking for rare vintages or special bottles, and had the deep pockets to afford them. At the mention of his name, the secretary on the other end of the line put him straight through.

Chen wasted no time on pleasantries. 'This is a lucky day for you,' he said to his client. 'I did well in Bordeaux. I got six cases, and I can promise you they're the only cases in Hong Kong. Now, in view of our long relationship, not to mention our deep friendship, I've put aside two cases for you at $75,000 per case. That's U.S. dollars, of course.'

He paused to let the news of his generosity sink in. 'What? How does it taste? What's that got to do with it? Come on, my friend. You know as well as I do this isn't wine for drinking; it's for buying and selling. An *investment*. My other clients here would sell their mothers for this wine. Hold it for a year, two years. The way it's going, you could double your money. No, I'm afraid that's not possible. Just the two cases. The others are promised to Beijing and Seoul. Yes? Good. You won't regret it.'

Chen put the phone down, blew a celebratory smoke ring, and crossed a name off the short list on his desk. Perhaps he should raise the price to $80,000. This was going to be an interesting couple of days. He put in a call to Beijing.

*   *   *

On the other side of the world, Roussel had, as usual, returned to his pink palace for lunch. He was a preoccupied man, picking at the salt pork and lentils of his favourite *petit salé*, saying little, hardly touching his wine. His wife Ludivine, accustomed to seeing a clean plate and an empty glass at mealtimes, came to the natural conclusion.

'It's your stomach, isn't it?' she said, with the conviction of a wife long familiar with the vagaries of her husband's digestive system. 'Too much cheese last night. You need a purge.'

Roussel shook his head and pushed his plate away. 'My stomach? No, that's fine.'

'So what is it?' She reached across the table and patted his hand. 'Come, Clo-Clo, tell me.'

He sighed, and let his body slump back in the chair. 'It's the vines. You know, the little patch.' Ludivine nodded. 'Well, yesterday we had the *oenologue* from Bordeaux come to look at the property, *un monsieur très snob*, someone arranged by Nathalie Auzet.'

'What did he say?'

'Oh, nothing much. Nothing good, anyway. I think that was the problem, because this morning Monsieur Max told me he was going to find someone else and get a second opinion. And you realize what that means?' Roussel traced circles on the table with his wineglass, his face the picture of dejection.

Ludivine did indeed realize what it meant, and had been half-expecting it for years. She came around the table and stood behind him, massaging his shoulders. '*Chéri*,' she said, 'it was bound to end sooner or later. We've had some good years because of those vines—the house, the cars, more than we could have imagined when we first got married.' She bent to kiss the top of his head. 'I hate to see you like this.' With a final squeeze of his shoulders, she cleared away the plates and was about to take them to the sink when she stopped, setting the plates back on the table with a rattle that made her husband start. She tapped a finger with considerable emphasis on the table. Her voice was equally emphatic. 'You must tell him, Clo-Clo. You must.'

Roussel sat staring at her, chewing his lip and saying nothing.

She reached out for his hand, and her tone softened. 'He seems very *sympa*, the young man. He'll understand. Better that he should find out

153

from you than from someone else, no?' She answered her own question by nodding vigorously. 'Much better.'

* * *

The mid-afternoon air was still, and thick with heat. Max was on a ladder, wrestling with a tangle of wisteria that was trying to creep uninvited into the house through an upstairs window. Christie had gone off in search of an English-language newspaper, and Madame Passepartout, her cat crisis over, was hanging out the washing on a makeshift line she had strung up in a corner of the tennis court.

The calm of the moment was broken by the clatter of Roussel's van coming to a stop in the courtyard. As was his invariable habit, Tonto was the first to get out, rushing across to bark at the ladder before sniffing it with great deliberation and cocking his leg against it. Roussel scolded him half-heartedly as he peered up at the figure perched above him, silhouetted against the sun-bleached pale blue of the sky.

'Monsieur Max, do I disturb you?'

Max came down the ladder, and the two men shook hands, Roussel tugging at one ear while he searched for words. 'I must speak to you,' he said, 'and there is something I must show you. It's about the vines.' He jerked his head toward the van. 'We can go together now, if you have the time.'

They drove without speaking in the direction of the village, and then turned off to follow a narrow track that ended in front of a long, windowless barn built into the side of a gentle fold in the land, its

154

double doors barred and padlocked. 'The *cave*,' said Roussel. 'You haven't seen it before.'

Max shook his head. 'I thought you took the grapes straight down to the *co-opérative*.'

'Not all of them,' said Roussel. 'That's what I want to talk to you about.'

He parked the van in front of the barn, and Max stood watching Tonto roll in the dust, squirming with pleasure as he rubbed his back on the grit while Roussel unlocked the barn doors and slid them open. He went into the gloom and turned on a light before beckoning Max to follow.

The temperature inside the *cave* was cool, almost chilly after the heat outside, and the air smelled slightly humid; tannic and musty. The floor was rough concrete, divided down the middle by a wine-stained drainage channel. On either side of the channel, raised up on plinths of concrete, were rows of barrels, marked in chalk with a scribbled code meaningless to anyone except the wine grower. Standing in one corner next to the door was a rickety tin table with a scattering of papers, a couple of dingy glasses, and a long glass syringe with a rubber bulb the size of a fist at one end. On the wall, hanging from a rusty nail, was a calendar illustrated with photographs of young women in the throes of some private ecstasy, draped over tractors.

Max looked around with interest, wondering if he was expected to say anything as Roussel wiped the glasses free of dust with a handkerchief and pulled two elderly wooden chairs up to the table. He gestured to Max to take a seat and half-closed one of the doors to lessen the glare. Finally, with a sigh, he took off his cap and sat down.

'Monsieur Max,' he began, 'as you know, I have worked on the vines at Le Griffon for thirty years, ever since your uncle bought the house. Many times over the years, I asked him to replace the vines, which were old and tired even before he arrived.' He looked down at the table, twisting his cap in his hands. 'But, for one reason or another, it was never the right moment: Next year, he used to say, we'll do it next year.

'There was one parcel, the parcel beyond the wall, which I thought could produce good wine.' He paused to shake his head, correcting himself. 'No, I was *sure* it could. It had the right stony soil, the right exposure, the right slope, not too big, perfect. I told your uncle—this was more than fifteen years ago—but he wasn't interested, or he had no money left after repairing the roof; there was always something. In the end, I decided to take out the old vines and replant the land myself. Ludivine and me, we had a little money saved.' He looked at Max for a few moments in silence, his eyebrows raised, waiting for a reaction.

'I should think the old boy was delighted, wasn't he?'

Roussel's hands continued to strangle his cap. 'Well, I never told him exactly what I'd done. He thought I had just used ordinary vine stock, but I wanted something better, something special. He had no idea I replanted with the best Cabernet Sauvignon and a little Merlot. Nobody did. These things are complicated in France. The regulations, the authorities from the agricultural ministry *qui se mêlent de tout*, who want you to declare every twig and fallen leaf.' He shrugged. 'Impossible. It was easier to say nothing.'

156

Without warning, he got to his feet, picked up the syringe from the table, and walked over to the barrels. Max watched as he knocked out the bung from one of them, inserted the syringe, and drew off several inches of wine. Coming back to the table, he squeezed the bulb carefully and half-filled both glasses, holding one of them up to the light.

'*Bon*. Go ahead. Taste it. Remember that it's still young.'

Max picked up the glass, conscious of Roussel's intent stare and his own shortcomings as a wine connoisseur. But once the wine was in his mouth, sending powerful and delightful signals to his palate, even he could tell that it was a different drink altogether from ordinary Luberon wines. He wished he could remember some of Charlie's ornate vocabulary, and was so impressed he forgot to spit.

'That's amazing,' he said, raising his glass to Roussel. 'Congratulations.'

Roussel seemed hardly to hear him. 'Nobody down here makes wine like this,' he said. 'And yet I realized that there was a problem: I couldn't sell it—not legally, at any rate, because the Cabernet and Merlot vines hadn't been declared. So I went to Maître Auzet for advice, thinking that she could find *une petite lacune* in the law. She's clever like that.' He took a mouthful of wine and chewed on it for a few seconds before spitting it into the drainage channel. 'That's when it started. Instead of a loophole, she found a buyer; someone who would take all of it, every year, and pay cash—good money, no paperwork, no tax, no questions asked. I couldn't resist. My wife, my daughter, my old age . . .' He looked at Max with the mournful, guilty

157

expression of an old hound caught *in flagrante* with an illicit lamb chop.

Max leaned back in his chair while he took in what Roussel has just said: Nathalie Auzet, *notaire* and *négociante*. No wonder she looked so prosperous. 'Who does she sell it to?'

'I don't know. I've never met the buyer. Nathalie said it wasn't necessary.'

'Well, where do you send it? Paris, Germany, Belgium?'

Roussel shook his head. 'Who knows where it goes? The truck comes once a year—in September, just before I start the *vendange*, and always at night. The wine from the previous year is transferred from the barrels, and I get my cash the following week. From Nathalie.'

'But the truck. Surely it has a name on the side? A company, an enterprise of some sort?'

Roussel's hand dropped down to fondle Tonto's ear. 'No. That's not normal, I know, but in an *affaire* like this, one doesn't ask too many questions. All I can tell you is the truck that picks up the wine has licence plates with a 33 registration.' He cocked his thumb over his shoulder, in a vague northerly direction. 'The Gironde.'

Max shook his head. 'How long has this been going on?'

'Seven or eight years, maybe a little longer. I don't remember exactly.'

'What I don't understand,' said Max, 'is why you're telling me all this. I might never have found out.'

Roussel stared at the shimmering horizon through the half-open doors of the *cave*, his eyes

158

narrowed, his dark brown face immobile, etched with deep lines. His head might have been cast in bronze. He turned back to Max.

'Your uncle was more interested in his books and his music than the vines. Even so, there were many times I almost told him, but—well, I paid for the vines, I planted them, I nursed them. I buy new oak barrels—the best French oak—every four years. No expense is spared. Everything is correct. And your uncle never suffered; it wasn't like stealing. It seemed fair. Not strictly honest perhaps, but fair. And now it's all changed, with you wanting to improve the vines, bringing in all these *oenologues* . . .' He finished the wine, swallowing this time, and put the glass down carefully. 'To tell you the truth, Monsieur Max, I knew someone would find out. I thought it best to tell you myself.' He resumed the mournful expression as he waited to see how his confession had been received.

Max was silent for a few moments. And then: 'You say it was Nathalie Auzet's idea?'

Roussel nodded. 'She's no fool, that one. She took care of everything.'

Two surprises for Max in the space of half an hour. The vineyard was not what it seemed. The glamorous *notaire* was not what she seemed. As for Roussel: Was he genuine, or was he playing some game of his own? Could the wine be sold legally, or would there be horrendous penalties? There were complications galore, far too many for any kind of instant decision.

'Well,' said Max, 'I'm glad you told me. I know it wasn't easy. Let me think about it.'

*   *   *

159

The afternoon had drifted into a still, warm evening under a lavender sky shot through with streaks of pink, promising another glorious day tomorrow. The tantalizing whiff of cooking came through the open windows of houses in the village. Christie had managed to find a three-day-old copy of the *International Herald Tribune*, and was giving Max belated news of the outside world, mostly the summer antics of politicians, as they walked toward Fanny's. Passing the *boules* court, they paused to watch the next throw. As always, it was an all-male event.

Christie found this puzzling, coming as she did from a country where women's participation in sports now extended to boxing—and soon, no doubt, to sumo wrestling. 'You've been coming down here a long time,' she said. 'Do you know why it is that you never see women playing?'

'Never thought about it,' Max said. 'You just don't. Hold on.' He went over to an old man, dark and wrinkled as a well-cured olive, who was waiting his turn to throw, and repeated the question. There was a cackle from the old man, and he said something to Max that provoked a ragged chorus of cackles from the other players.

Max was smiling when he came back to translate. 'You're not going to like this. But he said women should be home cooking dinner. Oh, and he said he could teach his dog to play *boules* better than any woman.'

Christie's face, her shoulders, her whole body stiffened with indignation. 'We'll see about that. Watch this, buster.'

She stepped onto the court, taking a *boule* from

160

the startled old man, and went up to the pitching mark drawn in the dust. The players fell silent. She crouched down, took long and careful aim, and let fly, scattering the other *boules* and scoring a direct hit on the *cochonnet*.

Turning to the old man, now even more startled, she tapped herself on the chest. 'St. Helena junior bowling champion, 1993.' Reversing the direction of her hand, she then tapped him on the chest. 'And you can tell your dog to eat his heart out.' The old man watched her leave the court, raising his cap to scratch his head. How times have changed, he thought to himself. How times have changed.

As soon as they reached the restaurant, Christie went to wash the dust from her hands, giving Fanny the chance to ask Max a question that had occupied her for several days: 'The little American girl—she's your *copine*?'

'No, no, no,' said Max. 'Just a friend. Too young for me.'

Fanny smiled and ruffled his hair as she gave him the menu. 'You're quite right. Much too young.'

Christie came back to find the look of dismay still on his face, but put it down to hunger. 'So tell me,' she said, 'where were you this afternoon?'

As they worked their way through the meal—a vegetable terrine followed by breast of Barbary duck, served, as it should be, with the skin crisp—Max reported on his expedition, and Roussel's revelations.

Christie's immediate reaction was smug satisfaction. 'I knew it,' she said. 'You can never trust a woman with hair that colour. What a piece of work. You can be sure she's robbing old Roussel

161

blind somewhere along the line.'

'You're probably right. I'd really love to find out where the wine goes. If we knew that . . .'

Christie mopped up some of her gravy with a piece of bread, a French habit she'd acquired unconsciously. 'She must be working with someone. Has she ever said anything that made you suspicious? Did you see anything in her office?' A smile of pure mischief. 'I guess you never made it to her bedroom.'

Max cast his mind back to the previous Sunday, when he had waited for Nathalie in her living room. What can you discover in ten minutes? He thought of the good furniture, the vintage carpet, the signed Lartigue photographs, the expensive volumes on painting and sculpture, the wine book he had leafed through. The wine book.

'There was one little thing, a wine label she was using as a bookmark. odd sort of name, which of course I've forgotten. But I did make a note of it when I got back to see if I could find some of the wine. Apart from that, nothing. Are you going to have cheese?'

They ate on in thoughtful silence, broken eventually by Max. 'The simplest thing would be to blow the whistle on her—I mean, the wine belongs to the property, and she and Roussel have been stealing it. Get her to confess. What do you think?'

Christie snorted. 'Confess? Her? *That broad*? Don't hold your breath. It would be her word against his, and she's some kind of lawyer, isn't she? Forget it. No, I think it would be better to wait and see if we could find out who she's been working with. Then you get them all.'

'I don't know about Roussel, though,' said Max.

'He may be a bit of a rogue, but I've developed a soft spot for him. And he did look after the old boy. Sorry, your father.' Max put down his wineglass and tapped his head. 'That reminds me. I had a call just after you'd gone out this afternoon from Bosc—you know, the lawyer we went to see in Aix.'

Christie rolled her eyes. 'Let me guess.'

Max nodded. 'You're right. The grey area is now so grey it's almost black. Much more complex than he had originally thought. Extensive investigation in France, probably a trip to California to consult authorities there, no stone to be left unturned, all that stuff. Months of research. He sounded very cheerful about it.'

Even before Max had finished speaking, Christie's head had been shaking slowly from side to side. 'Why am I not surprised?' she said. 'I used to live with a lawyer, remember? God, it's like—well, as my ex once said when he'd had too many beers, it's like milking a mouse. You know? Trying to squeeze something out that isn't there. They all do it.' With a look of high disdain on her face, she reached for her cigarettes.

'Calvados?'

'Absolutely.'

Leaving the restaurant, they saw that an after-dinner *boules* game—or perhaps the same game—was being played by the light of moth-freckled street lamps. The contestants looked identical to those playing earlier: the same wiry, wizened old men, still wearing their caps, the same endless flow of loquacious dispute. One of them saw Christie and nudged the man standing next to him. As she passed, he shook one hand vigorously from the wrist, as though he'd burned it, and gave

163

her a smile that glinted with gold fillings.

'What does that mean?' said Christie.

Max thought for a moment. 'One-nil to California, I'd say.'

Fifteen

Max was still dripping from the shower when his phone rang. It was Charlie, a joyful Charlie, sounding like a prisoner who had just received word of his reprieve.

'One more day of this nonsense,' he said, 'and then I'm yours. I'll be over tomorrow. All I have to do today is survive a lecture on offshore mortgage opportunities for those lucky buggers with seven-figure incomes, followed by what will no doubt be a thrilling Q & A session on the tax implications of secondary residence ownership. Want to come?'

'Slow going, is it?' said Max.

'I've had more fun at funerals.'

'Charlie, I've got some good news for you on the wine front—well, I think it's good news. It would take too long to explain now; things are a little complicated here. But I'll fill you in when I see you tomorrow.'

'Can't wait. Oh, by the way, I've got some smoked salmon and Cumberland sausages for you. I stuffed them in my minibar, so they should be OK. Couldn't think of anything else you'd like, apart from Kate Moss, and she's busy.'

Max was smiling as he put down the phone. The call had reminded him that Charlie—one of those rare and precious people who are consistently cheerful—was just about the only part of his previous life in London that he missed. He went to find Madame Passepartout.

She received the prospect of another guest—a special guest, as Max had described him—with avid curiosity mixed with mild alarm at such short notice. A gentleman from London, undoubtedly a person of quality and consequence, possibly even an English *milor*, and she was supposed to have everything *comme il faut* in twenty-four hours. There were a thousand things to do, possibly more: towels, sheets, flowers, a decanter of cognac for the bedside table (it being well known that the better class of Englishman is partial to his nightcap); and then the mattress must be turned and aired, the windows made to gleam, the old armoire given a thorough polish, and all traces of insect life removed.

She stood with her hands on her hips, catching her breath after this breakneck recitation, while Max tried to reassure her. Perhaps he had inflated Charlie's credentials. 'Actually, he's just a very old friend,' he said. 'He's not expecting the Ritz.'

'*Mais quand même!*' Madame Passepartout chose to be unconvinced, looking at her watch and almost pawing the ground in her eagerness to prepare for Charlie's coming. 'It would oblige me, Monsieur Max, if you and mademoiselle were to remove yourselves from the house today, so that I can work without distraction. The weather is most agreeable. I suggest a *pique-nique*.' The suggestion was delivered in a tone of voice that did not invite any discussion.

To Max's surprise, the thought appealed to

Christie, who had come down to the kitchen and was groping her way toward her first cup of coffee. 'Great,' she said, from the depths of her early-morning coma. 'Love picnics.' Within ten minutes, they had been ejected from the house and were standing by the car, equipped with a map, a corkscrew, and absolutely no clear idea of where they were going.

Inspiration came while they were in the village. They had bought the ingredients for a simple lunch and were getting bread when Christie's eye was caught by something pinned to the baker's notice board. There, among the photographs of missing cats and details of second-hand domestic and agricultural articles for sale at *prix d'ami*, was the card of a farm outside the village offering horses to rent for what were described as *pique-niques hippiques* in the Luberon.

'Is this what I think it is?' Christie asked Max. '*Pique-nique* I can just about work out, and there's a picture of a horse, so I guess it's horseback picnics, right? How terrific.'

'Can you ride?'

'Sure. Can't you?'

Max shared Oscar Wilde's view that horses were dangerous at each end and uncomfortable in the middle, and remembered his first and, so far, last attempt at riding. The horse had shrugged him off even before he was settled in the saddle, and had then stood looking down at him, lips drawn back in a ghastly yellow-toothed smile utterly devoid of sympathy. 'I tried it once,' he said. 'But the horse won.'

'Come on,' said Christie. 'It's just like riding a bicycle. Nothing to it.'

166

Half an hour later they were standing in the paddock next to two amiable and outwardly docile horses. The farmer had given Max a rough, hand-drawn map of the bridle paths—although, as he said, the horses knew them so well they could find their way blindfolded. Christie swung up into the saddle, smooth and easy, as Max put a tentative foot in the stirrup.

'No, Max. Other side. You always mount on the left.'

'Why?' The horse turned his head and gave Max a reproachful look.

'I'm not exactly sure,' said Christie. 'But you just do. I think it's got something to do with your sword. You know? So it doesn't get tangled up with your legs?'

'Of course,' said Max. 'My sword. Silly of me.' He scrambled into the saddle, and, without any urging, the horse set off at an unhurried, stately walk.

It wasn't long before Max had forgotten his fear of heights and was feeling, if not relaxed, then slightly less tense, and was even beginning to enjoy the unfamiliar but increasingly pleasant sensation of sitting on a large, living creature in motion. He breathed in the smell of warm horse and old leather, shifted his weight in the creaking saddle, tried to appear nonchalant, and started to pay more attention to the scenery. They were in single file, going upward all the time, the horses picking their way slowly along the narrow stony path through a tangle of broom and boxwood, their hooves crushing the rosemary and thyme that seemed to grow out of every rock. The views, carpeted in different shades of green, became more

167

and more spectacular as they climbed toward the top.

Two hours of gentle riding took them to the highest point on the Luberon, marked on the farmer's map as the Mourre Nègre, more than thirty-five hundred feet above sea level. The loudest sound was the soft whiffle of the horses' breath. They hadn't seen or heard a soul since they started off.

Christie tethered the horses in the shade of a scrub oak while Max unpacked the bread and sausage, the cheese and fruit, and a bottle of red wine, warmed by its proximity to the horse until it had reached the temperature of a well-heated room. He stretched to ease the stiffness in a back that had been held more or less rigid during the ride up, and looked around.

It was impossible not to be affected by the extraordinary peace and beauty of the surroundings, the total absence of human sounds, the enormously long views. To the north, he could see Mont Ventoux, the blinding white gravel on its crest looking like a permanent snowcap; to the south, the massive bulk of Mont Sainte-Victoire; and far beyond that, the silvery glint of the Mediterranean. Christie joined him, and they stood for a few moments without speaking, listening to the breeze.

'Roussel comes up here when he's hunting. He told me he'd often seen eagles,' said Max. 'Wonderful, isn't it? London seems a million miles away.'

'Don't you miss it?'

'London?' He thought for a moment before shaking his head. 'No, not a bit. Odd, isn't it? I'd forgotten how much I liked it here. Before, when I used to come out, I never really wanted to leave, and it's the same now. It feels like home.' He grinned at her. 'And I used to think I was a city boy.'

They found a spot where they could sit side by side looking south, their backs against a sun-warmed rock, and Max opened the wine and poured it into paper cups while Christie made primitive sandwiches. 'So,' she said, passing him half a baguette bulging with slices of sausage, 'are you going to stay?'

'I hope so. I don't know that I'll be able to, but I'd love to. It suits me down here—the lack of pressure, the little details of ordinary life, the chance to spend so much of the year out of doors; I even like the French—well, you know that . . .' He shrugged, contemplating the huge sandwich that he was holding with both hands. 'We'll see. How about you?'

Christie took her time to reply, and when she did there was an almost apologetic tone to her voice. 'I'm not ready for that yet. There's too much of the world I haven't seen. You won't believe this, but until a couple of years ago, I was one of the ninety percent of the American population that doesn't have a passport. You know? We travel, but we stay at home. And I guess we miss a lot. London, Paris, Prague, Venice, Florence—you name it, I haven't been there. I'd really like to see as much as I can while I'm over here.' She took a mouthful of wine and stared into her paper cup. 'So I guess I'll be moving along pretty soon.'

Half-dreading the answer, Max asked the question that had been on his mind almost from

169

the moment Christie arrived. 'So what do you think we should do about the house?'

'I've thought about it a lot. I guess you have too.' She put up a hand to stop Max from replying. 'First of all, I didn't come here for a house; I already have my mother's old house, and that's now worth about ten times what she paid for it. No, I came because I wanted to get away for a bit after breaking up with Bob—and, you know, to see if I had a long-lost dad. But I'm not ready to settle down yet, and certainly not in France.' She saw Max begin to smile. 'I mean, it's great, but it's not for me. Perhaps it's an acquired taste. In any case, your uncle wanted you to have the house. So you know what?' She raised her paper cup in a toast. 'It's all yours.' It was her turn to smile at the look on Max's face. 'Actually, it's just a way of getting out of spending good money on that creep of a lawyer with his waggling eyebrows and his dirty mind. I mean, the nerve of the guy.'

Max cast his mind back to that afternoon in Aix—it seemed so long ago now—when they had been to see the lawyer, and the remark that had outraged Christie. Something about romance. 'Don't be too hard on him. The French always think that sex conquers all. Look at Madame Passepartout—she's been trying to get us into the same bedroom from the moment you arrived, and it wasn't to cut down on the laundry.' He fished a startled grasshopper out of his wine with his finger before taking another mouthful. 'They don't mean to be offensive, but it's like a national sport. It's in their genes.'

'Like crazy driving and weird plumbing.'

'Exactly. But listen—you should think about the

house. It's a big decision.'

'Max? Don't push your luck. Remember what happened the last time you argued with me?' Christie yawned and stretched out on her back, resting her head on the canvas bag that had held their lunch, and Max looked out across the haze of afternoon heat toward the sea.

'I hope you like old Charlie,' he said. 'He's been such a good friend to me. If we can work out something with this wine that Roussel's been making on the side, he'd love it. Château Charlie. I can see him now, gargling away and coming out with all that overblown language—promising, promising, do I detect a *soupçon* of autumn leaves, of pencil lead, of truffle, of toasted apricots? You haven't really got anything against Englishmen, I know. It's just me. Charlie's different. You'll like him.'

But there was no reply. The sun, the wine, and the fresh air had done their work. Christie was fast asleep.

Max contemplated his future, suddenly much more rosy, and felt his spirits lift. In the space of a few days, he had inherited a house—now, thanks to Christie, free of any uncertainties about ownership—and a vineyard producing good wine. Good enough, at any rate, to attract the interest of Nathalie Auzet and her partners in crime, and possibly good enough to pay the costs of running the property. Liking Roussel as he did, he was glad that the old scoundrel knew nothing about the wine once it had left his *cave*.

Or appeared to know nothing.

He heard a very faint, almost equine snuffle at his side. Christie had changed position and was

171

now curled up, with an ant making its way across the smooth honey-coloured skin of her cheek. Very softly, he brushed the ant away and looked down at her sleeping face with a mixture of gratitude and, somewhat to his surprise, faint stirrings of affection. She'd been a good sport in a strange and difficult situation. He might even miss her.

Sixteen

'I borrowed this from an acquaintance in the village who is *très anglophile*,' said Madame Passepartout, who was showing Max the wonders she had achieved in what was to be Charlie's bedroom. 'It will make your friend feel instantly at home. Regard the dogs.' She pointed to the bedside table.

There, next to the decanter of cognac and a small vase of freesias, was a framed photograph, in full colour, of a smiling Queen Elizabeth. She was perched on a couch, possibly in her private sitting room at Windsor, with an entourage of corgis spread out on the carpet like a living fan at her feet.

Max considered the photograph, feeling sure that Charlie would think he'd gone mad. 'Such attention to detail, madame,' he said. 'My friend will undoubtedly be ravished.'

It was the morning of Charlie's arrival, and Max had spent the past quarter of an hour dutifully admiring the bedroom's high state of polish and perfection. He had to admit that Madame Passepartout had done wonders: the down-at-the-heel cushions and the maroon curtains with their

172

rather sinister blotches had been flogged until not a speck of dust remained on them, every hard surface had been buffed and made to shine, the tiled floor rejuvenated with an application of water and linseed oil and elbow grease. A small rug had been placed by the side of the bed to protect Charlie's delicate feet from direct contact with the floor. And there was the royal portrait. What more could a guest want?

Madame Passepartout interrupted Max's flow of praise with an upraised finger. 'Does he like to dance, your friend?'

Max had seen Charlie in action on the dance floor dozens of times. His feet seldom moved beyond a shuffle, but his hands were always busy; a form of slow-motion body search. Curiously, the girls never seemed to mind. 'Yes,' said Max, 'although he prefers music that is not too fast. It's his arthritis.'

'*Ah bon?* Well, tonight there will be music of every speed. It is the village *fête, un repas dansant.* There will be an accordion band, and a *diji* from Avignon who will play the more modern tunes. With records,' she added, in case Max was not fully up to date with contemporary developments in the world of music, 'as in a discothèque.'

Max nodded. 'I hope you'll be going, madame.'

'Of course. Everyone in the village will be there.' She raised herself up on tiptoe and executed a surprisingly accomplished pirouette. 'Everyone will dance.'

For a brief moment, Max thought of Fanny, of dancing with Fanny under the stars. He looked at his watch. 'I'd better go. He's supposed to be arriving in the village quite soon, and he won't

173

know how to find the house.'

*   *   *

In fact, Charlie had been so anxious to get away from everything and everyone connected with luxury real estate that he had made an early start from Monte Carlo, and had already reached the village. Pulling up in front of the café, he stepped out of his large rented Mercedes and looked around the square with cheerful interest.

There was no mistaking him for a native of Saint-Pons. He was dressed very much *à l'anglais*: a double-breasted blazer with a multitude of brass buttons, pale grey flannels, a glaringly new Panama hat—all in all, an apparition from another world, and one the locals were studying with sidelong glances of discreet curiosity. Catching the eye of one of them, an elderly woman, Charlie raised his hat. *'Bonjour*, my dear, *bonjour.'*

Alas, that was very nearly the full extent of his French vocabulary. He had progressed a step beyond the traditional English method of communicating with foreigners—that is, to speak English very slowly and at maximum volume—but it was only a short step, and frequently unintelligible. Indeed, it was a language that had never been heard before in Saint-Pons, or anywhere else, for that matter: basically English, but with an 'o' or an 'a' or sometimes an 'oo' added to the end of a word to give it that authentic continental flavour, with the occasional Spanish or Italian flourish thrown in for added confusion.

Leaving the car in front of the café, Charlie went inside to attend to what had suddenly become a

174

pressing need. 'Por favor, madame,' he said to the woman behind the bar, 'toilettoes?' She looked up from her paper and jerked her head toward the back of the café. Charlie hurried off with a thankful sigh.

When Max got down to the village, he found the square teeming with activity in preparation for the evening's revels. Half a dozen men were on ladders, stringing coloured lights through the branches of the plane trees; others were arranging the rows of trestle tables and benches that took up much of the square; and a third group, scowling, unshaven, noisy and irritated, had just jumped out of a huge truck that was loaded with scaffolding and wooden planks. These were to be transformed into a stage for the band, but unfortunately—and this was the cause of the scowls and the irritation—the truck was unable to reach or even get close to the area reserved for the stage. The way was blocked because some cretin had parked his Mercedes in front of the café. The driver of the truck leaned into the cabin, put his hand on the horn, and left it there.

The cretin, having completed successful negotiations for a cup of coffee to be served to him on the terrace, emerged, jaunty and relieved, from the door of the café as Max arrived. Their pleasure at seeing one another was cut short by a bellow from the truck driver.

'If that were my Mercedes, Charlie, I think I'd move it before they use the truck to shove it out of the way.'

'Oh God.' Charlie went over to the car, waving his hands in what he hoped were apologetic gestures. 'Pardonnay, pardonnay. Frightfully sorry.'

175

And with that, he backed the Mercedes out of the square, narrowly missing a trestle table and the café dog as he went.

Madame came out with a cup of coffee, and looked in vain for the man who had ordered it. She turned to Max, shaking her head. 'I'm always getting caught like that,' she said. 'They come in, they do their business, they disappear. As if I were running a *pissotière*.'

Max explained the problem, and ordered coffee for himself and, by way of a peace offering, for the men with the truck. He sat back and tilted his face up to the sun, smiling at the thought of having Charlie stay for a few days. It would be fun to introduce him to a different kind of life, especially with a pretty girl to keep him on his toes. The Panama hat would have to go, though. It reminded Max of the uniform worn by a certain kind of Englishman that he detested—loud, pink and bumptious—which Charlie certainly was not.

'Sorry about that.' Charlie had returned, stripping off his blazer and draping it over the back of his chair before sitting down. 'You're looking well, you old bugger. Suits you down here. But I thought you said this was a quiet little place where nothing happened. What's going on? You must have told them I was coming.'

The men from the truck were starting to erect the scaffolding framework that would support the wooden stage. Immediately in front of it was an area left clear for dancing, with the tables and benches lining the remaining three sides of the square. 'Tonight is the annual village knees-up,' said Max. 'Dinner, dancing, fairy lights, the works. Maybe even balloons. I'll get tickets for us from the

176

café before we leave. You don't know how lucky you are—you'll meet everybody from the mayor to the baker's daughter.'

At the mention of what he took to be a young and no doubt voluptuous woman, Charlie rubbed his hands and looked hopeful. 'Better polish up my French. You never know.'

'How's your American?'

Charlie gave Max a speculative look. 'Is there something you want to tell me?'

Max went through the story of Christie's arrival, including the visit to the lawyer and the episode with the cast-iron skillet. 'Ah,' said Charlie, 'I was going to ask you about your head. You were forcing your attentions on the poor helpless girl, were you? What a nasty brute you are. A slave to testosterone. You should be ashamed of yourself.'

'If you must know, Charlie, she's not my type—she's a blonde. You know how I feel about blondes.'

Charlie raised a finger. 'You were just unlucky with my sister.' He shook his head, and added, 'Weren't we all? Actually, I've known some very pleasant blondes. Did I ever tell you about the one I found kipping in a flat in Eaton Square when I went round to take the measurements?'

Max brushed the sleeping blonde away. 'As it happens, I've rather got my eye on a young lady from the village.' Realizing how prim he was sounding, he hurried on. 'Anyway, Christie's terrific. I'm sure you'll like her.'

'Pretty?'

'Very. And she knows a bit about wine. You'll be able to have a good old gargle-and-spit together.'

They ordered more coffee, and Max went on to

177

describe what he'd learned from Roussel's confession in the *cave*. Charlie's eyebrows, never at rest for long, went up and down with each revelation. 'Sounds to me,' he said, 'as though you could be on to a little winner with that wine. I'd love to have a taste of it.'

'And I'd love to know who's buying it. I've asked Roussel to draw off a couple of bottles and bring them over to the house. It's young—only been in the barrels since last October. But you'll get an idea of what it's like.'

While they were talking, a small, exuberantly coloured van—*Monsieur La Fête* painted in Day-Glo pink on its frog-green side—had managed to nose its way through the square to park by the stage. Then the driver, perhaps Monsieur La Fête himself, finished hooking up an amplifier and microphone to the loudspeakers he had attached to the scaffolding. He stood back to light a cigarette before throwing a switch on the amplifier. The square was instantly filled with electronic screeches and burps, scattering the pigeons and causing the café dog to raise his head and howl. The driver made some adjustments to the controls and flicked the microphone with his index finger. '*Un . . . deux . . . trois . . . Bonjour Saint-Pons!*' More screeching followed. The dog pursed his lips, retreated into the café, and found a haven of relative peace in the space beneath the pinball machine.

'Nothing like it,' said Charlie. 'The blessed tranquillity of village life.'

When they arrived back at the house, Madame Passepartout was hovering in the doorway, eager for her first glimpse of the young English *milor*. For an awful moment, Max had the feeling that she was going to curtsy, but she made do with a simper and a handshake.

'Enchanto, madame,' said Charlie, raising his hat, 'enchanto.' Another simper from Madame Passepartout, and the beginnings of a blush.

They took Charlie upstairs to his bedroom, where Madame Passepartout fussed with the pillows and made a point of carrying out invisible adjustments to the decanter and the royal portrait on the bedside table, in case Charlie might not have noticed them.

He put his suitcase on the bed and opened it, taking out a tangled pile of dirty laundry, a side of smoked salmon, and two packets of sausages. 'Here—you'd better put these in the fridge before they go off,' he said, giving them to Max.

'I shall take these.' Madame Passepartout swooped on the laundry and gathered it up in her arms. 'Does monsieur like his shirts and handkerchiefs with a little starch, or *au naturel?*'

Charlie beamed and nodded in amiable incomprehension. 'Splendide, most kind,' and Madame Passepartout, with a parting remark to Max that she had prepared a simple lunch of *crespeou* and salad for them, swept out of the bedroom to consign the laundry to the uncertain care of the ancient washing machine in the scullery.

Max shook his head. 'You'll have to get used to this. I'm afraid she thinks you're some kind of toff.' He sat on the side of the bed while Charlie unpacked what was left of his clothes and started to put them in the armoire. 'We'll have lunch, and then I'll give you the guided tour.'

'It looks pretty good so far. Definitely a château,

I'd say. Minor château, of course, but with château-like qualities, and that's what counts these days, rather than the inconvenience of the real thing; the feeling of being in a house that might have a ballroom, without the bother of the ballroom itself. Does that make sense? In any case, here we are with an early eighteenth-century gem whose original features have been carefully preserved through the generations. Imposing, of course, and standing in its own cultivated grounds, secluded but not isolated. I can see the sales brochure now. The guys in Monte Carlo would rip your head off to get their hands on this. Oh, I forgot.' He unrolled a pair of trousers and produced a bottle of Laphroaig. 'Still drinking whisky, I hope. Now then. Where's the beautiful lodger?'

Christie had spent the morning with guidebooks and a map of Europe, trying to decide where to go next. London? Venice? Paris? She looked up from the kitchen table as the two friends came in.

'Christie, this is Charlie.'

Max saw Charlie's eyes widen. He smoothed back his hair and held out his hand. 'Lovely to meet you. Thank God I won't have to dance with Max tonight.'

Christie giggled. The two of them stood smiling at one another without speaking while Max went to fetch glasses, and a bottle of wine from the refrigerator.

Madame Passepartout came out of the scullery and studied the couple, still silent, still smiling. Clearly pleased at what she saw, she tiptoed over to where Max was uncorking the bottle. 'Monsieur Max,' she said, in the muffled boom that for her passed as a conspiratorial whisper, 'perhaps they would like to have lunch alone.'

'What? Nonsense. I haven't seen Charlie for ages. We've got lots of catching up to do.'

A sniff from Madame Passepartout. It took a woman to recognize these things.

*   *   *

It had been Max's intention to spend lunch going over the business of Roussel's wine in greater detail, but he was instead treated to an example of Charlie's sales technique—selling himself, of course, but under the guise of promoting the charms of London compared with Venice or Paris. 'Did you know,' he was saying to Christie, 'that at this time of year there are more tourists than pigeons in Venice? True as I sit here. Also, one false step and you're in a canal, being run over by gondolas. Damned dangerous place. As for Paris, well, the whole city is closed for the summer; you'd be lucky to find the subway open. The Parisians are all down here on the coast, or in one of their little spas, bathing their livers in fizzy water. Now, London has it all: the theatre, clubs, pubs, shops, restaurants, Beefeaters, Buckingham Palace, Notting Hill—think of the postcards you could send home—a climate that is absolutely guaranteed to do wonders for the female complexion, taxi drivers who speak English . . . well, of course, everybody speaks English.'

'Wow,' said Christie. 'Fancy that.' She reached across the table and rescued Charlie's napkin from his salad, tucking it back in the top of his shirt.

'Seriously, that's a big advantage, particularly the first time you visit a place. And the other big

181

advantage is that you have a contact who knows London inside out, and who'd be delighted to show you around.' He leaned back in his chair and tapped his chest. '*Moi*. And I have a spare room.'

Charlie was for once managing to keep his eyebrows under control, and his expression innocent. Watching the two of them smiling at one another, Max felt it was as though he weren't there. He also thought that the spare room would probably stay empty. He broke the silence with a loud sigh of mock relief. 'Well,' he said, 'that's a load off my mind. Now that you two have settled your travel arrangements, do you think we could talk about the wine?'

Max went through it all again, and came to the same conclusion: They could confront Nathalie Auzet and try to extract a confession from her, which Max thought was unlikely and Christie dismissed as an impossibility. Or they could wait for the mystery truck to come back in September.

'Then what?' asked Charlie. 'Ask them nicely where they were taking the wine? Tell them to hang on while you call the police?' He shook his head. 'And another thing: how do you know Roussel hasn't already told Nathalie Auzet that the game's up?'

Max had to admit that was possible. 'He told me he wouldn't say a word, but I suppose we can't be sure of that.'

Christie was frowning at the empty wine bottle on the table in front of her. 'Wait a minute,' she said. 'Max, didn't you say you'd seen something at Nathalie Auzet's house? Some kind of label?'

Max nodded. 'You're quite right. I remember making a note of it, but God knows where I put it.'

He stood up. 'Why don't you show Charlie round while I go and have a look.'

Madame Passepartout had abandoned her observation post at the kitchen window to come out and clear the table, and she watched with an approving eye as Christie and Charlie left the courtyard, their heads close together in conversation. 'It is as I thought,' she said with great satisfaction. *'Un coup de foudre.'*

Max spent a frustrating hour going through the pockets of all his clothes and the various piles of lists and papers that he had stuffed into the chest of drawers and in the back of the armoire. Eventually, he found what he was looking for, scrawled on the back of his English chequebook. It was no more illuminating now than it had been when he'd written it down.

He went downstairs to find Charlie returned from his tour of the property in a high state of excitement. 'It's sensational,' he said to Max, 'all you need to do is a bit of work on the house—and put in a pool; must have a pool—and you'd be sitting on seven figures. That's sterling, of course.' He looked around, a real estate agent's gleam in his eye. 'You're protected at the back by the mountain, and there's a cushion of land surrounding the house, so there's no problem with neighbours. Why, if you . . .'

Max held up a hand. 'Charlie, before you get carried away and put in a helicopter pad, take a look at this. Does it mean anything to you?'

Charlie looked up from the chequebook, tapping it against his free hand. 'It rings a bell,' he said, 'but I can't be sure.' He looked at his watch. 'London's an hour behind, isn't it? Billy would know. Let me see if I can catch him.'

Christie watched him go into the house, with the smile that had scarcely left her face since she'd met him.

'I'm glad you two have hit it off,' said Max. 'I've known Charlie for twenty years. We were at school together. He's one of the best.'

'He's awfully cute,' said Christie. 'Is he always like this?'

'Cute?' Max grinned at her. 'I don't know about that, but he never changes—it's one of the reasons I like him so much. You'll have a lot of fun in London.'

At Christie's urging, Max began to tell her about the London he thought she should see, from the Tate Modern and the National Portrait Gallery to Harvey Nichols and the Portobello Road market, adding a few things she should avoid like the plague: plastic pubs, Piccadilly on Saturday night, anything masquerading as doner kebab. He was moving on to the sometimes bizarre attractions of Soho when Charlie returned, shaking his head.

'No joy, I'm afraid. His secretary said he's off playing golf with God—I think that's the unofficial name for the wine buyer from the Connaught. Anyway, he'll be back in the office tomorrow.' He tossed the chequebook back to Max. 'Now then, about tonight. I don't want to look like the visitor from outer space. What are we all wearing? I want to blend in.'

Max looked at him: rumpled winter-weight flannels, black city shoes, a blue-and-white-striped Jermyn Street shirt open at the neck, a broad, ruddy face; resolutely, eternally, unmistakably English. Even his hair was English. 'You didn't

184

bring a beret, did you? That might help.'

Seventeen

In the course of an exploration that had taken him into the far reaches of the cellar, Max had come across a bottle of rather old, very fine champagne, and had kept it aside to celebrate Charlie's arrival. He was now dusting off the bottle before putting it, for want of anything better, into one of Madame Passepartout's plastic buckets, which he had filled with ice cubes. The contrast between the homely blue of the bucket and the dark, sober elegance of the bottle fell a little short of perfection, but at least the wine would be chilled. He settled the bottle into its nest of ice and twirled the long, slender neck between his hands.

Although he had a great deal to learn and a long way to go, he was discovering how much he enjoyed the many small pleasures associated with wine and its various rituals—pleasures that he had never had time to appreciate during his life in London. There, wine had simply been good or disappointing, cheap or expensive, without any particular history, something that was served up in bars and restaurants with anonymous efficiency. Here it would be different. Here he would be involved in the entire process, from grape to bottle, and he looked forward to it with very keen anticipation. Wine would be his work. And as Charlie was fond of saying every time he buried his nose in a glass, there could be no more noble calling.

'Well?' said Charlie. 'What do you think?' He had come out of the front door and was standing in the courtyard, arms spread wide, waiting for comments. His hair was still wet from the shower, brushed straight back, and he was wearing a short-sleeved shirt, decorated with bright green marijuana plants, outside a pair of white cotton trousers. 'I picked this up last year in Martinique,' he said, smoothing down the collar, 'from a guy on the beach. It's called a spliff shirt. *Très cool*, he said—at least, I think that's what he said.'

'Cool's the word, Charlie,' said Max. 'No doubt about it. And you can roll it up and smoke it, too. What a shirt.'

Max returned his attentions to the bottle, twisting off the wire around the neck and easing the cork up a fraction. Keeping his hand over it, he could feel it pressing up against his palm, almost as though it were alive and trying to escape. Little by little, he allowed it to push upward, until it came out of the bottle with no more than a muffled, bubbly sigh.

Charlie had been watching, nodding with approval. 'That's the way to do it,' he said. 'I can't stand people who wave the bottle around and pop the cork like a bloody Scud missile. Terrible waste of champagne. What have you got there, anyway?'

Max pulled the beaded bottle from the bucket. 'An '83 Krug. I found it hidden away in a corner—Uncle Henry must have forgotten about it.'

'Good for him.' Max poured the wine, releasing its delicate, slightly toasty bouquet. Charlie inhaled deeply, with closed eyes, then held the glass up to his ear. 'It's the only wine in the world you can hear,' he said. 'The music of the grape. Cheers.'

They sipped for a moment in silence, the rush of bubbles prickling their tongues. 'Seriously,' said Charlie, 'you think the shirt's OK? Nonchalant but not too loud—that's what we're after. Casual elegance, Cary Grant on his day off, that sort of thing.'

Max nodded toward the front door. 'Here's your date. Ask her.'

Christie was wearing the same black dress—pressed to perfection by Madame Passepartout—that she had worn to the Roussel dinner, and the same exhilarating scarlet high heels, this time with matching scarlet toenails peeping through the cutout at the front of each shoe. Charlie let out a long, appreciative whistle.

Christie bobbed her head in acknowledgement. 'Like the shirt, Charlie,' she said. 'Very cool.'

Max handed her a glass of champagne. 'A toast,' he said. 'Here's to the man who made this possible: Uncle Henry, God bless him.' Their glasses raised, the three of them looked at one other—smiling, each with private and delightful expectations of the evening to come.

The level in the bottle and the setting sun dropped at an approximately equal pace, and it was dusk—a soft and rosy dusk—by the time the three of them reached the village. The square was crowded, a cheerful hum of greeting and conversation mingling with the music coming from the loudspeakers. Extra tables had been set out on the café terrace, and the accordion band, four impressively moustached gentlemen in their best black trousers, embroidered waistcoats and white shirts, were drinking a pre-performance pastis.

Children chased each other around, and sometimes through, the forest of adult legs. Dogs loitered, more in hope than expectation, beside the long open barbecue where a *méchoui* of spit-roasted lamb and *merguez* sausages the colour of dried blood were sizzling above the coals, watched over by the chef from Chez Fanny.

Max made his way through the crowd to the makeshift bar where Fanny herself, protected from collarbone to knee by a demure apron, was pouring glasses of the *vin d'honneur* with a liberal hand. 'This is a bit of a change for you,' he said, pointing to the apron.

Without speaking, Fanny performed a slow turn and looked at him over one shoulder, her eyebrows raised. Beneath the apron was an almost backless wisp of lavender-coloured silk, with little more than a suggestion of a skirt below. 'Better?' she said.

Max swallowed hard and ordered three glasses of wine. 'I hope you're not going to be stuck behind the bar all evening,' he said. 'A girl's got to eat. Can I save you a place?'

'Eh, Fanny! The drinks are flowing like glue.' Guichard the postman and his wife, both heavily scented, had pushed up to the bar and were panting for refreshment. '*Bonsoir*, Monsieur Skinner. Are we going to see an Englishman dance tonight?'

Max picked up the glasses and went off, encouraged by a parting wink from Fanny, to find Christie and Charlie, who had been watching him from a table in front of the café.

'What's so funny?' Max said, looking from one smirking face to the other.

'Nothing,' said Charlie. 'Nothing at all.'

'They've been circling each other for days,' said Christie. 'You should watch out, Max. I think she's decided to go for it tonight.'

'You two,' said Max, shaking his head. 'Vulgar speculation. I was merely being polite to a charming young lady who, I might say . . .'

'. . . is wearing a dress the size of a handkerchief,' Charlie added. 'I think Christie's right.'

They sipped their wine—which Charlie pronounced to be young and playful, but essentially good-hearted—while they watched the parade passing in front of them. The evening had attracted people from surrounding villages as well as some other, more distant foreigners: Germans the colour of polished mahogany, their speech sounding harsh and guttural against the background of softer, more mellifluous French; the American cyclists they had seen in the market, now dressed like wealthy teenagers in that particular kind of cotton that never seems to wrinkle, with silver-tipped belts, pristine pneumatic sneakers, and, of course, baseball caps with sporting or military motifs; a group of gypsies, lean and swarthy and all in black, slithering through the crowd like sharks among a shoal of tropical fish; a sprinkling of Parisians, pastel cashmere sweaters draped over their shoulders to ward off the eighty-degree evening chill. But, as Christie remarked, there didn't seem to be any English.

'Ah,' said Max, with the knowledgeable air of an old local inhabitant of ten days' standing, 'they're mostly on the other side of the Luberon—Gordes, Ménerbes, Bonnieux, the golden triangle. I'm told it's a lot more social over there than it is here,

189

soirées every *soir*. Right up your street actually, Charlie. Apparently they love talking about property prices.'

A few tables away, the accordion band, fortified by a final pastis, had gathered up their instruments and were now filing onto the stage. The rap singer being broadcast over the loudspeakers was cut off in mid-expletive, and the space in front of the stage began to clear. Over behind the bar, Fanny had removed her apron and was slipping it over the head of the relief bartender, an ancient, diminutive man who stood motionless, hypnotized by the proximity of the *décolleté* being presented to him at nose level.

Charlie gave Max a nudge. 'Better get in quick before young Lochinvar over there asks her to dance,' he said as he and Christie stood up. 'We'll go and find a table.'

But getting Fanny to the table was a slow, convivial process, marked by frequent stops while she embraced friends and clients of the restaurant, watched by wary and sometimes not wholly approving wifely eyes. Fanny in the restaurant, taken up with all her duties, was somehow safe—charming and highly decorative, but safe. Fanny freed from her professional responsibilities, in a dress that could make even the best behaved husband think of a weekend in Paris, was not a sight any wife would welcome, especially during an evening of wine, music and dancing. Max felt he had done well to cover the distance between bar and table—no more than fifty yards—in ten minutes.

Christie and Charlie had secured four places and a litre jug of wine at one end of a long table facing the stage. Charlie was at his most gallant when introduced to Fanny, springing to his feet, bowing over her hand, and murmuring enchanto, enchanto, with even more than usual enthusiasm. But this was unfortunately lost beneath the riffs and flourishes of the accordion band tuning up, and it wasn't until she asked how long he was staying in Saint-Pons that his language problem became evident.

Fanny turned to Max. 'He has no French, your friend?'

'About four words. I'm the official interpreter for this evening.'

And interpret he did, passing on Fanny's comments about the villagers taking their places at nearby tables, a kind of informal who's who of Saint-Pons. 'Over there is Borel, the mayor since twenty years, a sweet man, a widower. He has ambitions toward the widow Gonnet—there she is at the next table—who works at the Bureau de Poste, but he is *très timide*, a man of great shyness. Perhaps the music will encourage him. Now, at the far end of our table is Arlette from the *épicerie*, and her husband. As you can see, she is very large, and he is very small. It is said that she beats him.' Fanny giggled, and paused to sip her wine. Max inhaled her scent, and controlled an impulse to brush back her hair and kiss the nape of her neck.

'Those two don't look like locals,' he said, nodding toward an expensively dressed couple who were standing off to one side, heads tilted back, looking down their noses at the crowd.

Fanny sniffed. 'The Villeneuve-Loubets, very *prétentieux*. They have a house in the 16th in Paris and an estate not far from Aix. She says she is

191

descended in a direct line from Louis XIV, which I can believe. She looks exactly like him.' Another giggle. 'They're friends of Nathalie Auzet. They deserve each other.'

'I take it you're not too fond of Nathalie.'

Fanny looked at Max and tilted a bare brown shoulder toward him in a half-shrug. 'Let's just say we have different interests.'

Max was wondering if Nathalie would put in an appearance when a heavy hand clapped him on the shoulder. He turned to see Roussel in his Yves Montand outfit, and Ludivine, resplendent in deep purple. Fanny clearly liked both of them, and when they moved on to find their places, she said to Max, 'There is a good man. He was very kind to me when I was starting the restaurant, and he did his best to take care of your uncle . . . oh *merde*. Here comes the octopus.'

Max looked up to see a thickset man in early middle age bearing down on the table, the beginnings of a leer on his florid face. 'That's Gaston—he supplies meat to the restaurant,' said Fanny. 'A beast, but his meat is always good. I'm going to have to dance with him.'

'*Bonsoir ma jolie!*' The man stopped in front of the table, ignoring Max, twirling one finger in a circle and swaying his ample hips. 'They're playing a *paso doble* just for us.'

With a transparently false smile and an apologetic squeeze of Max's shoulder, Fanny allowed herself to be led onto the floor, with some quite unnecessary assistance from Gaston's hand in the small of her bare back.

Christie noticed Max's disconsolate face. 'If that's the competition,' she said, patting his arm, 'I don't think you have much to worry about. Listen, is it OK if we leave you? Charlie says he's the Nureyev of the *paso doble*.'

Max was doing his best not to watch Gaston's wandering hands when he heard a familiar screech, and Madame Passepartout, spectacular in a dress of lemon yellow with peppermint-green feather earrings, appeared at his side. 'You cannot sit alone, Monsieur Max. You must dance. *We* must dance.' Max glanced around in desperation, but there was no escape. And so, feeling some of the reluctance that Fanny must have felt, he took to the floor with his bird of paradise.

Reluctance was soon forgotten. She danced wonderfully well, light and precise in her steps, adapting herself to his mistakes, leading when he lost his way, whirling him around when whirling was called for, and generally making him feel like a much better dancer than he actually was. After the first few minutes, he was sufficiently as one with Madame Passepartout to relax and take some interest in the other dancers on the floor. And here, a wide and not always orthodox selection of styles could be seen.

The youngest dancer of all, a little girl of perhaps seven with coal-black ringlets, was learning the steps the old-fashioned way, by standing on the feet of her grandfather and clutching him round one thigh to avoid falling off in mid-*paso*. As the old man shuffled, he kept one hand on her shoulder while the other held a glass of wine. Beyond him, Max could see Fanny, her body arched backward in an effort to keep Gaston at bay. When she saw Max, she rolled her eyes to heaven, and gritted her teeth. Gaston took this as a

193

smile of pleasure; his leer broadened.

The Roussels, in complete contrast, were showing the village how the *paso doble* should be danced: bodies close, backs straight, shoulders square, little fingers cocked. At each change of direction, both heads would snap around at precisely the same instant, as though they were being jerked by an invisible cord, and Ludivine would mark the turn with a backward flick of her heel. Max pointed them out to Madame Passepartout, no mean flicker of a heel herself, and she nodded. 'In their youth they won medals,' she said. 'Pay attention to your feet, Monsieur Max—on the balls, on the balls.'

On the balls he continued, guided by gentle pressures from his partner, who was now steering him around the perimeter of the floor. And it was at the far edge, where the shadows were at their thickest, that he caught sight of Christie and Charlie: entwined, almost motionless, lost to the world. Madame Passepartout gave a small 'aah' of satisfaction, and swept Max back into the light, a feathered earring brushing his chin as she turned.

He delivered Madame Passepartout to the friends at her table, thanking her for the lesson, and saw that Fanny had escaped to the barbecue and was filling two plates. He came up behind her, and felt her flinch as he touched her arm. When she saw it was Max, she smiled. 'Sorry,' she said. 'I thought he was coming back for more. What an *emmerdeur*. The only way I could get rid of him was to tell him I had to feed you.' She passed him a plate, the slices of lamb black and pink, the crust on the potato *gratin* golden brown. 'Although,' she said with an exaggerated pout, 'you seemed to be

194

having a good time with Mimi. Do you dance like that with all the girls?'

'Is that her name, Mimi? I didn't know.' It was, he thought, the perfect name for someone who danced like she did.

Getting back to their table, they found that Christie and Charlie were still off in the shadows; at last, Max felt he had Fanny to himself. 'You know,' he said, 'this is the first time since we've met that we've been alone—well, if you don't count the other hundred and fifty people.'

Fanny looked into his face, her dark eyes open wide. 'What other people?'

Max touched her cheek gently with the back of his hand, all thoughts of food forgotten. 'Do you know something, I think . . .'

'There is *nothing*, absolutely nothing, like a brisk *paso doble* to give you an appetite.' Charlie had returned, looking rumpled, slightly dazed, and extremely happy. 'You should give it a try.' He took his head out of the clouds for long enough to notice Max's expression. 'Oh. Damn. Sorry—I'm interrupting. Bugger.' He stood there, awkward and rueful, his whole body writhing in apology.

Fanny laughed, and Max felt her thigh press gently against his under the table. 'What does he say?'

'I think he's worried our dinner's getting cold.' Max looked at the almost comical concern on his friend's face. 'Come on, Charlie, sit down. What have you done with Christie?'

The happiness returned to Charlie's face. 'She's getting us some food. Lovely girl. What a great evening.' He beamed at Fanny. 'Bello fiesta—ah, here she comes now.'

195

Christie put the plates on the table and sat down, shaking her head. 'That lawyer woman is here, in case you're interested. I thought she was going to ask me to dance.' Charlie looked puzzled. 'Max, you tell him.'

While they ate, Max explained—in both languages, for Fanny's benefit—and they looked around to see where Nathalie Auzet was sitting. Fanny saw her first, at a table with the Villeneuve-Loubets and a slim, fashionably dressed middle-aged man whom she described with a sniff as Nathalie's *accessoire*. In fact, Max was pleased to see her. It was unlikely that she would have come if Roussel had said anything to her about the wine. But the wine could wait until tomorrow.

The accordion band had finished their first set—and a rousing set it was—and were back at the café laying into the pastis while the disc jockey tweaked the sound system. A moment of static, and then the tempo changed abruptly. All at once, the square was filled with the sound of Diana Krall's slow, smoky, infinitely seductive voice. The language was English, the message universal, more like a murmured mating call than a song:

> *There may be trouble ahead,*
> *But while there's moonlight and music*
> *And love and romance,*
> *Let's face the music and dance.*

Max stood up and took Fanny gently by the wrist, feeling the throb of her pulse against his fingertips.

Christie grinned up at them, and winked. 'Dance like there's nobody watching.'

196

And this they did, under the mostly approving eyes—Gaston being an exception—of *le tout village*.

Eighteen

The arrival of Madame Passepartout at the house the following morning was unusually late and unusually muted; even stealthy. One dance too many, one glass too many the night before had led to an overall feeling of fragility, and this led in turn to a more tentative approach to the chores of the day. Shutters were eased open rather than flung wide, and the vacuum cleaner, that splitter of tender heads, was left for the time being in the scullery closet.

The house was still, and apart from an occasional distant groan from the plumbing, silent. Had it been audible, a louder sound by far would have been the furious working of Madame Passepartout's curiosity. She and her friends, like the rest of the village, had observed with close attention the dancing of Christie and Charlie, of Fanny and Max. Certain conclusions had been reached. Madame Passepartout, in view of the privileged position that gave her access to every corner of the house, had been delegated by her friends to confirm those conclusions—purely out of benevolent interest, naturally.

She stood in the centre of the kitchen, thoughtful but irresolute, seeking inspiration. What reason—what plausible reason—could she find for opening bedroom doors and counting heads? She glanced at the kitchen clock and saw that it was nearly ten-thirty. And then the perfect course of action occurred to her, prompted by the memory of an article she had once read in *Télérama* magazine. It was an interview with a well-known English film actor, described as *un vrai Cockney*. According to him, every Englishman's favourite way to start the day was early-morning tea in bed—proper tea, so strong you could stand a spoon up in it.

Madame Passepartout filled the kettle and prepared a tray: teapot, cups and saucers, bowl of sugar, small jug of milk (a bizarre addition, but apparently loved by the English). She found a packet of Earl Grey teabags that probably dated from the days of Uncle Henry, and brewed tea in what she hoped was the English fashion, leaving two bags to steep until the liquid in the pot attained the colour of creosote.

Climbing the stairs, she hesitated for a moment on the landing before turning left, toward the bedroom that had been prepared for Charlie. She knocked on the door, her head cocked. There was no sound, no response of any kind. She knocked again, then pushed the door open.

She saw the usual bachelor's muddle of discarded clothes tossed onto an armchair in the corner. But of Charlie himself, not a sign. The bed had not been slept in, the cognac left untouched. The queen smiled her royal smile from the framed photograph, and Madame Passepartout found herself smiling back. The young couple were doubtless elsewhere. It is as I thought, she said to herself.

It seemed to her a pity to waste a freshly made pot of tea, and so she decided that a visit to Max's bedroom was called for. But it was the same there.

All she saw was another empty room, another bed that hadn't been slept in. As she returned to the landing, considering her next step—would it be indelicate to try the American girl's room? No, of course not—she heard the sound of a car pulling up outside the house. She went down the stairs as quickly as the tray would allow, and was barely back in the kitchen when Max came through the door—tousled, unshaven, carrying a baguette and a bag of croissants, his face shining with happiness.

'What a morning!' he said, and, much to Madame Passepartout's surprise, kissed her soundly on both cheeks. 'How are you today, dear madame? I've just been down to the village—beautiful, beautiful day. Have you recovered from all your dancing?' He put the bread and croissants on the table, and saw the tray of tea for two. 'What's this? Room service?'

'It was for Monsieur Charles, but he was not in his room.

'*No!* Really? Maybe he got lost on the way home.'

'But his car is outside.' Madame Passepartout assumed her most innocent expression. 'Where could he be?'

'Your guess is as good as mine, madame.' In fact, he said to himself, your guess is probably exactly the same as mine. 'Did you by any chance try the young lady's room?'

'Of course not. The very idea!' An eloquent sniff at the very idea, and a swift change of subject. 'And you, Monsieur Max. How was the evening for you? If I may say so, you show considerable promise at the *paso doble.*'

'Ah, but I was in the arms of an expert.' And,

199

remembering the other arms he had been in until half an hour ago, he had the grace to blush.

Madame Passepartout was by now more or less satisfied with her investigations; she could report back to her friends not one but two empty bedrooms. She started to prepare coffee, and as the glorious smell of freshly ground beans filled the kitchen, she passed on to Max her personal souvenirs and impressions of the evening. There had been an incident—perhaps Monsieur Max had not noticed—when Gaston the meat supplier, who everyone agreed was prodigiously drunk, had attempted to fondle Maître Auzet's *derrière*, only to have his face slapped with such force that one could see the imprint of her hand on his cheek. The Americans had ended the evening on a wave of wine and popularity, having donated their baseball caps to the members of the accordion band by way of applause. The baker's daughter—well, the less said about the baker's daughter and that young gypsy the better. And the mayor had at last plucked up the courage to dance with the widow Gonnet. Altogether, a most satisfying fête.

Max was only half-listening, his thoughts still with Fanny, when Charlie—also tousled, also beaming—shuffled into the kitchen clad only in a pair of boxer shorts striped in the salmon and cucumber colours of the Garrick Club. 'Ah, there you are,' he said to Max. 'Looked for you everywhere last night.'

'Unavoidably detained, Charlie. You know how it is. Have a bun.'

The two friends sat at the table with their coffee and croissants, grinning at one another like men who had won the national lottery—but, being English, not about to exchange any intimate details. It wasn't necessary; their expressions said everything. Eventually Madame Passepartout threatened them with the vacuum cleaner and expelled them from the kitchen.

'God, it's good to feel the sun on your back,' said Charlie. They were finishing their coffee in the courtyard, the pigeons strutting back and forth with the self-important air of politicians at a party convention, the sound of the fountain cool and refreshing in the warm morning air. Charlie nodded at the *bassin*. 'Got any fish in there?'

Max looked at the dark, impenetrable green surface and shook his head. 'For all I know, there could be half a dozen sharks, but the water's so mucky you'd never see them. I'm going to drain it in the autumn and give it a clean; maybe put some carp in, and a few water lilies.'

There was a thoughtful look in Charlie's eye. 'So you've made up your mind. You're going to stay on.'

'I'm going to give it a try, yes.'

Charlie clapped him on the back. 'Good for you. I'd do the same myself. Now, what's the plan for today? I thought I might take Christie down to the village for a spot of lunch.'

Max looked out across the vines, for once deserted. Roussel must have overdone the *paso dobles* last night and danced himself into a state of exhaustion. 'Do you think you could call your friend Billy?' he said. 'See if you can get any joy on that wine?'

Nearly two hours passed before Charlie reappeared, this time with Christie, both of them

201

glowing, fresh from the shower and looking a little sheepish. They found Max finishing a phone call. 'I've booked a table for you,' he said. 'Well, for us, actually. Fanny doesn't speak any English. I thought you might need a bit of help with the menu.'

'Oh, I'm sure we could'—Charlie was cut short by Christie's elbow in his ribs, but recovered himself admirably—'that would be great. Do you know, I was down in Cannes once—this was years ago, before my French had improved—and I ordered the only thing I thought I recognized on the menu, something called an *omelette norvégienne*. And I asked for some French fries to go with it. The buggers gave it to me, too. They never told me it was a pudding.'

*   *   *

Jean-Marie Fitzgerald added up the figures for a second time, taking a moment to enjoy them before closing the small, now rather worn notebook in which he had recorded details of his wine sales over the past several years; details that were best kept well away from official eyes. He swivelled round in his chair and, from the bookshelves behind his desk, selected a cracked, leather-bound volume of Molière's *L'Avare*, its pages hollowed out in the middle to provide a convenient but discreet hiding place for the notebook.

It was all most satisfactory. The euros had accumulated in the account in Luxembourg to the point where Fitzgerald was a wealthy man. Another year or two like this one, and he would be sitting on a cushion of money for the rest of his life, with more than enough for a pied-à-terre on Park Avenue and a house and a boat in the sunny, delightfully tax-free Bahamas. The sooner the better, he thought. He was tired of Bordeaux and its incessant preoccupation with wine—although, as he had to admit, wine had served him well. Wine, and the more gullible side of human nature.

He could see only one problem that might interfere with his otherwise well-ordered and prosperous future: the Englishman, who had shown a little too much interest in the vines for Fitzgerald's liking. This year's vintage would be safe; tests and investigations would delay an *oenologue*'s report until well after the *vendange*. But after that? If only the Englishman could be persuaded to sell.

Fitzgerald made a note to talk to Nathalie. As he well knew, she could be extremely persuasive.

*   *   *

When Christie, Charlie and Max reached the village, they saw very little trace of the previous evening's festivities. The strings of coloured lights were still there, hanging like tropical fruit among the leaves of the plane trees, but the trestle tables, the benches and the stage were all gone, dismantled and loaded up overnight on the truck that would take them to the next fête. A sprinkling of tourists lounged on the café terrace, and from inside came the slap of cards that punctuated the never-ending game played by four ancient gentlemen at a table in the back. The square was empty except for one or two hurrying figures, clutching bread and late for lunch. Normality had returned to Saint-Pons.

It would have taken a keen observer to notice any difference in the way Fanny treated Max from any other well-liked client. She might have nuzzled his cheek for a second or two longer than usual when they were exchanging kisses, and her thigh was touching his shoulder while she was standing by the table taking their order. The same keen observer might also have detected an extra twitch to her hips as she walked away. But on the whole she was, as Charlie remarked, a model of discretion, and a girl you could very definitely take home to meet your mother. 'Now then,' he said, taking a creased envelope from his pocket and smoothing it on the table, 'this mystery wine.' He held his empty glass out to Max to be filled as he looked down at his notes. 'Billy had a job getting the details, but he knows his stuff. I'm sure he's got his facts straight, even if they're a bit hard to believe.

'First of all, we can't afford it. It's not at all widely known, except to hard-core connoisseurs with what Billy calls ample funds. It's part of a fairly recent phenomenon in the business—garage wines, Max, remember?—tiny vineyards with very limited production. Well, they've taken off like mad in the past few years, and they're fetching prices that would make your eyes water; just the thing for wine snobs with more loot than sense.' He paused to sip his wine and look at Max. 'Actually, it's exactly what I was talking about when we had dinner in London. Pity Uncle Henry didn't leave you a bit of land in Bordeaux.

'Anyway, the wine from this particular vineyard is selling for serious money: thirty or forty thousand dollars a case—that's wholesale, if you can get any. And you'd be lucky to get any because the production is never more than a few hundred cases each year. Almost all of it goes to Asia, a dribble to the States, a dribble to Germany, but none to France. Don't ask me why. And they're keeping it very close to the chest. Tasting is strictly by invitation only, and you have to deal with the sole representative. Let's see now'—Charlie turned over the envelope and squinted at the scribbles on the back—'yes, here we are. I suppose it's a bloke, but you never can tell with French names. Someone called Jean-Marie Fitzgerald.'

Max, in mid-swallow, almost choked. '*Who?*'

'But we *met* that guy.' Christie leaned across to check the name on the envelope. 'How many Jean-Marie Fitzgeralds can there be in Bordeaux?'

Charlie looked from one puzzled face to the other. Max described Fitzgerald's visit to the vineyard, and that made three puzzled faces around the table. 'If it *is* the same guy,' said Christie, 'what was he doing down here pretending to be . . .'

'. . . an *oenologue* recommended by Nathalie Auzet,' said Max. 'Who we know is up to something.'

They had been neglecting their first course, and ate in thoughtful silence until the last scrap of *jambon cru* and the last sweet scoop of Cavaillon melon was finished. 'I'm just thinking out loud,' said Max, 'but suppose Roussel's wine—our wine—that Nathalie Auzet pays for in cash and arranges to have shipped out by truck every year—suppose that's going to Fitzgerald.' He was distracted by Fanny's breast brushing his ear as she

205

bent forward to take away his plate. Coming back to earth, he went on: 'And suppose he bottles it, sticks on a fancy label, and jacks up the price.'

Charlie consulted his envelope. 'I got the right name, didn't I? Le Coin Perdu—that's what was on the label you saw.'

Max nodded, leaning back in his chair. 'What a scam. But if you could pull it off you'd make a fortune. The best Luberon wines fetch twenty or twenty-five dollars a bottle. Give the same wine a Bordeaux label, keep it exclusive, make up a convincing bit of history, and the sky's the limit.'

Christie shook her head. 'People would know. They can't be that dumb.'

'Don't bet on it,' said Charlie. 'You'd be amazed. This is the wine business, remember? The emperor's new clothes in a bottle.' He nodded his thanks as Fanny put a plate of *moules farcies*, fragrant with butter, parsley and garlic, in front of him. 'Look, say you put the word out very discreetly to one or two of the top buyers and let them in on the secret of this fabulously exclusive wine—well, their clients aren't likely to argue. The emperor's new clothes in a bottle,' he said again as he speared a mussel, clearly pleased with the description. 'And you've got human nature working for you, don't you see? Pick your man, appeal to his ego, flatter him rigid, tell him how much you admire his taste and his extraordinary palate. Then tell him that this is an unknown treasure—there's an old chestnut that's worked a couple of times in the property business, I can tell you—and you'd like him to be one of the lucky few to discover it. These people love to be the first to spot a great wine. And, most important'—Charlie jabbed the

206

air with his fork in emphasis—'you tell them to share the secret only with a few trusted clients. Publicity would spoil everything. Come to think of it, that's probably why they don't sell it in France. The frogs would ask awkward questions.' He raised his eyebrows at the other two. 'Well? It could work, couldn't it?'

It seemed wildly improbable. Although, as Christie said, it seemed more than wildly improbable—inconceivable, even—that a man would spend half a million dollars on a single bottle of wine. And yet it had happened. This was news to Charlie, and he jumped on it. 'There you are,' he said. 'Exactly what I've been saying. Common sense goes out of the window all the time in the wine business.'

'Suppose you're right about this,' Christie said. 'How do you prove it?'

Suggestions and countersuggestions went back and forth over the mussels and then the cheese. Max ruled out calling in the police, which would ruin Roussel as well as the others. A confrontation with Nathalie Auzet was raised again, and discarded for the same reason: she would simply deny everything, and for lack of proof she would get away with it. The more they talked, the more it became clear that they should concentrate on Jean-Marie Fitzgerald.

They were sitting with their coffee, watching the village come slowly back to life after lunch, when Max turned to Christie. 'Who's the richest man in the world?'

'I don't know. Bill Gates?'

'George Soros?' said Charlie. 'A Rockefeller, a du Pont, a Rothschild—no, wait a minute, what about the Sultan of Tengah? He's worth a bob or two.'

All Max knew about the Sultan of Tengah was that he was oil-rich—enormously, outrageously rich. He had vast real estate holdings in cities all around the world, he had forests in Canada, herds of bison in Wyoming, gold fields and diamond mines in Africa, gas holdings in Russia. The palace where he spent most of his time was rumoured to have four hundred rooms, each furnished with magnificent antiques. But apart from those few fragments of information, well known though they were, he was a mystery—rarely seen in public, never photographed, a reclusive Croesus.

'Perfect,' said Max. 'He'd be perfect. Charlie, you couldn't have come here at a better time. Here's what we'll do.'

Nineteen

'I can't do it with you two making faces at me,' said Charlie. 'I need to be alone. This is going to be an artistic performance. You're sure he speaks English? I'm not altogether confident in French.'

'Trust me,' said Christie. 'He speaks English.' She and Max shut the door behind them, leaving Charlie to himself in the cavernous, shabby sitting room. He arranged his notes and a pencil on the low table in front of his chair, and ran his thumb across the business card that Max had given him: simple and classic, the name of Jean-Marie Fitzgerald engraved in copperplate script. Charlie took a deep breath and picked up his phone.

'*Oui?*' The girl's voice—brusque and slightly ill-tempered—prompted Charlie to put on the plummy, upper-class drawl he normally reserved for his plummy, upper-class clients.

'Good afternoon.' Charlie let the words hang in the air for a moment to let the girl adjust to a foreign language. 'I'd like a word with your Mr. Fitzgerald, if he's available.' He spoke with exaggerated slowness and clarity.

But the girl's English was fluent, with the hint of an American accent. 'May I ask who's calling?'

'Willis. Charles Willis. In fact, I'm calling on behalf of my client.'

'And your client's name?'

'I'm afraid I'm not at liberty to divulge that—except, of course, to Mr. Fitzgerald.'

Charlie was put on hold, and he was treated to a couple of minutes of recorded chamber music while he reread his notes. Then: 'Mr. Willis? Jean-Marie Fitzgerald. What can I do for you?' Christie had been right, Charlie thought. The man spoke English with barely the trace of an accent.

'I hope you'll forgive me, Mr. Fitzgerald, but before we go any further, I must ask you to keep this conversation and any subsequent dealings strictly to yourself.' Charlie waited for the murmured reassurance, then continued. 'I act as the personal wine consultant and buyer for a very eminent client, a great connoisseur, a man for whom wine is one of the major pleasures of life. He is also a man of quite remarkable modesty and discretion, which is why I had to ask for your reassurance. But to get down to business: not long ago, word reached my client of your wine, Le Coin Perdu. He has instructed me to investigate, to taste,

209

perhaps to buy. And so, not entirely by chance, I find myself in France.'

Charlie could almost feel the curiosity coming down the line. 'Well, Mr. Willis,' said Fitzgerald, 'I should tell you that discretion is as important to me as it is to you. We never speak of our clients; our dealings are completely confidential. You need have no concerns, I assure you. And so I don't think you would be committing any breach of trust if you were to tell me his name. I must confess I'm intrigued.'

Here we go, thought Charlie. He dropped his voice to a level just above a whisper. 'My client is the Sultan of Tengah.'

There was a moment or silence while Fitzgerald tried to remember the estimate he had read somewhere of the Sultan of Tengah's wealth: a hundred billion? Two hundred? More than enough, anyway. 'Ah yes,' he said. 'Of course. Like the rest of the world, I have heard of him.' Fitzgerald had been doodling on a notepad, and jotted down the figure of $75,000 per case. 'May I ask where he lives?'

'He spends most of his time in Tengah. He owns the country, as you probably know, and finds it more agreeable to stay at home. Travel bores him.'

'Quite so, quite so. It has become very disagreeable. Well, I'm flattered that the reputation of our wine has travelled so far.' Fitzgerald had no precise idea of where Tengah was—somewhere in Indonesia, he thought—but it sounded distant. He scratched out the number on his pad and wrote down $100,000. 'Fortunately, we do have a few cases left.' The tone of his voice lightened, as though he had suddenly been struck by a most unusually happy idea. 'Perhaps I could suggest a tasting? A private tasting, naturally.'

'Naturally.' Charlie made rustling sounds with the paper on which he'd made his notes—the sounds of a busy man turning the pages of his diary. 'I could be with you tomorrow, if that's convenient. But let me say again that there must be no—how shall I put it?—talkative elements. The Sultan has an absolute horror of publicity.'

And that was that. After arranging the details, Charlie put down the phone and allowed himself a private jig of triumph around the sitting room before going out to find Christie and Max in the courtyard.

Charlie's expression told all. 'He fell for it,' said Max. 'I knew he would. I *knew* he would. Charlie, you're a hero.'

'I rather enjoyed it, actually. Didn't take him long to suggest a private tasting. But I hope to God you're right. What's the penalty for criminal impersonation in France? No, don't tell me. Anyway, it's all set for three-thirty tomorrow afternoon in Bordeaux.' And then the smile left his face. 'I hate to say this, but I've just thought of a snag. How are we going to know if it really is Roussel's wine? I certainly wouldn't be able to tell.'

Max grinned. 'Leave it to me,' he said. 'I've got a secret weapon.'

*　　　*　　　*

At Marignane airport early the following morning, a small group of passengers stood out from the usual clutter of briefcases and businessmen at the check-in desk for the Air France shuttle to

211

Bordeaux: Christie and Max, in jeans and light jackets; Charlie in blazer, flannels, striped shirt, bow tie and sunglasses; and, looking about him with an uneasy air, Roussel. But a formal Roussel this morning, dressed in the twenty-year-old black suit he had only previously worn at weddings and funerals.

In all his life, Roussel's travels had never taken him further than Marseille—a city which, being full of foreigners, he regarded with considerable suspicion—and this was to be his inaugural flight. At first, he had been reluctant to come; he was not anxious to take to the air, and there was also a good chance of an unpleasant confrontation in Bordeaux. But Max had explained the crucial part he would play, both now and in the future, and Roussel had done his best to conquer his misgivings. Even so, he stayed as close to Max as he could in these unfamiliar surroundings until the moment when they had to part company as Max passed alone through the security gate. Turning, he beckoned Roussel to follow.

Beep . . . beepbeepbeepbeepbeep. Roussel jumped, as if he'd been on the receiving end of a jolt of electricity. He was told to go back and try again; more beeps. The alarm on his face increased as he was taken off to one side, where a bored young woman swept his body with an electronic wand that came to rest with an agitated buzzing sound on his stomach. And there, tucked into his waistcoat pocket, was his old Opinel knife, a friend of many years and the peasant's constant companion in the fields and at table. With a frown of deep disapproval, the young woman confiscated the knife, tossed it into a plastic bin, and attempted to

212

wave him on his way.

Roussel's alarm turned to outrage. He stood his ground. That was his property; he wanted it back. He turned to Max, waiting a few yards away, and jerked an accusing thumb at the young woman. 'She has stolen my knife!' The other passengers waiting to go through security, curious and suddenly nervous, took a few steps backwards and watched as the young woman looked for the nearest armed guard.

Max came over and took Roussel by the arm. 'Best not to argue with her,' he said. 'I think she's worried you might use it to slit the pilot's throat.'

'*Ah bon?* Why would I do that, being myself in the plane?'

With some difficulty, Max steered him away from the security area and up to the bar in the departure lounge, where a fuller explanation, a pastis, and the promise of another knife—a Laguiole, even—did something to restore Roussel's good humour.

As the plane heaved itself off the runway, with the customary clamour and judder of machinery under extreme stress, Max noticed that Roussel's hands were gripping the arms of his seat so tightly that his knuckles showed white through the tanned skin. And thus they remained throughout the short flight, despite Max's efforts to convince him that the unnerving and totally unnatural experience of being thirty thousand feet above the ground in a tin tube was unlikely to end in death. It wasn't until he had celebrated his survival with another pastis at the Bordeaux airport that the colour returned to Roussel's face. He got into the rental car a more relaxed man. This was a form of transport he understood.

During the drive to their hotel in Bordeaux, Max and Charlie once again went over the plan they had worked out. The afternoon's tasting was to be for Charlie alone. He would be suitably impressed, and a price would be negotiated, subject to approval by his client, the Sultan. Because of the time difference, the call to Tengah couldn't be made from Bordeaux until midnight, and so a second visit would have to be arranged for the following day to deliver a bank draft and finalize shipping details. At this point, Charlie would be joined by the others, Fitzgerald would be confronted by Roussel, justice would be done, and the police could be called in. Nothing to it.

'All you have to remember,' said Max, 'is to make sure you come away with a sample this afternoon, so that Claude can taste it and compare it with the bottle he's brought.' He glanced at Charlie. 'You OK?'

Charlie nodded, but not with any great conviction. 'I think so,' he said. 'I just hope I can pull it off. It's one thing to do it on the phone, but . . .'

'Of course you can,' said Max. 'A master of disguise like you? I remember when you did Hamlet in the school play.'

Charlie frowned. 'But I was playing Ophelia.'

Max didn't miss a beat. 'Well, there you are. Had me fooled. This should be a piece of cake after Ophelia.'

There was a giggle from Christie in the back seat. She leaned forward and squeezed Charlie's shoulder. 'You'll be fine. You won't even have to wear a wig.'

They were staying at the Claret, a businessman's hotel Max had chosen from the Michelin guide for its appropriate name and for its convenient location just off the quai des Chartrons, a short walk from Fitzgerald's tasting rooms. Stopping to drop off their bags and pick up a street map of Bordeaux, they walked along the quai and found a café overlooking the broad curve of the Garonne. There, over ham sandwiches and a carafe of wine, Charlie rehearsed his performance for Christie, his audience of one. Max and Roussel talked, their mood quietly optimistic, about the future—a future that largely depended on the events of the next few hours.

The time had come. They agreed to meet back at the hotel, and Charlie, map in hand, set off for the cours Xavier Arnozan.

It was Fitzgerald himself who opened the door in response to Charlie's knock. 'Enchanted to meet you, Mr. Willis,' he said as they shook hands. 'I think you'll be pleased to hear that I have given my secretary the afternoon off. We are entirely alone. I thought that would make you feel more comfortable.'

'Most kind, most kind.' Charlie nodded his thanks with a faint smile, and followed Fitzgerald down the corridor to the tasting room. The sound of a Bach fugue came softly from concealed speakers. Bottles, glasses and silver candlesticks were arranged along the gleaming length of the mahogany table, a burnished copper *crachoir* at one end next to a tasteful arrangement of white linen napkins laid out in the form of a fan. It was the church of Bacchus, a shrine to wine. Charlie half-expected a priest to pop out of the woodwork

215

and give his blessing to the proceedings.

Fitzgerald took a slim crocodile case from his pocket, and passed Charlie a business card. He waited, clearly expecting a card in return.

Charlie had anticipated just such a moment. He aimed the two black barrels of his sunglasses at the other man, shaking his head slowly. 'My client sometimes carries discretion to the point of secrecy, Mr. Fitzgerald. He prefers that I don't advertise myself, and so I don't carry business cards. I'm sure you understand.'

'Indeed,' said Fitzgerald. 'Forgive me. And now, if you feel ready . . .' He extended an immaculate tweed-clad arm toward the table, inclining his head as he did so.

Charlie had an awful twinge of doubt. If this was a scam, it was a beautifully presented scam, and Fitzgerald—every aristocratic inch of him—appeared to be the genuine Bordeaux article. It was hard to imagine that he was a crook. And then Charlie had a mental image of some of his acquaintances in the top end of the London property business: charming, well educated, well tailored, glib—and more than capable of evicting their grandmothers in order to make a sale; villains to a man. Encouraged by this thought, he removed his sunglasses with a flourish and advanced toward the table as the fugue reached its plaintive conclusion and the room fell silent.

'If I may make a suggestion,' said Fitzgerald, 'we might start with the '99 before going on to the 2000—which I have to say is my personal favourite.' He poured wine into two glasses, and passed one to Charlie.

Hours of practice—at his wine-tasting course,

216

and during a final rehearsal the previous evening, in front of the bathroom mirror—had prepared Charlie for the all-important niceties of this all-important ritual. Holding the glass by its base, between finger and thumb, he presented it to the light of the candle's flame, his eyes narrowed in what he hoped looked like knowledgeable concentration.

'As you see,' said Fitzgerald, 'the robe is particularly fine, somewhere between . . .'

Charlie held up a hand. 'Please. I need complete silence.' He began to swirl the wine with a gentle circular motion of the glass, his head tilted to one side. And then, judging the bouquet to be sufficiently developed, he buried his nose in the glass, with graceful little waves of his free hand—a rather pretentious refinement he'd picked up in his course—to direct the fragrant air toward his cocked and waiting nostrils. He inhaled, looked up to commune with the ceiling, bent his head to inhale again, and issued a quiet hum of approval.

Raising the glass to his lips, he took some wine and held it in his mouth for several seconds before going through what he always thought of as the sound effects: he sucked in air; his cheeks went in and out like bellows; he chewed; he swilled; and, finally, he spat. In the silence of the room, the sound of wine hitting the copper bottom of the *crachoir* seemed unnaturally loud, almost shocking.

Fitzgerald waited, his eyebrows raised like two question marks.

'Excellent, quite excellent,' said Charlie. He decided to risk a compliment. 'I am reminded of Pétrus, but a more muscular Pétrus. And yet you say you prefer the 2000?'

The half-smile on Fitzgerald's face grew broader. 'You are kind enough to flatter me. But with the 2000, I think you will be surprised, even *étonné*. Permit me.' He took Charlie's glass, and replaced it with another, this one containing wine from the 2000 vintage. Once again, Charlie went slowly and deliberately through the tasting ritual while Fitzgerald watched like a cat that was one short jump away from the mouse.

Again the echoing splash of liquid on copper. 'Remarkable,' said Charlie, dabbing his lips with a linen napkin. 'My congratulations, Mr. Fitzgerald. This is a Bordeaux unlike any others I have ever tasted. A triumph.'

Fitzgerald allowed himself a modest shrug. 'We do the best we can,' he said. 'Organic fertilizer, of course, and the grapes are picked by hand *avec tri*—as you know, that's to guarantee the *état sanitaire*.'

What the hell was that? Charlie nodded wisely. 'Good, good.'

'And the vinification is always *avec pigeage*, as we say. Just as my grandfather used to do. Sometimes, the old ways are the best.'

What the hell was *pigeage*? Nobody had told him about that in the wine course. It sounded complicated and vaguely unhygienic. 'One can always tell,' said Charlie. 'God is in the details'—he inclined his head to Fitzgerald—'as we say. Now then. Perhaps we could move on to the more squalid financial details; for the 2000, I think. You're quite right. It has just that little more complexity, a longer finish, more—how shall I put it?—gravitas. And I'm sure such excellence has its price.'

218

Fitzgerald, with only the faintest shrug of apology, said: 'One hundred thousand dollars a case.' He smiled. 'That would include delivery to anywhere in the world.'

Charlie recovered sufficiently to wave aside such a minor matter. 'As far as delivery goes, I'm sure the Sultan would want to send one of his planes. He considers the security in commercial airlines far too lax for valuable shipments.' He consulted the ceiling again, deep in thought, before speaking. This time, his tone was brisk and businesslike. 'Very well. I intend to recommend that my client take a position with this wine. Let me see now. Would ten cases be possible?'

'You would be stripping our cellar, Mr. Willis.' Fitzgerald did his best to appear reluctant, a man loath to part with his treasures. 'But yes, we can just manage ten cases.'

'Splendid.' Charlie looked at his watch. 'The time difference is nine hours, which is a little inconvenient, I'm afraid. I won't be able to place the call until quite late tonight. However, I can use the rest of the afternoon to arrange a bank draft. Crédit Suisse is acceptable, I would imagine?'

Indeed it was. Fitzgerald's thoughts were already turning to the silver Lamborghini he had coveted for many years.

'Shall we meet here again at ten o'clock tomorrow morning?' said Charlie. Putting on his sunglasses, he stopped on his way to the door. 'Oh, there is one small service you could do for me.'

By this point, Fitzgerald would happily have stood on his head stark naked and whistled the Marseillaise if that had been required. 'If it is in my power, I should be delighted.'

219

'Do you think I might take that opened bottle of the 2000 with me? I'd like to have the taste fresh in my mouth when I make the call tonight. It would give an extra *je ne sais qui* to my recommendation.'

'*Quoi*,' said Fitzgerald, unable to resist correcting the foreigner adrift in his language. 'By all means. Let me find you a cork.'

Closing the front door behind Charlie, Fitzgerald went back to the tasting room, poured himself a glass of wine, and sat down to better enjoy the prospect of tomorrow's million-dollar cheque. Maybe he should start thinking about a bigger apartment in New York, and a bigger boat in the Bahamas. He took a sip of wine. It really was very good; almost as good as he said it was.

*   *   *

Charlie collapsed in the first bar he came to and ordered a large brandy, high and lightheaded with elation. Even though he'd been acting the part, he had the giddy feeling that he had indeed just committed a million dollars of someone else's money to buy one hundred and twenty bottles of wine. Superb wine, without any question; but was it Roussel's wine? He gazed at the bottle Fitzgerald had given to him, worked out its approximate price, and marvelled that anyone would pay so much for it. The emperor's new clothes came to mind again.

The others were waiting for him in the lobby of the hotel: Max pacing up and down, Christie trying to concentrate on a copy of the *Herald Tribune*, Roussel idly turning the pages of *L'Equipe*. As Charlie came across to join them, their eyes went at once to the bottle in his hand.

'There you go,' he said, putting it on a low table in front of them. 'At current prices, that will cost you about eight thousand dollars. I'm giving you a discount because I've had a couple of mouthfuls. Very nice too.' He sat down and pulled off his bow tie as he fielded a barrage of questions from Christie and Max, while Roussel took out the cork and applied a thoughtful nose to the neck of the bottle.

Max interrupted his reflections. 'Claude,' he said, 'put the bottle down, because I think you might faint. Fitzgerald is asking a hundred thousand dollars per case for this wine. Your wine.'

Roussel's eyes opened wide in astonishment, and he shook his head slowly from side to side. The world had gone mad. A hundred thousand dollars was more than he had been getting for an entire vintage. Anger would come later, but for the moment he was in a state of shock. *'Tu rigoles, non?'*

'No, I'm not joking. Now, what we need to know is whether or not it really is your wine, and you're the only one who can tell for certain. You did bring that other bottle, didn't you? To compare the two?' Max looked into his face and was relieved to see a confident nod. 'Good. Why don't you get it, and we'll meet you in the bar.'

The bar was just off the hotel lobby, dedicated to the local beverage, *dégustations* encouraged. It was still too early for the daily invasion by parched businessmen who had not had a drop to drink since lunch, and the barman was happy for a little distraction. By the time Roussel had returned with the second bottle, tasting glasses, paper napkins, and an empty ice bucket for anyone who chose to

221

spit had been arranged on the table in front of them.

They sat silent and expectant, all eyes fixed on Roussel as he poured the wine, held it to the light, swirled, sniffed, and tasted; swallowed, tasted again, considered.

'*Bon.*' He sucked his teeth and nodded several times. 'This is my wine.'

Max leaned forward and put his hand on Roussel's arm. 'You're sure, Claude? Really, really sure?'

Roussel stiffened, his face indignant. '*Beh oui.* I have known this wine since he was a grape. It is my wine.' He poured wine from the second bottle, tasted, and nodded again. 'My wine.'

There was a collective sigh of relief, audible even to the barman, who had been watching and listening with avid attention. It took only the briefest of signals from Max to bring him over to the table; and seeing their smiling faces, he came with an expectant air. Happy customers, in his experience, drank and tipped much more lavishly than those who came to his bar simply to drown their miseries. '*Je vous écoute, cher monsieur.*'

'I think my friends deserve some champagne. A bottle of Krug, if you have one chilled.'

Krug would certainly be possible. Was there a special cause for celebration? The barman hovered, his eye fixed on the two unmarked bottles of Roussel's wine. This being Bordeaux, unmarked bottles were of particular interest.

'A very promising vintage,' Max told him. 'We're going to drink to its success.'

Christie waited until the barman had gone in search of champagne before speaking. 'No

222

disrespect to Claude's nose,' she said, 'but don't you think it would be smart to have an analysis done, just to be totally sure?' She looked at the faces around the table. 'You know, like a wine DNA? There must be dozens of places here in town where they do that.'

According to the barman, indeed there were. What's more, his brother worked at one of them, and, following a quick phone call, he agreed to send a messenger over to pick up the wine so he could do the analysis that evening.

With that settled, the toasts were proposed: to Roussel for making the wine, to Charlie for his virtuoso impersonation, to a giggling Christie for reasons that Charlie preferred not to disclose, to a prosperous future. By the time they went up to their rooms to change for dinner, the mood of the group was as effervescent as the champagne bubbling through their veins.

That mood was to be dampened, but only slightly, and not for long. Their new best friend the barman had recommended a bistro in the rue Saint-Rémi—posters from the 1920s and long silvered mirrors on the walls, dark red moleskin banquettes, traditional good solid food—and they were deliberating over the menus when Max noticed that Roussel had fallen quiet.

'What is it, Claude? Something wrong? You're not worried about the wine?'

Roussel tugged at his ear and pushed his menu aside. 'I spoke to Ludivine before we left the hotel—you know, to tell her—and she said that Nathalie Auzet had called this morning.'

'What did she want?'

'She didn't say. Ludivine told her I was away,

and she said she'd call again tomorrow. Perhaps something about the contract for the *métayage*. I don't know.'

Max waved a dismissive hand. 'Don't let it spoil your dinner. We'll deal with her when we get back. Come on—what's it to be?'

Dinner was long and increasingly convivial, followed by one last glass in the hotel bar to celebrate the results of the analysis. This confirmed the findings of Roussel's nose, much to everyone's relief.

It was well past midnight by the time Max got back to his room, where he found the little red eye of the message light blinking on his phone. Madame Passepartout had called: to remind him, no doubt, that he'd promised to bring her back a box of *canelés*, the small caramelized cakes—a Bordeaux speciality—that she loved with a guilty passion. He made a note on his pad before undressing, then took a bottle of Evian with him into the bathroom; a long shower and a litre of water last thing at night was a more effective cure for a hangover than any number of aspirin in the morning. The moment his damp head touched the pillow, he was asleep.

*   *   *

The ringing of the phone jolted him into semi-wakefulness after a night of delightful dreams—Fanny, wine, the future, Fanny—and he winced as the familiar screech came down the line.

'Monsieur Max! *C'est moi*.'

Max cast a bleary eye at his watch: eight o'clock. He wished Madame Passepartout a good morning and fumbled for the Evian bottle.

She was *désolée* to disturb him, but she thought he should know that Maître Auzet had come to the house wanting to see him. On being told that he was away, she had demanded to know where he was. Imagine! The impertinence! Such ill-mannered curiosity! *En plus*, when asked, she had refused to say why she wanted to see him. An obstinate and difficult young woman. Needless to say, her questions had not been answered, and she had been told to come back later in the week.

Madame Passepartout paused at the end of this break-neck recitation for Max to comment, and seemed disappointed that he had nothing indiscreet to say. He promised to bring her back a large box of *canelés*, and put down the phone, a thoughtful man. But whatever the problem was, it would have to wait.

The four of them left the hotel after breakfast, a subdued group that moved slowly and talked quietly. The previous night's alcohol had something to do with this, of course, but also the thought of the confrontation that lay ahead had taken the edge off their high spirits. It's one thing to know a man is a crook and a liar, but quite another to tell him so to his face. Would he break down and confess? Deny everything and call the police? Lose his temper and start throwing bottles at them? Nobody was taking any bets.

They arrived at the house in the cours Xavier Arnozan as the tolling of a distant bell marked ten o'clock. Charlie squared his shoulders, adjusted his bow tie, and knocked on the door. The sound of footsteps could be heard coming down the corridor, and the door was opened to reveal a

225

young man in a dark suit, stocky and impassive.

'I have an appointment with Mr. Fitzgerald.' Charlie's voice sounded firm and confident, despite his surprise.

The young man neither smiled nor spoke, but stood back to let them in before leading them down the corridor and into the tasting room.

The long mahogany table was bare except for an ashtray. A chair behind the table was occupied by an older man with a long, bony jaw and his hair cut *en brosse*. Like the young man, he too was wearing a dark suit. As they watched him select and light a cigarette with studied deliberation, they heard footsteps behind them, and turned to see two uniformed policemen taking up their positions on either side of the door. The man behind the desk frowned, and spoke for the first time. 'You two can wait outside,' he said to the policemen, with a flick of his finger, 'and close the door.'

'Where is Mr. Fitzgerald?' Charlie made a brave attempt to bluster. 'This is most irregular.'

The man behind the table held up a hand. 'Who among you speaks French?' Max and Roussel nodded. 'Good. You can translate for your colleagues. My name is Lambert. Inspector Lambert.' He left his chair and came round to perch on the corner of the table, squinting at them through the smoke from his cigarette. 'Word reached us yesterday of your . . . activities, and I must tell you that here in Bordeaux we are not amused by this kind of adventure. To misrepresent the good name of our wines, to attempt this despicable substitution, to profit from fraud and breach of trust—these are crimes of a most serious nature, and the penalties are extremely severe.' He

226

ground out his cigarette in the ashtray and went back to sit behind the table. Looking up at the row of frozen faces in front of him, he nodded and said again, 'Extremely severe.'

'*Putaing*,' said Roussel.

'Bloody hell,' said Charlie, who had understood the gist if not the detail of Lambert's remarks.

'I can explain everything,' said Max.

*　　*　　*

'Thank God you called when you did,' said Fitzgerald. 'You know, I was sure he was genuine: he did all the right things, said all the right things. And an order like that, on the other side of the world, well away from France—it was perfect. Although I suppose I should have smelt a rat when he didn't even try to negotiate on the price. But we can all make a mistake.' He shrugged, and his face brightened. 'Fortunately, it wasn't fatal—thanks to you, my dear. Have some champagne and tell me again what made you suspicious. Our last conversation was a little rushed.'

Their table overlooked the enclosed garden of the Hotel Bristol, green and refreshingly cool in the heat wave that had turned Paris into an oven. Nathalie Auzet sipped her wine before replying. 'Mostly luck. As you know, I had to talk to Roussel about this year's shipment, and when I found out he'd gone away, I thought it was odd. He hates to travel; I've never known him to spend a night away from home. And his wife wouldn't give me a number where I could reach him. So I went to see Skinner, and nobody was at the house apart from that nosy old boot of a housekeeper. That's when I called you, and when you told me you'd just had a private tasting for an Englishman . . .' She stared into her glass, and shook her head. 'It's such a pity Roussel lost his nerve and had an attack of honesty. It was a wonderful scheme.'

Fitzgerald leaned across to touch her hand. 'Never mind. It served us very well. Enough, more than enough, to set you up in California, and me in New York. What a convenient country America is if you want to disappear. And we'll be there by this time tomorrow.' He turned to the third person at the table, a man with a long, bony jaw and his hair cut *en brosse*. 'How about you, Philippe? Did you enjoy pretending to be *un flic*?'

A smile softened the angles of the man's face. 'Easy work,' he said, 'and the pay's good.' The wad of hundred-euro notes Fitzgerald had given him was so thick he had had to divide it between two pockets. 'It's funny. Once they saw the boys in those uniforms, they didn't ask for any proof of identity. I suppose you believe what you see.'

'What you *think* you see, Philippe,' said Fitzgerald, 'what you *think* you see. Very much like wine. Tell me, how did you leave it with them?'

'Skinner and Roussel put up quite a good case, I have to say. A court would probably let them off with a slap on the wrist and a fine. But I don't think they'll cause any trouble. I told them we would be launching a full-scale investigation into this so-called Monsieur Fitzgerald and his wine dealings, and that we'd be in touch. I let them think they might avoid prosecution if they behaved themselves and cooperated when the time came. My guess is that they'll keep their heads down for the next six months and hope for the best.'

228

'*Chapeau*, Philippe. You did very well. And now I think we deserve to indulge ourselves.' Fitzgerald barely had time to raise his hand before there was a flurry of waiters at his shoulder. 'The foie gras here is superb. And I believe they may let us have a glass or two of Yquem to go with it.'

Twenty

It wasn't long before Max began to suspect that he'd been had. The first, most glaring clue was the overnight disappearance of Maître Auzet, which was to be the subject of fascinated speculation in the village for months, possibly years, to come. She had left no forwarding address at the post office, which the village took as a sure sign of irregular or possibly criminal behaviour. Had she run off with a lover? Or was there—a thought always accompanied by a morbid but delicious shiver—something more sinister? A *crime passionnel* that would account for her empty office and shuttered house? Rumour was rampant—she had been spotted in Marseille, a light had been seen in her house, she had absconded with clients' funds, she had forsaken this wicked world and joined the Sisters of Mercy. There was a fresh story every day. As one of the old men in the café said, it was better than anything on television.

Max and Roussel, for obvious reasons, kept their theories to themselves, hoping that in the way of these things, interest would fade. Eventually, they told one another, the case of the missing *notaire* would become just one of many unexplained

229

incidents in the nine-hundred-year history of Saint-Pons.

Max discovered another disappearing piece in the puzzle when he tried to contact Fitzgerald in Bordeaux, only to find that his phone number had been discontinued. But what finally confirmed the deception was another call, this one made at the urging of Roussel.

Because he was a principal in the original scheme—even, it could be argued by the state prosecutor, the instigator—Roussel was an extremely worried man. Again and again he turned over in his mind the penalties he might face if the authorities chose to enforce them: back taxes (with copious interest) on the money he had made, fines for not declaring that income, bankruptcy, possible imprisonment, his family destitute, his life in ruins. During the days that followed the events in Bordeaux, one could almost see the black cloud over his head as he went through the motions of tending the vines. He lost his appetite, hardly spoke to his wife, snapped at his dog. At last, when he could bear it no longer, he persuaded Max to contact the Bordeaux police; knowing the worst, he felt, would somehow be better than fearing it.

The two men sat in the kitchen while Max called information for the number in Bordeaux, and, after some delay, was put through to Inspector Lambert.

'*Oui?*' It was the clipped, impatient voice of an overworked man.

'It's Monsieur Skinner here. Max Skinner.'

'Who?'

'You remember? We, ah, met last week in Bordeaux.'

'No, monsieur. I'm afraid you're mistaken.'

230

'You are Inspector Lambert?'

'Yes.'

'I'm sorry, but is there another Inspector Lambert in Bordeaux?'

'No.'

'Are you sure? It was only last week that . . .'

'Monsieur'—the voice was now sounding exasperated—'Lambert is a common name. I happen to know that there are approximately sixty-seven thousand families in France with the name of Lambert. However, I also know that there is only one Lambert in the Bordeaux police department, and that is me. I'm sure you have something better to do than to waste my time. Good day, monsieur.'

Roussel had been leaning forward intently, chewing his lip, trying to guess at the other half of the conversation. Max put the phone down and shook his head, the beginnings of a grin on his face. 'That crafty sod.'

'Who?'

'Fitzgerald. He must have set it up. Lambert, or whatever he's really called, was no more a police inspector than I am. The whole thing was a fraud.' Max couldn't stop shaking his head, like a man who's just been shown how the white rabbit gets into the magician's hat. 'We've been conned,' he said. 'Isn't that great? We've been conned.'

The frown disappeared as hope began to dawn on Roussel's face. 'But the policemen . . .'

'Claude, you can rent anything nowadays, especially uniforms. Remember, we didn't ask for any identification. You don't, not in a situation like that. No, I'm sure of it. The only people who know what's been going on are us and Fitzgerald and his friends. And they're not about to tell anyone, are

231

they? I mean, if it all got out, what are the penalties for impersonating a police officer? I think you can relax. *We* can relax.'

Roussel got to his feet and came round the table, his arms spread as wide as his smile. '*Cher ami. Cher ami.*' He plucked Max from his chair, clasped him in an embrace that threatened to crack his spine, whirled him off his feet as if he were no heavier than a sack of fertilizer, and kissed him on each cheek.

'Steady on, Claude,' said Max. 'Put me down. I'd better call Charlie and tell him the good news.'

*   *   *

The rest of the summer passed under blue skies, with only the traditional mid-August storm as a temporary relief from the heat. There was hard, unremitting work in the vines and in the *cave*, with Fanny providing food and sweet consolation at the end of each long, blistering day. Max learned to drive a tractor and, as the shining season of autumn came, to pick the grapes and sort them according to size without bruising them. His face and arms turned the colour of a pickled nut; his hands developed a thick carapace of rough skin; his clothes became dusty and faded; his hair grew shaggy. He had never been happier.

Madame Passepartout took enormous pleasure in the postcards that arrived regularly from London, particularly those featuring members of the royal family. It appeared, to her great satisfaction, that Christie and Charlie were carrying on what had begun under her very eyes in Saint-Pons.

It became a litany. 'I should never be surprised,' she would say to Max without fail every time a new postcard arrived, 'if this doesn't end in something more permanent. A ceremony at the Mairie would be most appropriate, *non*? I must think of something to wear. Of course, Monsieur Max, you will be the *témoin de mariage*.'

And even taking into account his friend's past success at avoiding matrimony, Max was inclined to agree.

He and Roussel, with the help of a loan arranged by Maurice at the local Crédit Agricole, were planning to uproot the tired old vines during the winter and replace them with Roussel's Cabernet and Merlot mixture. Working with a cousin in the building trade, they had made much-needed changes to the *cave*, scrubbing it out, white-washing the ceiling and walls, and installing a simple stone bar just inside the door. They levelled the track that led to the barn and put up a plain but handsome sign on the road for passers-by who might want to stop for a *dégustation*.

As for their pride and joy and hope for the future, the wine from the stony patch, it was no longer called Le Coin Perdu. Instead, they had decided to use the name of the property, with a presentation suitable for an exceptional wine. The corks were long, the capsules were lead, the bottles were *feuille morte*, that particular and expensive type of glass that prevents the penetration of harmful ultraviolet rays. And the label was a model of classic understatement: Le Griffon. Vin de Pays du Vaucluse. M. Skinner et C. Roussel Propriétaires. Their ambition was to join that other distinguished *vin de pays*, the Domaine de

Trévallon, as one of the very few non-appellation wines worthy of a connoisseur's consideration.

These were early days, of course, but the indications were encouraging. Several good restaurants, one as far away as Aix, had agreed to put Le Griffon on their lists; this despite its price, which was very high by Luberon standards. Next year, when May came around, Max and Roussel planned to enter the wine at Mâcon, to see if it could win a coveted medal. But already the word of mouth was good, and growing.

Unfortunately, it had not yet reached the group of Americans who came to the *cave* one bright October morning while Max and Roussel were in the back, stacking cartons ready for delivery. Roussel went to greet the visitors at the bar, setting out a line of glasses, pouring the wine and wishing them a *bonne dégustation* before returning to his cartons.

Max couldn't resist eavesdropping.

'Hey, this is pretty good.' There was a murmur of agreement from the other members of the group. 'You know, it's got that Bordeaux taste. I bet there's some Cabernet in there somewhere.'

'Do you think they ship?'

'Sure. Everybody ships.'

'Where are the prices? Oh, right, this little card here. It's about one for one with the euro, isn't it?'

A moment of silence. Then: 'Jesus! Who do these guys think they are? Thirty bucks a bottle!'

*   *   *

'For a minute or two,' said Max, 'I thought they were going to try to haggle. But then they had a whip-round and bought a couple of bottles between them. That's when I began to think the vineyard motto ought to be Get Rich Slow. Actually, it was a historic moment, because it was our first American sale. Mondavi had better watch out.'

He picked up his glass and looked past Charlie at the faces around the long table that had been set up under the plane tree in front of the house. When Fanny had learned that Christie and Charlie were coming over from London for the weekend, she had offered to close the restaurant and cook her specialty for lunch: she would make the first cassoulet of autumn. The guest list reflected her opinion that one needs a crowd for cassoulet—as well, of course, as the correct weather. And in this, she couldn't have asked for better: October was coming to an end with a series of spectacular, Indian summer days—cool in the morning, cool at night, warm enough in the middle of the day to eat outdoors, but not too hot to stifle the appetite.

In fact, jackets were already coming off as the guests paused after a first course—nothing serious, in view of what was to come—of quails' eggs spread with tapenade, *brandade de morue* on toast, and crudités. The Roussels were there, with daughter and dog. Madame Passepartout, in dazzling autumnal hues of red and gold, had brought her special friend Maurice, his shaved head, silver earring, and tattooed forearms marking him out as one of the region's less conventional bank managers. Fanny had invited her chef and his wife, and, to make up a round dozen, young Ahmed, who helped in the restaurant's kitchen.

Charlie had turned away from Max to resume his efforts to pass on to the Roussels some of the basic curiosities of the English language. 'There is no sex in English, you see,' he was saying, 'no *le* and *la*, which makes life much easier. *Plus facile.*'

'No sex,' repeated a thoughtful Roussel. 'But much cricket, *non*?'

Max left them to plunge ever deeper into the thickets of English grammar, and followed his nose into the kitchen, where Christie and Fanny had just removed from the oven a vast, deep-sided earthenware dish. It sat on the kitchen table, the size of a cartwheel, with a golden crust of breadcrumbs covering the top.

'*Voilà*,' said Fanny, '*le vrai cassoulet de Toulouse.*' Max looked at her and smiled. He couldn't imagine any other woman who could look desirable while wearing oven gloves. She took them off and ran her fingers through her hair.

Max bent over the dish and breathed in the heavy, rich aroma, humming with the promise of cholesterol. 'God, that smells good. What did you put in it?'

Fanny started to count off the ingredients on her fingers: 'White beans, confit of duck, garlic sausage, salt pork, breast and shoulder of lamb, duck fat, baby onions, loin of pork, *saucisses de Toulouse* (of course), tomatoes, white wine, garlic, a few herbs...'

'Max,' said Christie, 'stop drooling and do something useful.' She gave him Fanny's oven gloves. 'Careful when you take it out. It's heavy.'

The dish was greeted with a round of applause when it reached the table, and Christie was given the visitor's privilege of making the first ceremonial incision in the crust, releasing a fragrant sigh of steam. Plates were passed and filled, the wine was tasted and admired, the cook was toasted, and then, as frequently happens when cassoulet is served, silence descended on the table.

Madame Passepartout was the first to recover her voice. Emboldened by her second—or even her third—glass, she stretched over and tapped Max on the shoulder. 'Well?' she said to him in a whisper that carried the full length of the table, nodding toward Christie and Charlie, 'when are they going to announce it?'

'I think they're waiting for you and Maurice to go first.' Madame Passepartout bridled. Maurice seemed to be hypnotized by something in his cassoulet.

Max called across to Charlie, 'Madame here is dying to know if your intentions are honourable,' and was rewarded by a blush from Christie and a broad beam from Charlie. Translations didn't seem to be necessary.

*   *   *

It was almost five o'clock before the evening chill set in and guests began to disperse. Christie and Charlie put on sweaters and went for a stroll in the vines. Others went down to the village, to recover in the café; or to nurse their stomachs in front of the television; or, in Roussel's case, to take a nap before dinner. Max waved the last of them good-bye and went inside. He lit a fire in the kitchen and put on the Diana Krall CD that Fanny had bought him as a memento of their first dance on the night of the village fête. As he was rolling up his sleeves and contemplating the mountains of post-lunch debris, he heard footsteps behind him and felt

Fanny's arms slip around his waist.

He had to tilt his head to hear the whisper in his ear. 'I don't think you're going to do the dishes.'

'No?'

'No. You're going to do something else.'

He turned so that they were face-to-face. 'Well, we could dance.'

Her hands moved slowly up his back. 'That would be a start.'